**"UNLESS YOU DO WHAT I SAY, WE WILL BLOW THIS HOSPITAL TO KINGDOM COME, AND THE SPARKS WILL IGNITE FIRES OVER THE ENTIRE WORLD!"**

This was Commandant Rosario speaking, broadcasting his message to the doctors and patients of Manhattan Jewish Hospital, and to the Mayor and assembled police force of the city of New York.

Already he and his devoted, dedicated followers had taken control of the vast institution.

Already corpses lay in bloody heaps in the rooms and corridors.

But this was just the beginning of what was going to happen as his master plan of terror moved into its next and even more horrifying stage. . . .

## INTENSIVE FEAR

*It will hold you hostage, too!*

## Big Bestsellers from SIGNET

# INTENSIVE FEAR

## NICK CHRISTIAN

A SIGNET BOOK
NEW AMERICAN LIBRARY
TIMES MIRROR

NAL BOOKS ARE AVAILABLE AT QUANTITY DISCOUNTS
WHEN USED TO PROMOTE PRODUCTS OR SERVICES. FOR
INFORMATION PLEASE WRITE TO PREMIUM MARKETING DIVISION,
THE NEW AMERICAN LIBRARY, INC., 1633 BROADWAY,
NEW YORK, NEW YORK 10019.

SIGNET TRADEMARK REG. U.S. PAT. OFF. AND FOREIGN COUNTRIES
REGISTERED TRADEMARK—MARCA REGISTRADA
HECHO EN CHICAGO, U.S.A.

SIGNET, SIGNET CLASSICS, MENTOR, PLUME, MERIDIAN AND NAL
BOOKS are published by The New American Library, Inc.,
1633 Broadway, New York, New York 10019

First Printing, August, 1980

1   2   3   4   5   6   7   8   9

PRINTED IN THE UNITED STATES OF AMERICA

# 1

Fanny Altheimer lay peacefully in her bed in the Morgenstern Pavilion of the Manhattan Jewish Hospital. The pain of her recent surgery had been numbed by an injection from the floor nurse. The room was a bright and cheerful one, on a private floor. It would serve her in good stead in the days to come. She had been in the Intensive Care Unit for three days after her operation. Her doctor estimated that it would be another day or two before she could have visitors, and two weeks before she could go home.

Mrs. Altheimer was sixty-three years old and, except for the aneurism that had been removed from an artery in her chest four days earlier, in excellent health. She came from a large and wealthy family. As soon as the initial trauma of her successful surgery had passed, there would be a flood of flowers, and then of people. It was late April, and the park was green, with buds already opening to the sun.

As a result of her still fragile condition, her more or less constant stupor from morphia, and the normal loss of fluids from massive thoracic surgery, Mrs. Altheimer's life was being sustained by a combination of nutrients and drugs fed to her from a bottle hanging on a stainless steel pole above her head. At the neck of the inverted bottle a nylon valve controlled the steady drip of the fluid into a clear plastic tube, which ended in a needle inserted into the large vein on the back of Mrs. Altheimer's right hand.

An efficient figure in the starched light green uniform of the hospital's nonprofessional staff stepped through the door. She neatly swept up the wrapping of the intravenous set that had been left on the dresser top, then emptied the wastebasket into the large rolling cart outside of the door and put a new plastic lining into the basket, spraying it carefully with disinfectant to maintain the highest possible level of antisepsis.

She put the basket back in the room next to Mrs. Altheimer's bed. As she was leaving, she grasped the plastic tube about halfway up its length, gave it a pinch, then walked out humming cheerfully, to continue her chores in the next room.

The nurse's aide had not squeezed the tube hard enough to damage it. Nor, for that matter, to leave a mark. Nonetheless, the momentary interruption in the gravitational flow of the liquid had caused a vacuum. A bubble of air from the small chamber below the bottleneck, where the fluid dripped into the tube, was drawn into the plastic a few inches below the bottle. As a result, there was no further movement in the tube, pressure built up in the bottleneck, and the drip stopped.

It is not necessarily fatal for a patient receiving an intravenous infusion, or even a blood transfusion, to have the flow interrupted. It occasionally happens spontaneously, especially when a patient struggles with the intravenous set in delirium. It is a matter of time, however.

As it happened, Frances Hoffbauer, R.N., who was covering M446, was otherwise occupied across the hall, applying suction from the built-in wall socket to the throat of a sixteen-year-old girl who was just down from a nose job. She had been in the Recovery Room for the better part of three hours, but the aftermath of the breaking and resetting process had left a constant drip of blood and mucus at the back of her throat. So, despite her semi-comatose condition, she pushed the call button next to her bed every five minutes.

It was a half hour before Nurse Hoffbauer got around to taking another look at Mrs. Altheimer. She moved into M446 in her usual brisk fashion, took a quick look to see if there had been any additions or deletions by an attending physician since she had last been in the room, and then, with an experienced hand and eye, scanned the patient.

In seconds she determined that Mrs. Altheimer's condition had worsened: respiration shallow, pulse faint, a bit of temperature. She looked up at the bottle of dextrose and saline and saw that there were no bubbles. She tapped at the vein in which the needle was implanted, hoping to jar the vacuum and to resume the flow. When that proved unsuccessful, she tried turning the small nylon faucet on and off. She tapped her foot on the shining vinyl floor in impatience. She would have to put in another vein set.

As she turned to leave, Mrs. Altheimer's body gave a little heave; her heart began to flutter and pound in the irregular destructive pattern of fibrillation.

As Nurse Hoffbauer hurried out of the door toward the nursing station, she bumped into Usdan Poonjiajee, M.D. The doctor, a rotund, hairy little man with a gaudy maroon turban, was a resident in cardiovascular surgery from Goa, the former Portuguese colony on India's west coast.

He followed Hoffbauer into M446, took one look at Mrs. Altheimer, and bellowed, "Emergency cart." He pulled the dressing gown away from Mrs. Altheimer's ample bosom, placed the heel of his hand over her heart, and rocking to a rhythm he alone could hear, his eyes closed in concentration, began to exert a downward pressure.

By the time the cart arrived, Mrs. Altheimer had taken matters into her own hands. The fibrillation had stopped, and both her pulse and respiration had regularized. Dr. Poonjiajee wiped his sweaty forehead with a large handkerchief, and administered two injections. He phoned through to Mrs. Altheimer's private physician. After a brief discussion, they decided not to return her to Intensive Care, but rather to order around-the-clock private nursing. Dr. Poonjiajee called the Nursing Office, gave instructions, then hung up and turned to Hoffbauer. "You wait here till the Private comes up. It won't be but a few minutes. And be a good scout, Hoffbauer, put in another vein set yourself."

In all, no one had been really discomfited by the episode. Mrs. Altheimer lived to receive her visitors, and to enjoy her view of Central Park without even knowing how close to death she had wandered. Both the doctor and the nurse had the satisfaction of knowing that they had managed the routine of lifesaving with efficiency and aplomb.

The nurse's aide and the organization that she represented were not unsatisfied either. While Mrs. Altheimer had not died, the opportunity for her death had been improved. And in the course of time, repetition invariably produces results. Slowly but surely, in a pattern so carefully planned that it appeared to be entirely random, the mortality rate at one of the world's great teaching hospitals had been driven toward the point of unacceptability.

# 2

Detective Sergeant Arnold Ross glanced at his watch for the third time in as many minutes. It was eleven-thirty in the morning on an odd Tuesday in the beginning of May. Where the hell were all these people going?

Ordinarily, even stuck in traffic, Ross would have been pleased to be behind the wheel of his new car. For the thirty-nine-year-old bachelor, the red Porsche 924 represented both a symbol of status, and a practical tool in the pursuit of young ladies, which was among his hobbies.

Despite his somber mood, Ross managed a smile. In the two months since he had purchased the car, replacing a run-down, old Chevy, his co-workers in Homicide Zone Four of the New York City Police Department had not let a day pass without remarking on the efficiency of the car, and on the purpose for which it was intended.

The traffic moved a few yards and Ross fell back into his brown study. The Belt Parkway winds from the Battery Tunnel's Brooklyn end around the borough skirting the harbor, and under the Verrazano Bridge, which hurdles the Narrows to Staten Island, then continues on past Coney Island to the Rockaways. After an interminable fifteen minutes, just after the entrance to Jacob Riis Park, the traffic suddenly thinned, and Ross went through the changes into fourth gear. He glanced at the parking lot in front of the beach and muttered to himself, "Them fuckers must all be on welfare," then stepped on the gas and began to weave through the pattern of cars before him. As he drove, he clenched his teeth in rhythm with his hands, muscles knotting in his square jaw, the scar at the corner of his mouth drawing white against darker skin.

Arnie Ross was afraid. As he drove along the parkway to the exit at Farragut Avenue he squeezed his fists, gnarled and scarred from karate, till he lost the feeling in his crabbed fingers.

4

He stopped at the corner of Eighty-eighth Street to compose himself for a moment. Only a dozen blocks from Jamaica Bay, the smell of the salt water was strong in the air. Grass sprouted in the little plots in front of the small one- and two-family houses that predominated in the clean middle-class neighborhood.

He put the car in gear again and turned the corner, stopping before the red brick house with quasi-colonial white clapboard trim, where he spent a sizeable portion of his time. A fig tree leaned from the back yard, dangling its branches above the narrow driveway that separated the Hernandez house from that of their next-door neighbor's. The Cristalis were very old-country. Ross could hear their few chickens clucking faintly from the coop on the other side.

Ross killed the engine and put on a smile. Though he was very broad across the chest and shoulders, and thick through his middle, Ross was agile, rotating his body easily from the low bucket seat and standing without the use of his hands for support. There was no fat in the hundred ninety pounds spread over his five-foot-ten-inch frame.

He walked purposefully to the door, rapped lightly and called out, "Anybody home?"

From the living room beyond the hall, Ross heard a woman's voice reply clearly. "We're here, Arnie. I'll be out in a minute."

Margarita Hernandez appeared in the hall smiling stiffly. Ross could see that her eyes were bright with tears, suppressed with great effort. He glanced at the floor.

"I thought people only had two legs," he said. He could see two small bare feet protruding below the hem of Margarita's skirt, beside her own legs. A ragged diaper trailed on the floor behind them.

"All except Puerto Ricans," Margarita said. "We have four, two big ones and two little ones." There was a squeaky giggle, and a tiny girl in pink pants darted around her mother and grabbed Ross around the knees. "Hi, Uncle Arnie, gi'me a kiss."

Ross lifted the child effortlessly toward the ceiling with one hand, then lowered her slowly toward his face. He made a great show of puckering his lips, and gave her a loud, wet smack on the end of her nose. "All women," he remarked, "regardless of age, find Ross irresistible." He put the child down and kissed her mother lightly on the cheek.

Margarita Hernandez was two years younger than Ross, but it looked like ten. She had a strong Latin face with an aquiline nose and piercing black eyes. A slender body on long legs set off a full bosom. She wore a peasant skirt and sandals. She was cleaning house for her five children and her husband, Detective Sergeant Luis Hernandez, Ross's partner.

Their eyes met for a moment, then they glanced away. Ross licked his lips, drew a breath and asked, "Is she ready?"

Margarita's nostrils pinched together as she fought off the tears again, then she nodded. "She's in the kitchen."

Ross followed Margarita through the living and dining rooms into the kitchen, with the little girl playing about his feet. When he entered the room, he relied on a policeman's self-control.

*"Qué pasa, Mama?"* Arnie said to the old woman hunched at the table.

The woman attempted a tired smile. *"La Pulia, me hijo."* Termites, she said. That's what she always said.

"You ready to go for a spin in my new car? You're not afraid of your reputation in the neighborhood?"

She smiled again and reached out for his hand. He held it still as she used it for support, trying to pull herself upright from the straight-backed chair in which she was sitting. She sat back again. Holding his features expressionless, Ross put his hand under her elbow and lifted her like a feather till he felt that she had her balance. Then he said, "Step this way please, my lady."

Four months ago, Carmelita Lopez Hernandez had been a rotund hundred and sixty-pound bundle of energy. Despite her almost seventy years, she had been a tireless guardian of her only son, his wife and her five grandchildren—and, parenthetically, of Arnie Ross. As Ross guided her through the door, he wondered at the awesome changes that her illness had wrought. Her skin was flaccid and wrinkled, and where he held her upper arm, where once there had been abundant flesh over strength built from a lifetime of hard work, the tips of his thumb and forefinger almost touched. The pumpkin face with the high Indian cheekbones was drawn and the expression slack; the bright eyes were dulled with pain. Arnie opened the car door and lowered her to the seat. She must have lost fifty pounds, he thought.

He went back to the door where Margarita stood with the little bag holding Mama's few possessions. She handed him the bag, then bit her knuckle and turned without a word into the house where the little girl sang cheerfully to herself.

"So, Mama, still think you can ride around the neighborhood in this kind of car and nobody will talk?"

She reached out and patted his hand. "I think my reputation is safe." She winced at a wave of pain. "Papa is waiting for me, as he waits for all of us."

"Even me, Mama?" Arnie said, pulling away from the curb, and toward the highway back to the city.

"You know Papa always believed that God would forgive you for being Jewish because you were a good boy."

"Arnie, he used to say, maybe we can make you an honorary Puerto Rican, and then you can go to Heaven."

They drove quietly for a while with their memories, then Mama added, "But I'm sure it would be much easier if you found a nice girl, got married, raised a family."

"Well, Papa and Felipe are going to have to wait a while for all of us—including you. So don't talk silly," Ross said confidently. "And besides, I'm always finding girls."

Mama sniffed, then turned to look out at the neighborhood spinning by. After a few minutes, she dozed off.

# 3

When Arnie Ross was eleven years old, his father had stumbled through the door of their third floor walkup in Yorkville and announced to his wife, son and daughter, "You know what's moved into this building? Motherfuckin' spics, that's what. Worse'n niggers. Garlic and peppers. Can't even speak no fuckin' English." Then he passed out on the couch.

Eddie Ross was a small-time numbers runner and third-rate gangster. He beat his wife and his children when he was home, which thankfully was not often. He drank and caroused and bullied and boasted, provided almost no money, and the poorest possible example. When Arnie was not quite twenty, Eddie Ross committed some indiscretion, so his employers blew his legs off at the knees with a shotgun. Arnie had reached Bellevue just in time to watch the last of his father's life leak into the stained sheets.

But by that time, Arnie's course had already been set. He had the good fortune to find surrogate parents in the Hernandez family on the ground floor. His mother sank deeper and deeper into a welter of self-pity, and gave up the ghost shortly after Eddie Ross died. His older sister changed her name and left town as soon as she was able. He had not seen or heard from her since. But when Arnie Ross had graduated from Bronx High, he and his best friend, Luis Hernandez, applied to the Police Academy. Together they enrolled in City College, in the evening program, while taking what odd jobs they could to make some money. In time, they passed through the academy near the top of their class and, after seven years of struggle, they earned their college degrees.

The traffic to the city was much lighter than it had been on the way out. It was a little before one when Ross pulled up to the toll plaza of the Brooklyn Battery Tunnel, paid his seventy-five cents, and headed in to Manhattan. Mama Hernandez slept peacefully, her chin on her chest.

Ross emerged from the tunnel, drove past the World Trade Center and the Battery, and headed uptown on the East River Drive. The highway was almost empty, and an occasional pleasure boat skipped by on the river. At the Sixty-second Street entrance, Ross heard the throb and howl of a police siren. He wheeled to the right side of the road and watched as a blue and white squad car careened around the corner, red lights flashing, and sped northward. He automatically reached out to flick on the police band radio hanging under the dash, and leaned on the accelerator.

There was an altercation in progress in a bar on Ninety-sixth and Second. Ross wondered idly why a patrol car from the Twenty-third Precinct was on Sixty-second Street. He shrugged. Probably shopping, or cooping. Maybe they had found a new place to park the car and sleep.

The operator at Police Radio Control squawked some more information and instructions, and the noise caused Mama Hernandez to stir and moan softly. Ross eased up on the gas, and turned off the radio, watching the squad car pull away.

Ross exited at Ninety-sixth Street and headed west. He came to a red light at the corner of Second Avenue, and watched as the two patrolmen pushed a young man with his hands cuffed behind him from a bar toward their waiting car.

Catching every traffic light, Ross worked his way crosstown. Ninety-sixth Street is the line of demarcation between the white, affluent Upper East Side of New York, and the southern border of black Spanish Harlem. An invisible wall separated the sedate, handsome, ten or fifteen storied, granite-faced apartment houses on the south side of the street from the old law tenements and six-story tax payers, with their ugly jumble of exposed iron fire escapes on the north.

At Lexington Avenue, Arnie turned right, and passed the first of the buildings of Manhattan Jewish Hospital. At the end of the complex, Ross pulled up in front of the Morgenstern Pavilion and shut off the engine. As a uniformed doorman approached with a look of protest on his face, Ross flipped down the driver side visor, with its placard identifying him as a Detective Sergeant of Police. The doorman slowed and returned to his post in resignation.

Ross reached out and gently shook Mama Hernandez' shoulder. "Mama, we're here."

She shivered slightly and nodded. "All right, Arnie. I'm coming."

He helped her from the car, and supporting her with one hand, carried the little suitcase toward the door. The uniformed man stepped forward to take the case, holding the door and watching sympathetically as Mrs. Hernandez struggled toward the steps.

"Why don't you wait a minute, and let me get a wheelchair," he asked. "Then you could ride up the ramp in style."

Mama straightened her back and lifted her shoulders. "I can walk just fine, thank you." Clenching her teeth and leaning on Arnie, she carefully negotiated the several steps to the door. He led her to an office marked Admissions. There were two women sitting at paper-cluttered desks. The nearest motioned to him. Mama Hernandez, spent from her effort, sat heavily in the wooden chair at the side of the desk.

"Are you her son," the woman asked.

"A friend," he squeezed Mama's shoulder, "but you could say a son." He pulled up another chair, and sat down. "This is Carmelita Hernandez. She's a patient of Dr. Rogovin's. He said that we would be expected."

The woman checked a list and said, "Yes. A private room. M443. All taken care of. Mrs. Hernandez," she pulled out a sheaf of snapout forms, "have you ever been a patient in this hospital before."

It took a moment for the question to sink in. "No. I never been sick. I never been in a hospital. I had my boys at home. But that was in Puerto Rico."

The admissions clerk looked down at the papers. There were so many questions to be answered, and the little brown lady in front of her was so tired and ill. It would be like pulling teeth. "Sir," she addressed Ross, "can you help out with this a little bit? It'll go faster, and she'll be upstairs where they can make her comfortable that much sooner."

Arnie's memory was jogged by the questions, and the answers came easily to him. Her date of birth, her place of residence, other details were all at the tip of his tongue.

"And family history," the clerk said. "Husband, sons, daughters; I need dates and places of birth."

"Felipe Hernandez, husband," when Arnie mentioned the name, Mama looked up. "He died on October 8, 1971, here, in New York. He was born in Santos, Puerto Rico on January 6, 1904." Arnie remembered Papa Hernandez trying to explain in his comic English the meaning of Three Saints Day. Sixty-seven years of kindness, and hard work, and love: from a job washing dishes for ten cents an hour, to the day he fell asleep forever in the chair behind the counter of his immaculate grocery store.

"Sons. Felipe Hernandez, died October 22, 1953." Big brother, fresh out of Brooklyn College, with his shiny new ROTC commission. Second Lieutenant Felipe Hernandez, Junior, age twenty-two, dead on Porkchop Hill. Bronze Star for heroism awarded posthumously, framed beside his graduation picture over Mama Hernandez' dresser.

"Luis Hernandez, born Santurce, Puerto Rico, April 3, 1939. Detective Sergeant of Police." Arnie gave the address.

The clerk looked up at Ross as if in reproach. He replied brusquely to the unspoken question. "Sergeant Hernandez is testifying at a murder trial."

She stared for a moment at the geometric planes of Ross's face, the straight, narrow-lipped mouth with the white scar running up from the corner toward his right eye, and another above the brow, disfiguring it, the nose a jutting angle, then she looked away. "That's all I need, Mr. . . ."

"Sergeant Ross."

"Sergeant Ross. If you and Mrs. Hernandez will just wait here a moment, I'll have a nurse's aide come to get her."

"Can I go up with her?"

"You'll have to wait for at least a half hour. She has to be undressed and checked, and there are tests that have to be done. All part of procedure," the girl said primly. "And by the way, is she going to sign the financial responsibility form?"

"I gave you her Blue Cross and Medicare cards."

"Yes, but well, we always require. . . ."

"I'll sign it." He scratched his name on the piece of paper. The girl took it from him and reached for the phone at the same time.

As they were waiting, Ross asked, "Is Dr. Rogovin in the hospital?"

"Is he expecting you," she asked with respect. Rogovin was a member of the Medical Board, and was reputed to be the next Director of the Department of Medicine, and Physician-in-Chief.

"Ask him," Ross snapped. The woman looked at Ross's eyes and picked up the phone. In a moment, she turned back to him and said, "He's not in his office, but his secretary is going to have him paged." Ross was starting to make her nervous. There was an anger hovering just below the surface of his composure. She would be pleased when he was gone.

The telephone rang. "You can go up whenever you want, Sergeant Ross. Do you know where his office is? It's in Leibner, that's just across the way from the big new building in the center. Just take the passageway at the back of the entrance hall and follow the signs. It's quite a way. Oh, good," the clerk looked up, "here we are."

A plump, rather attractive girl with Latin features appeared at the door with a wheelchair.

"I'm here to take Mrs. Hernandez up to the fourth floor."

"Well, here she is," the clerk said, cheerfully. The nurse's aide reached out to help Mrs. Hernandez, Ross stood abruptly between them. "I'll do that," he said. He lifted her by the arms to a standing position, and helped her around to the wheelchair.

"I want to walk, Arnie. I don't want to go in that thing."

"Come on, Mama, sit down. That's the way everybody goes upstairs," he said sternly. "Isn't that right, Nurse?"

"Oh, yes, lady. There ain't nothing to be afraid of. *Ven acá.*" Come here, she said in Spanish. Tired and resigned, Mama Hernandez fell into the chair. The girl smiled and said, "Don't you worry, mister, I'm going to take good care of her."

Ross walked with them to the elevator, waited for it, and after kissing Mama on the cheek and watching the door close, he went down the corridor to the internal passageways that connect the pavilions of Manhattan Jewish Hospital.

The elevator stopped once on the second floor, then went on to the fourth. The plump girl rolled the chair out into the hallway, the small suitcase balanced professionally on one of the handles. She stopped at the nursing station and told the duty nurse, "This is Mrs. Hernandez," handing her a packet of computer forms that she had received in Admissions. "M443. Shall I take her down and prep her?"

The duty nurse glanced through the papers and a medical chart that was already prepared and on her desk. "Why don't you do that. Get her into a dressing gown." She checked another typed sheet. "Nurse Hoffbauer's covering her station this shift. She's down there now, and she'll do a workup right away." She leaned forward. "Dr. Rogovin," she said the name in italics, "has personally been here to request that she be looked after."

The girl smiled. "Big brass, huh? Not to worry." She turned down the hall toward the room with the same cheerful confidence she had when she had pinched the intravenous tube in Fanny Altheimer's arm.

# 4

Dr. Saul Rogovin chewed at the stem of his pipe with distaste, and wished for the hundredth time that he had not had to give up cigarettes. It was not a matter of health, he thought, at least not in the immediate sense, but rather of political wisdom. It does not do to preach the evils of cigarettes to patients when there is one dangling from the corner of your mouth. It sets a bad example that might be ill-considered by one's colleagues.

Saul Rogovin wanted his colleagues to admire and respect him, to think and speak well of him. More than anything in the world, Saul Rogovin wanted to be Physician-in-Chief of the Manhattan Jewish Hospital. He put the pipe down on his desk and stood to look out of the window across the concrete courtyard at the soaring skyscraper of the Rosenstein Pavilion, built from the funds accumulated by that family from the sale of prophylactics to the lovers of America. The building thrust itself toward the sky, towering over its neighbors, a monument to the growth and progress of the hospital where Rogovin had worked virtually his whole career.

Rogovin shook the heavy gold identification bracelet on his wrist nervously, and brushed at the pompadour of graying hair above his high forehead. His long, handsome face, normally wreathed in an ingratiating smile, was tense with concern. Above and beyond his preoccupation with his own ambitions, Saul Rogovin was profoundly worried about the state of affairs at his hospital. That is how he thought of it—his hospital; not so much in the sense of possession, as of responsibility. His hospital was suffering from a gently rising curve of patient mortality which, in Rogovin's mind, was beginning to take on disastrous proportions. With the improvement in facilities and equipment, with the addition of the medical school and the improvement in staff, it was inconceivable that things seemed to be slipping this way. The new administrative

14

director of the hospital, brought in several months ago after a successful career in the midwest, had already begun to ask questions for which Rogovin, and the other members of the Medical Board had few answers. It was rumored that the subject might even be brought up before the Board of Trustees, that august body of wealthy and civic minded citizens who both donated and raised the money that made the hospital possible. In the final analysis, they were the last word on the hospital's operations.

Rogovin's ruminations were interrupted by a knock on the door. "Come," he said, in a light tenor voice, unexpected from a man of his height. He pulled at the sides of his immaculate white coat.

Rogovin's secretary opened the door to admit Arnie Ross. Ross reached out his gnarled hand and took the doctor's. It had always been a source of wonder to Arnie that the six-foot-three-inch Rogovin had a high voice and the long slender hands of a woman. Ross noted that the carefully manicured nails gleamed with clear polish.

Rogovin shook Ross's hand firmly. For his part, he was glad to see the roughneck detective whose life he had saved on two separate occasions. "So how's the Jewish Bulldog Drummond?"

"I could be better. I could be worse. Chase any interesting ambulances lately, Saul?"

"Sit down, Arnie. How have you been, really?"

"I've got no big bitches, Saul, except for Mama Hernandez. How about yourself?"

Rogovin shrugged, the corners of his mouth turning down. "Last year, it was an unpleasant divorce. This year I have *tsouris* at the hospital. Do you think God is trying to tell me something?"

Ross smiled. "Speaking of divorce, have you changed girlfriends again?"

Rogovin laughed. Having shed his wife of twenty-six years, with a married daughter living in London, he had become something of a playboy. As he had said, "I can't believe I'm going to die, not after making all of this money, not after listening to Gladys's bitching, not without getting some decent ass.

"The truth, Arnie? I manage, but I get tired."

"What's the matter with the hospital, Saul?"

"Would that I could tell you, my friend. It's a technical problem."

"That a dumb homicide cop wouldn't understand?"

Rogovin shook his head ruefully. "Quite the contrary, Arnie. You would understand perfectly. Right up your alley, you might say. There are too many people dying around here."

Ross leaned forward in the chair. "You serious, Saul? I mean is there something here the department should be interested in?"

Rogovin said, "No, Arnie. It's a lot more complicated than that. And you keep your mouth shut, you hear? We don't need to have somebody getting panicky or blabbing about a hospital problem. I want your word that you won't mention this to anybody."

"Sure, Saul. But, if you need a little professional advice, I'm available."

"Speaking of professional advice, how's the old side holding up?"

Ross probed at the scar over his ribs on the left side. "No sweat, Saul. How long is it, six years now?"

"Something like that. I wish I had time to be a police surgeon again. I used to enjoy piecing you together." He reached out to touch the scar on Ross's cheek. "One of my nicest jobs. Won me the Betsy Ross award." There was a moment of silence while both of them remembered the dark night when Arnie Ross had kicked down the door of the narcotics dealers' room, busy proving—as always—that he was better than anybody else, even if he was Eddie Ross's kid. Rogovin had pinned the slashed cheek together in the dim light, among the three gut-shot bodies that Ross had left behind.

"Tell me about Mama Hernandez, Saul. What's the real story?"

Rogovin picked up his pipe and his professional manner in the same motion. "It's not cut and dried, Arnie. I don't want to lumber you with a lot of medical mumbo jumbo. The symptoms are clear; spots on the lungs, grossly enlarged spleen, certain lymph nodes swollen. . . ."

"What does it sound like? I, mean, what would you guess?"

"You know me better than that. I don't guess. I try to find out. You wouldn't guess about putting a killer away for life. Well, I don't guess about my killers either. All I can tell you is that she will get the best care that this hospital can provide, and that as soon as we know something, we'll notify Lou, or you. How is Lou? I'm surprised he's not here."

"He's in court today. He was the arresting officer in this Vargas thing."

"Isn't that the kid with seventy felony arrests?"

"Right. He had just turned eighteen, and was let loose on five hundred dollars bail by one of our good hearted assholes on the bench. So he went out and just for fun—and three bucks—strangled an eighty-year-old lady."

"They ought to hang the little bastard, Arnie."

Ross shrugged. It was his turn to be professional. "With a little bit of luck, he'll bargain down, and he'll be out on the street, totally rehabilitated in three years, just in time to find another little old lady." Ross stood and put out his hand. "I'm sure you have better things to do than talk to me, and I've got to go to work. Thanks, Saul. Please keep us informed. And if there is anything that I can do for you, you only have to ask."

Rogovin guided him to the door. "I'll keep that in mind, Arnie."

When the door closed behind Ross, Rogovin put the pipe back in the ashtray and sat down. How do you tell somebody you like that his best friend's mother—like his own mother, really—probably is dying of Hodgkin's Disease. Twenty-eight years a physician, and there was still no easy answer to that question. Rogovin picked up the pipe again. There was no sense in jumping to conclusions either. There was a lot of testing and work to do before coming to a conclusion, and many courses of treatment open, in any case.

As Rogovin began to write in his notebook, he briefly entertained the idea of taking Arnie Ross up on his offer. Maybe he shouldn't look askance at professional help. The phone rang, and with the resumption of hospital routine, the thought slipped away.

# 5

At four o'clock Detective Sergeant Luis Hernandez walked down the steps of the Municipal Court Building with his head down and his hands in his pockets. Fortunately, he had been able to avoid the crush of newsmen in the hall outside of the courtroom who had clustered around the District Attorney of Kings County, and the lawyer defending Armando Vargas.

As Hernandez crossed the street and walked uptown toward the square gray Department of Motor Vehicles building with its Depression-age NRA eagles frozen in flight on its corners, he felt a sudden urge to spit. Halfway through the testimony, which clearly illustrated that Vargas had lain in wait for his victim, and the coroner's conclusion that she had been purposefully and thoroughly throttled with a stocking, there was a change in plea, followed by a conference in chambers. Guilty was the new plea. Guilty was the verdict. Guilty of robbery, assault and *involuntary* manslaughter. Sentencing would not be for a month, but the maximum penalty was seven years. He'd be on the street in less than three. Two cheers for justice.

When Arthur Weinberg, the assistant district attorney who had tried the case, had reached out his hand, Hernandez—totally out of character—had slapped it away.

Hernandez gritted his teeth as he turned east toward the river. For a nickel, he thought, he'd walk the other three blocks to Police Plaza, and tell them where to stick their gold plated detective's badge. He could see the tall, awkward red brick building from where he stood.

Kicking at an imaginary can, Hernandez continued his walk till he came to the little square where St. Paul's Church, the oldest Catholic chapel in New York, stands surrounded by a wrought iron fence. He pondered a moment, then walked in. Luis Hernandez was not a religious man in the orthodox sense, but he believed there was a

God. He walked toward the altar, genuflected, then slipped into a pew and knelt on the padded board.

"God," he said, under his breath, "somehow it seems unfair to me. I spent a day in the courtroom that I should have spent taking my mother to the hospital. Because I felt it was my duty. Because that boy is bad to his heart, God. He's no good at all, and he should be off the streets forever. So how come, God, my mother, who should be a saint, is dying, and you let that little bastard off?" Hernandez drew a deep breath, stood and left. On the way out, he dipped his hand in the holy water, turned back toward the altar and crossed himself again. "Sorry, God," he said. "I guess I just lost my temper."

Hernandez headed for his car in the municipal lot on Baxter Street. As he walked, wrapped in his thoughts, a young woman passing in the other direction gave him a look of frank appraisal and tried to catch his eye. Hernandez was six-foot-three, slender, and remarkably handsome, with gleaming, even white teeth and large limpid brown eyes. His nose was short and straight, and his cleft chin perfectly proportioned to his face. Temperamentally, he and Ross were perfect opposites. Where Ross expended much energy controlling a vicious temper, and a wellspring of self-contempt, Hernandez was a model of calm self-possession, rarely raising his voice. Arnie passed his free time in his bachelor apartment rigorously exercising his stone-hard body, chopping at a sand-filled canvas dummy with the calloused edges of his hands and feet. Hernandez read, listened to music and played with his children. For exercise, he ran, loping for miles along the windswept edge of the bay, ordering his thoughts.

Officially, his shift finished at four, but once in his car, having regained his composure, Lou decided to drive up to the Twenty-third Precinct House, where H/Z 4—Homicide Zone Four—is headquartered, to see if anything special had happened during the day. Then, since it was located at 102nd Street, between Second and Third Avenues, he could easily drop over to the hospital to visit with his mother before going home.

It was only a quarter to five when he hit the Drive, too early for the heavy traffic, and he breezed uptown. He parked in front of the filthy, hundred-year-old brick building, and was greeted by the stench of the slums which surrounded it, made more pungent by the warmth of the day. He was pleased to see Arnie's Porsche.

Hernandez waved at the uniformed officer behind the desk and mounted the stairs toward the third floor where H/Z 4 is located. As he climbed past the second floor, Captain Anthony Caputo, the Precinct Commander, stepped out of his office.

"Hi, Lou. Hey, listen, I hope your mother's feeling better. I'll light a candle for her."

"Thanks, Captain, I appreciate it." He continued up the stairs. H/Z 4 had more than an occasional squabble with their uniformed landlords of the Twenty-third, especially with the Precinct Investigation Unit, which often felt that H/Z 4 was stepping on its toes. But when it came to trouble, dark blue was thicker than water, and cops stuck together.

There was no one in the holding pen outside of the office. Either the suspected perpetrators had been hauled downtown or to Riker's Island, or it had been a slow day with no customers for the wire cage that served as the local jail.

Hernandez opened the door to the squad room and looked around. Louie Fischman, his great gut hanging over his belt, was reading *Sports Illustrated*. Round, popeyed Charlie Spinelli, his own traveling partner, was talking into a telephone and taking notes. Marvin Baxter, the new boy, was tending the incoming call phone, and reading through a thick file. Hernandez had been keeping an eye on him during the six weeks since his assignment here, and he liked what he saw.

Baxter was a former St. John's basketball player, six-foot-four with shiny black skin and a shaved head. He was also a graduate of the John Jay College of Criminal Justice, a straight-A student. He seemed to have all the assets to make a good detective. They had given him to Arnie to break in. Hernandez smiled to himself. I hope he has a strong stomach for work, he thought.

He glanced into the Lieutenant's office, but it was after five, and Francis Xavier Flaherty, taking a privilege earned by thirty years of hard work, had already gone home.

The sergeants' office next door was his to share with Arnie Ross. It contained two file cabinets, three chairs, and two desks pushed together and facing each other in the middle of the room.

Arnie was tilted precariously in his springless office chair, with his feet in a drawer, squinting at a leaf from a file.

"Hi, Arn."

"Hi, Roach, how'd it go?"

"Three guesses."

"Misdemeanor. Two weeks at Disneyland."

Hernandez made a sour face. "Right the first time. Involuntary manslaughter. Seven max, out in three."

Ross shook his head in disgust.

"How did it go with Mama, Arnie? How is she? Did you see the doctor?"

"I spoke to Saul, but he just isn't talking. He says it's too soon to know, and he isn't going to guess."

Hernandez looked into Ross's eyes. "It's cancer, isn't it, Arnie?"

"Jesus, Lou, he didn't tell me nothing. Would I shit you about Mama?"

"What do you think, Arnie?"

Ross stood up and put his arm around Hernandez' shoulders. "Come on, Roach, go home. She's getting the best care possible. Saul promised he'd see to it personally, and he's one of the biggest cheeses there. And there isn't a better hospital in the world."

"I'm going to go over and see her. When are you off?"

"Midnight. I'll see you tomorrow. Give her my love."

"Yeah." He opened the glass door, then turned back. "Thanks, Arnie."

Ross waved his hand and picked up the papers.

When Hernandez left his mother, she was sleeping comfortably between sparkling white sheets. The room was big and bright and—thanks to her medical insurance, and Saul Rogovin's intervention—virtually free. He was almost happy when he got in the car to drive home. Arnie was right, she couldn't be in better hands.

# 6

Juanita Marques, the young nurse's aide who had tried to kill Fanny Altheimer, and who had brought Mama Hernandez to her room and tended to her needs so kindly, sat at the edge of the bed naked. Her hands clenched and unclenched involuntarily as she watched Rosario's rigid penis, fascinated as a mongoose watching a cobra weave before it. Though she was barely twenty-two, her breasts were so large and heavy that they fell nearly to her thick waist. Unconsciously, she ran the tips of her fingers down the stripe of black hair that descended from her navel to the thick curly mat of her groin. The lips of her vagina were everted and swollen, moist in anticipation.

"And you know that what you are doing is right, Juanita? That the cause is just? And you will do whatever is necessary?" The voice was deep and hypnotic. Juanita nodded her head. She licked her lips.

"Tell me, Juanita. Tell me with your voice."

"It's what you said, Rosario. They have to pay, pay, pay, for what they have done to our people. It's all a great plot to destroy us. Their medicine is a sham, a trick. We will show the world." She gasped, and reached out for him. He backed away. "Please, Rosario, please."

"And you will do anything, absolutely anything."

"Yes," her eyes began to roll.

He looked around at the others in the room, eight other girls ranging in age from twenty to thirty-five. "Yes," they said, their faces shining with perspiration. "Yes."

Rosario reached out for Juanita and pushed her back on the bed. He lifted her knees and plunged himself into her, thrusting slowly at first, then with increasing speed as she bucked against him until, finally, she screamed aloud three times and lay still, trembling with exhaustion.

Gonzalez withdrew his member, still erect and gleaming from her wetness. The other women clapped and cheered.

He walked past them, touching each of them lightly on the cheek, then walked out of the bedroom.

Once outside, the look of calm slid from his face like a mask, and his features contorted with pain. He slipped quickly into the bathroom and locked the door behind him. He turned on the cold shower and stepped under the blessed water, his testicles knotted, the muscles of his legs quivering. After a few minutes, the discomfort began to subside. He turned the faucet to increase the temperature, and began to soap himself. The increased warmth brought on a resurgence of the pain, and he vomited drily between his feet.

Another five-minute bout of cold water calmed him. He was able to clean himself and step out of the tub. As he dried himself with the towel, he looked in the mirror. He was five-foot-six, and weighed less than one hundred twenty pounds. His wretchedly skinny body was matted with black hair. His penis seemed grotesque and dispro-portionately large. His face was framed in long black hair, falling nearly to his shoulders, and covered with a thick beard and moustache. His nose was small and hooked. His forehead was low and wrinkled. Thick brows joined at the center above deep-set eyes that gleamed with fever, as though he were sick.

He dried himself thoroughly and stepped out of the bathroom into the hall, and to another room containing a single cot, a desk with a gooseneck lamp, a straight-backed chair, and walls lined with books and magazines. Pinned to the back of the door was a blueprint schematic map of the Manhattan Jewish Hospital. Gonzalez folded the towel neatly at the foot of the bed and opened the closet. He dressed and, as he always did before he left the room, he kissed a faded sepia picture that sat by the lamp on the desk. It showed a couple in their late thirties or early for-ties, with seven children ranging from toddler to mid-teens. They were all kneeling. In the background was a lake surrounded by palms and stands of tropical scrub.

As usual, Rosario Gonzalez left first, without saying goodbye. Then after a half hour, the women drifted out one by one.

By the time the last one had gone, Gonzalez had walked down from 117th Street and Second Avenue to Ninety-sixth Street and Lexington. He entered the Waldman Pavilion, walked past the sign that said "Please Check at

Information Desk," and through the door marked "Authorized Persons Only."

At the bottom of the stairwell, heading toward the utilities complex that serves the whole hospital, he passed a guard. The man looked up at the green uniform with "Manhattan Jewish" on the back and "Maintenance" printed on the sleeve top like a mark of rank. Above the pocket, "Rosario" was embroidered in script. "Hi, Rosie," the guard said, "how you doin'?"

"Just fine, Mac. Don't let 'em work you too hard."

They both laughed as Gonzalez walked down the corridor toward his station in the emergency electrical section.

# 7

Emily Stolzfuss climbed down from the Greyhound bus feeling dirty and uncomfortable. Including stops, the ride from York, Pennsylvania, had taken almost seven hours. It was just six P.M. She had gotten up at four-thirty that morning to sneak out to the barn and remove the suitcase she had hidden under some loose straw. Then, walking rapidly, because she knew that dawn would be soon upon her, she headed south from the large farm near Bird-in-Hand, in the heart of the Amish country. She skirted the little towns with the quaint names—Blue Balls, Intercourse, Paradise—that lay between her and her destination.

By eight she had walked almost ten miles. At the side of the road was a stretch of forest that ran a half mile, and was several hundred yards deep. She stepped off the road and walked into the woods. There she crawled under the low, sprawling branches of a spreading fir, pulling the case behind her till she was totally out of sight. She rested for a few minutes; then, looking around to make sure that she was absolutely alone, she took off the gray homespun dress and white apron that identified her as Amish.

By habit she folded them neatly and lay them against the base of the tree. Then she struggled out of the thick gray stockings and black heelless laced shoes. She opened the suitcase and looked at her treasure trove, two cotton print dresses, two pairs of stockings, two pairs of high-heeled black shoes, two pairs of bikini underpants, and a small box of assorted makeup. In a small purse at the bottom of the case was almost eighty dollars. She was going to New York and that cost $11.65 by bus, she knew. The rest would tide her over until she found a job.

Feeling the thrill of adventure, Emily removed her plain cotton and for the first time in her adolescent life, stood naked in a place other than the bathtub. Joyously, she raised her arms over her head and felt the breeze ripple the hair that had not been shaved since it had begun to grow three years earlier, when she was twelve. Her breasts were quite large, and the fresh air caused the nipples to harden. She closed her eyes and breathed in deeply.

Conscious of the time, she broke open the packages of panties and stockings and put them on. She regretted that she had no mirror, but she imagined how she looked. She pulled one of the dresses over her head and adjusted it so that the side seams were straight. It was a little snug, making her protruding breasts even more obvious, but she felt that wouldn't really matter. Leaving her Amish things behind, she walked back to the road and waited for a car to pass. In a few minutes, a group of tourists from New Hampshire rolled by and stopped for her. They were headed in her direction, and she was in York in plenty of time to catch the bus.

The Port Authority Bus Terminal at Eighth Avenue and Fortieth Street is among the most sordid corners of the universe. It is perpetually filthy, littered with the most distasteful human refuse that the Big Apple can provide. Drifters drink cheap muscatel from pint bottles in brown bags, as grifters and hoodlums look for the unwary—to grab a purse, a suitcase, to mug an old man. They hang around in men's rooms to expose themselves to little boys, or to ply their trade with a visiting fireman. But the most important stars of the Port Authority nightlife are the pimps.

These are not the macks with their customized Cadillacs or Lincolns. These are the two-bit variety pimps, hoping to add a runaway to their small stables, so they can eat three meals a day and maybe even afford an occasional snort of coke.

Eddie Biggs was just such an entrepreneur. He stood on the platform and watched Emily Stolzfuss climb down from the Pennsylvania bus, a little tired and sweaty, but young and fresh, with nice big, jiggly tits, with the nipples sticking out of the cheap cotton like signal flags.

Biggs watched her for a while. The dismal atmosphere of the place would numb her, and make her easier prey. She looked about, then headed for the ladies room.

"Shit. Fuck," Eddie Biggs said to himself. "If one of them old bull-dykes is hiding in there, she gonna chew her pussy off, 'fore it's any use to me."

But luck was with him. Emily had stepped inside, used

the john and washed. Her face was decorated like a Christmas tree with the dime store makeup from her bag. The lipstick, unblotted because she had never seen it applied, much less done it herself, was a thick crust on her lips. Her cheeks were clown-like circles of rouge.

Eddie Biggs, resplendent in a light gray suit, black shirt, white tie, with a floppy brim hat to match, sidled over on his $150 red-and-gray lizard shoes. The high, clear plastic heels had pennies embedded in them.

"Hello, sweetie, can I help you carry that bag?"

Emily was startled. In the first place, she had never talked to a black before in her life, though she had occasionally seen a black tourist. In the second, she didn't know anyone in New York, and didn't expect to be talked to.

"No thank you. It's not very heavy." She laughed shyly. "There isn't very much in it." She sniffed. He was wearing some kind of perfume. All the men she knew smelled of sweat or manure.

"Then why don't you let me buy you a cup of coffee."

"I don't drink coffee."

Shit. Fuck. Eddie Biggs thought. "Well, how about a hamburger and a glass of milk? You must be hungry."

Emily looked carefully at him. He seemed to be nice enough, and he was right. She hadn't had anything to eat since the previous evening.

They trotted across to the Burger King, and Eddie bought her dinner. He hoped that she wouldn't eat too much because he was down to his last five dollars.

He smiled at her in his most engaging fashion. She was prime, untouched white pussy. Eight, ten, even fifteen johns a night at an average of twenty-five, less the five dollar kickback to the hotel makes twenty. Hot shit! She could be worth maybe three, four hundred bucks a day for the six months she might last. And it wouldn't cost him but maybe five a day to feed her, and give her a place to sleep. What else would she need money for. And besides, he'd get to break her in.

By the time Emily had finished her hamburger, and listened to Eddie Biggs brag, it was nearly eight-thirty—her regular bedtime on the farm—and she was exhausted. She was strong, and used to physical labor, but the walk and the long day were telling on her.

"Listen, baby, you got a place to stay?"

"No, I just got here. And I'm really tired."

"Well, why don't you come stay with me. Just for tonight that is," he added as he saw alarm in her eyes. "You look all wore out."

Emily stretched, her breasts riding up in the dress. Biggs's eyes bulged. "I guess you're right," she said. "Thanks. But I can pay you. I have some money."

Shit. Fuck. Hot line, mama. "Don't you worry none. Say, what's your name?"

"Ah . . . Amanda. Amanda Jones."

"Right on, Amanda," he said. She laughed at the funny expression. "Let's be on our way." She followed after him, carrying the little bag. I'm on my way, Eddie Biggs thought. I'm twenty-three, and I ain't never had nothing but shit luck, but now I'm on my way.

# 8

Michael J. Connelly, M.D. Associate Professor in Neoplastic Diseases at Manhattan Jewish Hospital looked out at his class of one hundred first-year students with satisfaction. As all of his colleagues were aware, Dr. Connelly's hobby was the history of the hospital. The hour-and-forty-minute lecture would be a combination introduction to his department, which concerned itself with cancer, and the history of the hospital starting from day one. Some swore that it was all memorized.

While Dr. Connelly was talking, a tall, spare man named Alex Klinger was climbing the stairs of the Morgenstern Clinical Center. He was heading for the Neoplastic Diseases Department. In his back pocket was a dog-eared book that he had read several times. It had been given to him by the man he considered to be his intellectual father, Rosario Gonzalez. It was the life of Franz Fanon, a man of medicine, and an important figure in black revolutionary history. Cognizant of the futility of dealing with the white man on his own terms, Fanon the physician preached death and bloodshed as antidotes to white oppression. On the floor below the Department of Neoplastic Diseases, Klinger sat down in a waiting room near one of the administrative offices. He looked aimlessly through several of the magazines on the table in front of him, occasionally checking his watch. People who passed didn't seem to notice him.

"And so," Dr. Connelly continued, "that brings us to you gentlemen, or rather your immediate predecessors. The school officially opened in 1956, to admit twenty-five students. Prior to opening, over five hundred clinicians had been appointed to teaching positions, and finally over fifteen hundred physicians were on the teaching staff. As someone pointed out, in their search for teaching physicians, the Board left no Cohen unturned." He waited for polite laughter. "Now let's deal broadly with my specialty, neoplastic diseases—uncontrolled cellular growth. . . ."

A cleaning woman stepped out of the office into the room where Klinger was waiting and dropped a key into the magazine he was reading, without slowing her step. He waited until she had disappeared, then stood and walked back to the stairway. He continued up one flight till he reached the floor which contained the Clinical Center for Neoplastic Diseases. He walked down the hall with the same air of efficiency practiced by all others there, stopped at a door marked "Absolutely No Entry Except to Authorized Persons," slipped the key in the lock and stepped in. There were four sealed air circulation units operating a closed filter system. He lifted a corner of one of the seal guards with a stiff rubber spatula that would leave no marks. Immediately, the system began to suck in some of the unfiltered air from the crawlspace. Klinger reached into his pocket and pulled out a sealed plastic bag. He spilled the contents onto the ground beneath the open filter, resealed the bag, and put it back in his pocket. He wrinkled his nose. The dead mouse from the lab smelled of decomposition. He put his ear to the door. When he heard nothing, he left the crawlspace, closing the door behind him. There was no one in the corridor, so it was easy for him to slip down the stairwell to the next floor. He looked at his watch again and sat down at the magazine stand. When he heard footsteps in the hall, he slipped the key into a copy of *Time* magazine, rose, and strolled to the elevator bank. The woman who had dropped the key in the first place picked up the magazine and brought it to an office where she carefully wiped the key clean. She put it back in the safety box in which it was kept, and resumed her work.

"The risks are clear," Dr. Connelly was saying to his class. "If you apply such doses of medication in chemotherapy that will be effective against the neoplastic disease, cancers of whatever form, you chance lowering the resistance of the patient to a host of infectious diseases to which he was previously either partially or totally immune. One of the ways in which we have sought to circumvent this circumstance is the creation of a sterile environment. This has been accomplished by the establishment of four Laminar Air Flow Rooms. Here patients can be kept in sterile environments for weeks at a time while undergoing chemotherapy of such strength that if exposed to unfiltered air, they would be disposed toward infection."

The nurse at the station which monitored the condition of the Laminar Rooms was speaking to the next shift leader on the phone when she noticed the changing faces of the dials which tested the air on a continuous basis. At first, there seemed only to be a variance in pressure in Room 3, then a slight change in temperature. Then the bacteriological monitors which gauge the sterility of the air—by burning it in small quantities and reporting on the composition of trace gases—began to flicker ominously. There seemed to be a slight leak of flammable gas somewhere in the atmosphere. The nurse rang off immediately and studied the display. As she began to reach for the phone to call the Senior Staff Physician on duty, the alarm light flashed. There was contamination in Room 3 of a substantial nature which might threaten the lives of the two patients under treatment there.

She reached for the alarm button and called for another nurse down the hall. The whole floor was shut off from the rest of the Center. She was put through to Dr. Connelly, who was just finishing his lecture. He excused himself immediately and left the lectern to the buzzing of the class.

"What the hell is going on up there?"

"The biological contamination count is sky high in Room 3, Doctor."

"Give that to me in parts per billion," he snapped.

"It's in parts per million," she replied.

"I'll be right up. Move the patients out, strip them, get rid of everything they've been in contact with. Yes, I know one is on a vein set. Pull it and throw it away. Take beds out of sterile rooms." He stopped. "Are the other rooms holding up?"

"Yes, sir."

"Wait for me."

Connelly was forty, and a jogger. He took the stairs two at a time to the fifth floor. It took a minute to deactivate the special seal on the door and let him in.

Calm, despite the flush of perspiration on his face, he

directed the transfer of the two patients from Room 3 to Room 4, with the necessary sterile procedures.

"Well," he said, "now there are four of you. Soon you'll all be well enough to play bridge."

He stepped outside the door and stripped off his sterile clothing and mask, and left them on the floor. "What the hell happened?"

"We don't know, Doctor. All of a sudden we got . . . Well, we read you the instruments."

"Okay. Okay. You did a good job. Let's just hope that those poor buggers don't catch anything. Nurse, you'd better get the boss on the phone, and after that, get me Dr. Rogovin, will you." It wasn't till he was behind the desk in his office that Dr. Connelly noticed that his hands were shaking.

# 9

Eddie Biggs was uncertain about the proper logistics of his plan. Should he get a room in one of the sleazy hotels that hover above sex shops and electronic junk stores in the rotting buildings that line the Times Square area? That's where he would have Emily ply her new trade. Or was he better off in a place he knew, like his pad in Spanish Harlem? He sucked at his teeth and walked a half pace behind Emily, appreciating her unfettered buttocks.

"C'mon, baby. I'm gonna take you on another bus ride."

Emily put down her small burden. "Goodness, I hope it's not a long one." She yawned. "I just want to sleep. I'm so tired."

Eddie hesitated again. The hotels were nearby, but she was bound to make some commotion. He considered a cab, but he barely had bus fare. "It ain't far, baby. The bus stop is right up there. We go over to the East Side, and then uptown. You can do some sightseein'."

Emily saw precious little on both rides. Fortunately, they had no wait for the crosstown bus, and only a five minute delay for the Third Avenue bus which they took uptown. There were plenty of empty seats on both buses. On both rides, Emily fell asleep, her head on Eddie Biggs's shoulder. He shook her gently when they got to 108th Street, and led her off the bus. They headed west past a group of uniform red brick city-owned apartments to a block of rundown tenements on the other side of Lexington Avenue. Eddie was on his mettle, torn between enjoying the admiring stares of the stoop-sitters and penny-pitchers, and at the same time frightened that he might lose his catch, either to a bigger man, or to a patrolling policeman.

He drew a deep breath of relief when he mounted the brownstone steps and entered the tawdry building in which he lived. Emily wrinkled her nose at the smell of urine and unwashed humanity that pervaded the dank hall. She was used to the aromas of the barnyard, but her house was a shrine to her mother's cleanliness. She plodded wearily after Eddie Biggs, to the third floor. His room was in the rear of the building. He fumbled with several keys, and one by one turned three locks, reaching around the edge of the door to remove a bar that was attached to the floor and propped against the middle of the door.

The room was small with only one window that gave on an airshaft. A tiny extension contained a halfsized white icebox, and a miniature range with two burners. Both were yellowed and flyspecked. The door to the bathroom hung crazily from the top hinge. The seat on the commode was broken, and the tub was stained yellow and green by the metals leached from the constantly dripping faucet. A dresser was propped up in one corner of the room, a broken leg supported by three paperback books. A kingsized mattress was stretched out on an ancient iron bedstead that Eddie had rescued from the Sanitation Department. There was a small bedside table and a battered lamp.

Eddie Biggs flicked the wall switch, but only one of the three bare bulbs in the ceiling fixture was working. It cast gloomy shadows on the little room and its peeling paint. The tin ceiling was dented and scratched, down to bare metal in some places.

Emily stared in fascination as Eddie closed the door behind them. The only decorations were pictures from the centerfold of *Hustler*. Emily had never seen female sex organs before, not even her own. There were no mirrors in the Stolzfuss house.

Eddie replaced the locks on the door. In the few moments it took him to arrange the pitted iron bar, with one flat side in a slot on the floor, and a corresponding bend in a metal bracket on the door, Emily had fallen fast asleep. She had sat at the edge of the bed, and simply slumped over backwards, arms akimbo, mouth open, snoring softly.

Eddie lifted her skirt and smiled. Emily had nice, long, slim legs. He brushed the back of his fingers gently against the rough blond hair that ran patchily from her shins to the wiry curls that straggled from the close-cut panties and spilled down the inside of her thigh.

He squeezed his crotch. He had a hard-on. It'll wait, he thought. There'll be plenty of time in the morning, when old Amanda Jones—he chuckled at the name—finds out what's going down.

Eddie Biggs went to the drawer of the dresser and rummaged till he found a pair of old nylon stockings. He reached into the deep pocket of his jacket and pulled out a spring-loaded knife, pushed a button and released the four-inch stiletto blade. He cut each stocking in half, then pocketed the knife.

Carefully, he lifted Emily's legs from the floor and turned her toward the long axis of the bed. He found her surprisingly heavy, and even in sleep, her muscles were resilient and strong. Gently, trying not to wake her, Eddie Biggs tied the old stockings to the corners of the bedstead, and then to Emily's hands and feet. He left enough slack so that the tension wouldn't wake her, but she was held fast. He fastened her with slipknots which were loose enough to prevent irritation but, when she struggled, they would tighten painfully.

When she was secure, Eddie went through her bag. "Sheeit," he said aloud, clutching the roll of bills in his hands. He counted the thick wad. "Sheeit," he said again. Jew bankroll—all singles. Still, there were seventy of them, and that was seventy more than he had. He put the wad in the top drawer of the dresser, and pulled the knife again. He unbuttoned Emily's dress, then slit the narrow thongs that held the panties together. He pulled the cloth from under her and stepped back.

Eddie Biggs smiled, rubbed his hands together and stripped to his underwear. He hung his clothes carefully in the almost bare closet near the kitchenette. Then he flicked off the light and fumbled his way to the bed. He hopped nimbly over Emily's prostrate form, and huddled between her and the wall. Anticipating the morning and his improving fortunes, Eddie fell asleep.

# 10

Saul Rogovin didn't hear the alarm until he had pulled on his pants. The beeper that he always carried with him was in the inside pocket of his jacket, and that had been the first thing to hit the couch. Mary Dressler, now quiescent and naked under the covers across the room, was a some-time-moaner and sometime-screamer. He nodded appreciatively in her direction. She was absolutely terrific. He tucked in his shirt and pulled on his shoes and socks hurriedly, then tiptoed into the hall, closing the bedroom door behind him. It was half past eleven.

He strode to the phone in the kitchen of his four-room bachelor apartment on Park Avenue and Seventy-first Street and called the hospital.

"This is Dr. Rogovin."

"Good, Doctor. We've been trying to get you on your page since seven. Is is broken, sir?"

"Oh," he hesitated, "yes, I'm afraid it is. What's the problem?"

"It's Dr. Michael Connelly, sir. He says he must speak to you immediately."

"I have his home number. I'll call him right away."

"Oh, no, Doctor. He's on the sixth floor at Morgenstern. On the Neoplastics floor. He says it's very important."

"All right, transfer me."

"He asked that you use his private line, Dr. Rogovin."

Rogovin took down the number and hung up the phone. He scratched at his chin in puzzlement. What the hell was Connelly doing there in the middle of the night? The beeper continued its insistent call in his pocket. He thought for a moment, then dropped it from shoulder level to the floor. It stopped beeping. He stooped to replace it in his pocket after dialing Connelly and waiting for him to answer.

"Connelly."

"Mike? Saul Rogovin."

"I think you'd better come in, Saul."

"Right now?"

"I don't want to talk on the phone."

"Okay. Fifteen minutes. My office?"

"No, Saul. You'd better come up here. You'll be asked to put on sterile whites."

Rogovin licked his lips. "Contamination?"

There was a pause. "Right."

Rogovin didn't bother with his tie. He rushed out of the door without a thought of the blonde girl asleep in his room. He brushed past the doorman at the entrance to the building, almost bowling him over, and whistled down a cab.

He entered the hospital through the Morgenstern Clinical Center on the Lexington Avenue side. A uniformed guard stepped in front of him as he headed toward the elevator, then backed away as Rogovin flashed his identification badge. He tapped his fingers impatiently against the control panel as the car moved deliberately from floor to floor.

When he finally emerged at five, he was confronted by two more uniformed security police and detained until they had checked with Dr. Connelly, who followed them out of his office into the hall.

Rogovin said nothing until he was inside Connelly's office. "Mike, have you lost a screw? What are you doing?"

"I'm following Joe Nichols' orders."

Rogovin swallowed. Even being an old friend, one did not tamper lightly with the decisions of the Director of Neoplastic Medicine of Manhattan Jewish. Nichols was a brilliant theoretician, the center's leading voice in the war on cancer, and a major supporter of Saul Rogovin in the political infighting at the staff and management level. He was also highly temperamental and eccentric. Rogovin changed tactics, "Okay, okay. What's biting him now?"

Connelly snorted. "Biting him? I'll show you what's biting him. Step right this way." Connelly led Rogovin by the arm to the supply room at the back of the hall. "Come on, Saul," he said, handing him sterile overalls from a white cabinet. "And you'd better put these on, too." He gave him a sterile cap and a filter mask that fit over the nose and mouth, and a set of surgical gloves. Wordlessly, he donned a set of his own, then motioned to Rogovin and headed toward the Laminar Rooms.

"We've had a failure in the air system of one of the rooms."

"How did that happen?"

"I'll show you. Joe said he wanted you to see it yourself before he decides whether or not to come back. He's on his farm in New Hampshire. He'd planned to stay a week."

Rogovin was about to ask what was serious enough to interrupt a long-planned vacation when they arrived at the door of the service corridor. There was another security man standing in front of it. Rogovin pulled Connelly aside. "Who authorized all of these specials?"

"I asked Gaines in the Security Office."

"Did you tell him why? He'll be shooting his mouth off over all creation."

Connelly smiled. "I told him you had instructed me to call, Saul. He didn't say a word or ask a question. I'm not sure you realize how important you are."

Rogovin choked and turned back to the door, motioning the security man out of his way. Connelly took a key from his pocket, opened the door, and ushered Rogovin before him, then slipped inside himself.

Two reflector lamps had been set up in the corridor, which was splashed with white light. The relatively narrow space was occupied by two other people.

"Hello Saul," Dr. Morris Nassiter said through his mask. He was sitting on his heels with his back against the wall. "This," he gestured to an obviously younger man squatting next to him, "is Melvin Farbstein. It seems somebody has stolen one of his rats."

"Mouse, Doctor," Farbstein said.

"Oh, yes, mouse."

Rogovin wrinkled his nose at the musty odor. *"Und so weiter?"*

Nassiter stood awkwardly, perspiration gleaming on his bald crown, only partly covered by the cloth cap. *"Und so* is that the mouse is loaded with coliform bacteria— enough to give diarrhea to the entire Mexican Army."

Rogovin looked at the floor. They had put the dead mouse, stiff and bloated, in an airtight sterile container used to handle contaminants. Nassiter continued, "I've taken the precaution of having this entire floor and the walls washed and sprayed." Noting Rogovin's concern, he said, "By Dr. Farbstein. Not to worry. No one knows about our pet," he motioned at the box, "except for the people in here and, of course, Joe Nichols."

Connelly took Rogovin's arm and led him toward the air conditioning ducts. "Somebody," he said, "pried up that cover. Then dropped the mouse."

Rogovin nodded, hesitated, then said, "Can the mouse be left there in the box? Without harming anyone, or risking further contamination. Morris?"

The Director of the Microbiology Laboratories scratched pensively, then shrugged. "In that box he represents no threat."

Rogovin turned to Connelly. "Does that broken cover represent any threat to the patients?"

"No. The room is contaminated. It has to be resterilized. I think everything in it should be destroyed."

"Me too," said Nassiter. "I wouldn't want to think that anyone could come in contact with what our mouse had. Very unpleasant."

"Okay. This is the drill. There is to be no discussion of the matter with anyone. There are to be no written reports except the one that describes the failure of the system because of a mechanical fault in an air conditioning duct seal, and naturally, the report covering the movement of the patients, and any necessary medical records."

Connelly looked at him over the mask. "Are you saying you want this hushed up?"

"Absolutely. I want this to go nowhere."

"For Christ's sake, Doctor. Are you going to keep this from the Medical Board? I mean, this wasn't an accident, you know. What do you intend to do?"

Rogovin held up his hand in exasperation. "Dr. Connelly, please. What do you think this is? A movie? And to save my reputation I don't want to tell the police? What am I—Frederic March? What I am saying is that the mouse should be left where it is, in the box. The cover of the duct should be left the way it is. That's so the police can look. What I don't want is for anybody to get involved who doesn't need to be. Maybe what we have here is a crackpot. Maybe something worse. We don't know. So let's get professional help. I was a police surgeon for a long time. I have a few friends. Let's see if we can get to the bottom of this without getting the newspapers and the networks on our backs, and scaring the shit out of everybody."

The four physicians walked out of the hallway and locked the door behind them. "I want someone on this door until I say otherwise," Rogovin said to the guard. "If you need to take relief, then call someone." Then smiling, "We just want to make sure that none of the equipment in there is tampered with." The guard nodded indifferently.

The two biologists, Nassiter and Farbstein, threw their garments into a disposal chute marked with a red radiation-warning triangle, then headed toward the elevators. Rogovin and Connelly followed suit. "Listen, Mike, you call Joe and tell him to stay there, and that I'll call him tomorrow or the day after, as soon as I know something."

Connelly nodded, then looked up and said, "You wouldn't kid me, Saul—about the movie?"

Rogovin stopped smiling. "I'm scared to death. If we don't find out what this all about, we may have a recurrence. I'm going to call my friend right now."

Rogovin bid Connelly goodnight and watched him walk through the lobby to the street. Rogovin rode to the basement and wove his way through the labyrinthine corridors that wind around the basement of Morgenstern, around the base of the Rosenstein Tower and across into Leibner. He took the elevator up to his office. The floor was dark, except for a red safety light over the stairs. He flicked a switch and waited till the starters ignited the neon, then found his room. He sat down heavily behind the desk and thumbed through his personal address book. He dialed the number of the 23rd Precinct, and asked for Ross.

# 11

Rogovin and Ross sat together in the small diner on Madison and Ninety-seventh, stirring their coffee.

"You'd make a terrific detective," Ross said, around a bite of Danish. "You know that, don't you, Saul? I mean, it's not everyone who could claim not to have disturbed the evidence after having the scene scoured with disinfectants."

"You'd prefer an epidemic?"

Ross shrugged and finished the sticky cake. "Eventually, I'm going to have to report this, Saul."

"Eventually could be a while, not so, Arnie?" There was a touch of pleading in the voice.

"Aw, bullshit, Saul. I'll keep it under my hat as long as I can, for your sake. But you're telling me that you see this incident as part of something larger. If it is, you could be jeopardizing all of the people in the hospital by not having a full-scale investigation."

"Okay. Agreed. But let's say that this is some kind of freak . . ."

"Freak what, Saul? Somebody pried up the edge of that seal and dropped a dead mouse underneath it in the hope of contaminating the patients in that room. What's that? Unfortunate circumstance?"

Rogovin shook his head in agreement. "All right. Small odds that it could be coincidence. But let's say the mouse just got loose, and that the air conditioner seal was the problem of a forgetful worker—or even a nut—with no particular evil intent."

Ross waved his hand at the sleepy old man leaning against the counter and asked for a check. "You want to treat it that way? You think that's valid?"

Rogovin hesitated and said, "It seems as likely to me as the idea that somebody would be smart enough to know what that mouse was full of, and still dumb enough to open his cage and take him from the lab to the sixth floor of Morgenstern."

As they walked out, Arnie Ross lifted his scarred eyebrow and looked at Rogovin skeptically. "All right, Saul. I'll take a private, off duty look. You get all the crap that you find suspicious together in one pile, and I'll see if I can find a pattern. Maybe I'll ask Lou, too."

"Okay, Arnie. But please, no further than Lou. Not unless you talk to me first."

Ross motioned to Rogovin to get into the Porsche parked at the curb.

"I'll take a cab. It's out of your way. And Arnie, thanks."

As Ross pulled away from the curb, and Dr. Rogovin hailed a cab, Alex Klinger tossed fitfully in his disheveled bed. The girl sleeping with him woke up and asked, "Something the matter?"

He felt that he couldn't catch his breath, and after periods of quiescence, he was racked by violent intestinal cramps. His face had a gray cast, and he had begun to perspire, leaving his skin cold and clammy to the touch.

The girl got up from the bed. She was sixteen, and slender. Her name was Iris Alonzo. She had three brothers and five sisters.

"Thanks for fixing me the chili, Alex. It was great." She smiled. "So was the rest." She reached out to touch his face, then pulled her hand away. "Hey, maybe you better call a doctor, Alex."

He managed a smile. "I work in a hospital. I know too much about them. I'll be okay. See you soon."

"Right." She slipped out and closed the door behind her.

Maybe it was the goddamn chili, he thought. A spasm gripped him, and involuntarily his bony knees snapped up against his abdomen. His face was distorted in a rictus of pain. He felt a terrible need to move his bowels. Balancing himself carefully into a sitting position, he pushed at the bed with the heel of his right hand, clutching his belly with the left. He forced himself upright, and staggered toward the lavatory. Almost at the door he was doubled by a stab of pain. As the upper part of his body came forward, he hit his head on the door handle, cutting his forehead severely. As he fell to the floor, vomiting, he lost control and soiled himself.

# 12

Ross, dressed only in an athletic supporter, took two quick strides across the floor of his sparsely furnished bedroom, and leapt into the air, his body parallel to the ground. At the apex of his flight, he coiled his legs and snapped them out again. His heels struck the sand-filled canvas dummy at the base of its bottle-like neck. The top of the bag rebounded from the blow, almost doubling on itself. Ross turned nimbly in the air and landed in a crouch facing the bag, his blunt fingers crabbed like claws.

He straightened up and reached out to pull the head of the canvas dummy upright. Had it been a man, he would be lying dead, his jaw crushed and his neck broken. Ross glanced at the clock on the dresser. It was ten-thirty. He had been exercising for an hour. He showered quickly and dressed in slacks and a pullover wool shirt, then picked up the phone.

"Hernandez," the voice answered.

"Hey, Louie, want to waste a couple of hours?"

"I was going to visit Mama. I'm on four to twelve."

"You can do both at the same time, and in the same place. I want to go up to Rogovin's office."

"Does he know we're coming?"

"It's a kind of command performance. Look, why don't we meet in Mama's room? About an hour?"

"Suits me."

Ross straightened up his three-room flat, looked out of his tenth floor window onto Eighty-sixth Street to see what the rest of the world was wearing, then slipped on a blazer and went out.

Arnie nodded to the doorman as he strolled out into the fresh spring air. The new apartment had come with the new car. Maybe Mama Hernandez was right. Time to settle down and stop farting around. He patted at his stomach. He crossed the street and walked to First Ave-

43

nue, taking a short list from his pocket. He spent fifteen minutes in the D'Agostino's on the corner buying two full bags of groceries. When he was done, he walked quickly across the congested avenue and entered Everett's Liquor. Everett, a tall Brooklyn Italian named Vinnie, greeted him effusively.

"Catch any of my relatives today?"

"You know I'm not in the guinea business. Nothing but small-time shit for me." He looked up at the shelves. "I got no gin, no scotch, and no vodka."

"You're just shit outta luck, Arnie."

"Get somebody to stick this upstairs for me, will you?"

"Anything for the icebox?"

"Yeah, eggs, butter, milk . . ." Arnie waved cordially, said thanks and left. Vinnie would put the bags in his wine cooler, then when the delivery boy came in, he would have the bags and the liquor brought up to Arnie's apartment. As though afraid he would forget, Vinnie took out a massive ring, studied it for a moment and extracted Arnie's key.

Arnie walked back to his building and down into the garage to get the car. He headed east. There was an accident on York holding up the traffic so he went a block out of his way to East End. He saluted irreverently as he passed Gracie Mansion, the Mayor's official residence, then turned west on Ninety-second. He smiled in satisfaction. He had gone around the bottleneck. It took him five minutes to negotiate the rest of the trip to Manhattan Jewish Hospital. Musing aimlessly, he went a block past the Morgenstern entrance on Lexington Avenue. By the time he had awakened to his mistake, he had driven two blocks more, and decided to park the car and walk back to the hospital. Halfway to the corner, Arnie, looking down at the sidewalk, bumped into a man walking in the other direction. Only quick reflexes saved him from falling.

"Whyn't y'all watch out where the fuck you goin', man?"

Ross clenched his jaw in irritation and looked up. And up. The black man in front of him, dressed in smelly mismatched clothes, was the size of a bear. Ross stepped back and smiled.

"Sorry, sir."

"Y'all betta watch yo' ass, honky," the man sniffed, and continued down the street toward the station house.

Ross continued his walk to the hospital with a smile on his face. That was Sergeant Albert Ruggles of the Street Crime Unit who had almost flattened him. Ross made a note to ask Albert if he had heard anything about a nut with a hard-on for Manhattan Jewish Hospital.

The door of Mama Hernandez' room was slightly ajar when Ross arrived. He knocked softly, and when there was no response, he edged the door open, and peeked in.

A white-clothed figure was bent over Mama Hernandez, straightening a pillow under her head. From his angle, he saw a firm well-shaped rear end, and two long and shapely legs tightly encased in sheer white stockings. The nurse bent forward a little further, balancing on one leg. Her skirt rode up, and Arnie clucked in involuntary appreciation.

Startled, she turned and straightened. She was of medium height with red hair supporting a tilted nurse's cap. Bright blue eyes blinked behind octagonal tortoise shell glasses. A small freckled nose peeped out above a mouth compressed in surprise. Ross smiled and followed the impressive contours back toward the lovely legs. The elfin mouth fought a smile and the freckles collided in a blush.

Arnie whipped out his shield and said, "I am Detective Sergeant Arnold Ross, Nurse. I have come to take custody of the dangerous criminal in this room."

The nurse, who was in her early twenties, cocked her head and blinked wordlessly as Ross pulled a set of cuffs from his hip pocket and strode toward the bed.

He reached out for Mama Hernandez' hand. She opened her eyes when she heard the familiar voice. Seeing his hand, she took it. He clapped the cuff on her wrist.

"Carmelita Hernandez," he intoned, "in accord with the law of the State of New York, I am placing you under arrest. You have the right to remain silent until you have consulted an attorney, but whatever you say may be used against you in a court of law."

With a straight face, Mama asked, "What is the charge?"

"Overfeeding a police officer." He undid the cuff with a snap of his practiced fingers and leaned forward to kiss her forehead. He turned back to the nurse and smiled. "And what's your name, little girl."

"Little Red Rosenberg," she snapped with irritation. "And you're under arrest, too."

"Huh?"

"Yeah," she said over her shoulder as she stormed out of the room, "arrested development."

Ross shook with laughter and turned back to Mama. "They treating you good?"

She nodded. "Very nice, Arnie. Very nice. The doctor came to see me and told me there would be lots of tests and that I should be patient." She put her hand to the side of her neck. There was a swelling that Ross had not noticed before. He fought the look of concern from his face. She sighed and patted his hand. "I asked to see the priest. He's very nice."

The door opened again and Lou walked in. He was carrying a bunch of black-eyed Susans.

"You stop that," Mama said. "You stop spending your money like that."

Lou kissed his mother gently. "They didn't cost anything, Mama. They're from the garden. The kids picked them."

She nodded, suddenly tired.

They talked for a few minutes more with forced good humor, then the nurse returned. "Gentlemen, this nice lady is going to have some lunch and she needs some rest. It's time to go." She let them say goodbye, then ushered them firmly out of the door into the hall.

A few steps down the corridor, Ross said, "See you around, Red."

"Not if I can help it, you juvenile delinquent. And don't call me Red."

"What can I call you?" he asked.

She turned on her heel and walked away.

"Never mind," Ross said, "I'll think of something."

He was brought back to reality by Hernandez, leaning glumly against the wall. "I think she looks lousy, Arnie."

"You're not a doctor. You're a spic. There's a difference. Come on," he threw his arm over Lou's shoulder. "Let's go see Saul. Maybe he has a better educated guess."

# 13

It was probably true, between prayers on holidays and work the rest of the year, that Emily Stolzfuss had never slept so late in all her life. For Eddie Biggs, sleeping late was a way of life. He didn't wake until he felt the bed shake as Emily struggled to get up, unmindful of the bonds that held her wrists and ankles to the bedstead. She was cramped and uncomfortable, and had to go to the bathroom. She blinked and struggled some more, then stopped for a moment to survey her situation. Propping herself as best she could on her elbows, she saw that her dress had ridden up to her waist, and that the thick blond triangle of her pubis was exposed, her legs held apart by the thongs at her ankles so that she could see the hairs which straggled down the inside of her thighs and up toward her navel.

Eddie Biggs snorted stupidly and raised his head from the bed. He sat up and rubbed his eyes, looking at Emily both before and after, as if he were unsure that finding her were not a dream.

He smiled ingratiatingly and said, "Hello, baby," then put his hand gently on her crotch. "How you doin' this morning? You all ready to enjoy yo' first day in the big city?"

Emily, unable to continue in her upright position because her wrists were tied, fell back against the bed, looking at the ceiling, her heart pounding.

Thinking that her motion meant acquiescence, Eddie probed her, further spreading her lips and trying to penetrate her with his fingers. She was dry with fear and tension, and he succeeded only in hurting her. When she realized what he was trying to do, she wrenched her body away from him, yelling, "No, don't do that. You're hurting me." He twisted her thighs so that she was on her back again, and said, "Now we can do this nice or we can do it nasty. You are gonna thank me. You just gonna love it. Here, look at this. You gonna love it."

He pulled off his shorts in one motion, exposing his already erect penis. He reached his hand toward her groin again, bending forward to see what he was doing. She twisted her body forcefully, trying to escape his touch. Inadvertently, because she could not see what she was doing, her knee struck him in the forehead. The blow was numbing. Eddie was knocked from the bed and fell in a heap on the floor. He lay there, stunned.

Emily, shivering and white-faced with fear, struggled with all her strength against her bonds, succeeding only in making them painfully tight. She licked her lips and said, "I'm sorry. I didn't do it on purpose. Only you scared me. I just want to go. I . . . I'll pay you for the room, and pay you back for dinner . . . and the bus rides, too. Only please, let me go. Please. Please let me up." She was even too frightened to cry. "I . . . I have to go to the bathroom. Please, let me up."

"Bitch cunt," Eddie Biggs muttered from the floor. He propped himself on his elbow and gingerly touched the growing knot above his right eye. "Honky motherfuckin' bitch cunt." He pulled himself to his feet and walked into the bathroom. He cursed as he regarded himself in the fly-specked mirror, then washed his face in the tepid rusty water from the corroded faucet above the stained sink.

He walked to the dresser and took the long switchblade knife from the drawer. When he was within Emily's view, he pressed the button. The spring hissed, and the four-inch blade seated itself with a satisfying click.

Emily drew in her breath, her eyes bulging with fear. Eddie Biggs put the edge of the knife against her stomach and slid it slowly upwards till it touched the material of her dress, then in a single motion, holding the flimsy cotton taut with his free hand, he slit the garment to the neckline, then tore it away. Emily's breasts spilled from the torn cloth, nipples erect from the sudden contact with the air, her chest heaving in undisguised panic.

Biggs put the knife back on the dresser and pulled off his tee shirt. He was already aroused by Emily's nakedness, and fear. She looked aside at him, tall and thin, his black body runneled with perspiration, erect as a stallion in the breeding shed.

"You gonna be nice, now," he asked.

"Please, I have to go to the bathroom."

Both fear and the course of nature pushed at her bladder.

He walked towards her, incongruously dressed only in his socks. "Suck it." He thrust himself at her. She rolled her eyes and turned away. "Suck it," he insisted, raising his voice.

"No. Leave me alone. I have to pee. Please. Please. Don't hurt me."

He grabbed her hair and twisted her head toward him, but she struggled so hard he could not control her, despite her bonds. "All right," he said. "You can go right where you is at. You can piss and shit all over yourself. And then you gonna fuckin' clean it up. Cause you ain't goin' no place till you comes across. You got that?" He raised his fist in the air and brought it down like a sledge hammer just below her navel. Emily heaved, choking in pain, and on the edge of consciousness felt biting shame and a warm wetness trickling on her legs.

# 14

Abner Stolzfuss was in some ways a liberated Amish. While he hewed carefully to the traditions that his Mennonite forebears had brought with them from Germany two centuries ago, he was a shrewd businessman and a superior farmer who accommodated within that strict framework as much of the twentieth century as the Law and the Lord would allow. Thus, while he plowed with horses and mules, and traveled about in the gray box-like Amish wagon powered by a fine pacing mare, when it came time to go to York or to Lancaster to choose stock, or to buy forage, he would ride as a passenger in the truck of one of his suppliers.

Telephones and electricity were strictly forbidden in Amish households. In fact, tour guides in the area teach the millions of tourists, who come each year to be charmed by the Plain Folk and stuffed by their cooking, that the surest way to tell an Amish dwelling is by the absence of wires from the phone and utility poles which still line the byways of Lancaster County, Pennsylvania. On the other hand, the Lord did not inveigh against the Pennsylvania Bell Telephone Company itself. As it happened, the phone company chose to place a telephone booth on the country lane just opposite the door of Abner Stolzfuss's house—and with a remarkably loud bell that could be heard even within that strict Amish home.

Abner Stolzfuss drew the line of accommodation with the outside world in indelible ink just beyond the reach of his nine children. Of all of them, Emily was the most troublesome to him. She was a good enough worker, as his wife Rachel often said, and she didn't complain about her tasks or her long hours. She was no grumbler. Nor was she outwardly disobedient to her stern father, gaunt and gray and bearded in black homespun and hat.

Perhaps it was schooling. Abner Stolzfuss had been in

the forefront of the battle against the State of Pennsylvania in the matter of Amish schooling. There had been a compromise. Amish children would go to school through the eighth grade. But the schools would be Amish run, and for Amish only. The State Department of Education would inspect the schools and the curriculum regularly. There would be literacy, and a minimum of arithmetic and American history would be taught, but there would be no contamination from outside influences.

Emily had plunged eagerly into her lessons. She had been at the top of her class from the day she entered. Rather than rejoicing—as did other children—when school was over, Emily cried. Abner Stolzfuss remonstrated with his wife over the unseemly interests of her daughter and, on more than one occasion, he meted out corporal punishment to Emily as well. With the almost embarrassing burgeoning of her body, he had hoped that soon she would be suitably chosen and wed. A full belly and a household to care for would bring her back to earth.

Afraid of her emotions, Emily Stolzfuss had not written a farewell note to her parents the day she sneaked away. Her father was in evil temper when, upon arising at five and going to the room that served as both dining room and church hall for his family, he discovered that Emily was not about. He shouted mightily that if she were a slug-a-bed as he suspected, it would go hard with her. He sent one of her younger sisters scurrying to the bedroom to rouse her. The child already knew that Emily was not there. Afraid to say anything, Rebecca Stolzfuss, aged nine, ran to the room she shared with two of her older sisters and made a great show of turning back Emily's quilted comforter, and even looking under the rope-sprung bedstead. Then she ran back to the dining room.

"She's not there, Father."

"Was she there last night? The truth, child."

"Yes, Father."

He turned stern eyes down to the Good Book. "Let us pray."

For the bulk of the morning, a kind of low-level tension pervaded the Stolzfuss farm. Nothing was said. All chores were done according to the usual schedule, save those normally assigned to Emily. These were redistributed among the other girls by Mother Stolzfuss.

By noon, Abner Stolzfuss felt a genuine concern. He

called his eldest son Isaac, who was twenty, married, and already the father of one child.

"Isaac. Quietly, you will saddle the mare. My mare, Isaac. And you will look at every foot of this farm. You will miss no building, no hayrick, no fold or pen. Is that clear?"

Isaac, almost six-foot-four and weighing two hundred forty pounds, looked upon his father with awe. "Yes, sir." He started to turn away, then resolutely cleared his throat and turned back. "Father, do you think she might have run away?"

The old man looked at him sternly. "Let us hope that she would not bring shame on her household and a shunning on herself." He turned on his heel and walked back to the house.

It was nearly four when Isaac found his father uncharacteristically hunched over his ledgers, a job usually reserved for evenings, especially in the spring planting season.

Abner looked up at his son, dusty and perspired. "She's not on this farm, Father, unless she's playing cat and mouse with me. I've been over every foot." He wiped his brow and sat. There were almost four thousand acres to the Stolzfuss farm. For Lancaster County, it was a very large enterprise and, since it was fully paid for, probably worth several million dollars.

Abner Stolzfuss slammed the heavy book closed, raising dust from its ancient cover. Isaac took a step backward. "Hitch my cart. I'll want the new bay." Abner strode into the house to change his clothes. His son went to the barn and led the gleaming horse (rescued from the harness track in Philadelphia two months earlier) toward a ring in the stable wall. He tacked him, then harnessed him to the traces of the cart and brought him to the front of the house. His father appeared in a moment.

"Get Abraham and Joshua."

The three eldest sons of the Stolzfuss family appeared in five minutes, panting. "You," he pointed at Isaac, "will ride into Intercourse. Joshua, to Bird-in-Hand. And you, Abraham, toward York. Look for your sister. For the moment, you are to inquire politely, but without raising suspicion. It is perfectly possible that for reasons of her own, she has chosen to lark about without letting us know. If you find her, you may well tell her that I am sore displeased, but that . . ." he stopped and swallowed," . . . I would be grateful if she would return home so that we might discuss her unseemly behavior." They turned to leave, but he gestured and they looked back at him. "You might add that I do not wish to punish her . . . Only that I wish her to return." Isaac wanted to reach out to his father, but the gulf of a lifetime separated them. The brothers departed on horseback. Abner took his cart and moved smartly through the gate toward the county seat at Lancaster, nine miles away.

It was ten-thirty when the men of the Stolzfuss family, dirty and disheveled, gathered around the table among the guttering lamps and candles. The boys ate with gusto. Grim and hollow-eyed, the patriarch sat unmoving. They had not seen her. Nor had anyone else. He sent them off to bed, exhausted. He rose and took the great family Bible from its place in the sitting room, turned past the pages that marked the genealogy of his family since the book had been acquired over a hundred years ago, and to the parable of the Prodigal Son. When he had finished, his eyes were misted with tears. He rose to go to bed. In the morning he would return to Lancaster to see the police.

# 15

While Abner Stolzfuss sat in the corridor outside of the office of the Sheriff of Lancaster County, Pennsylvania, and his daughter lay sobbing and gagged, tied to a bed in a Harlem tenement, Lou Hernandez and Arnie Ross sat in the office of Saul Rogovin, M.D., listening intently.

Rogovin made a pyramid of his fingers on the desk. "As I told Arnie last night, Lou, I don't want to speculate. All we have is a few preliminary test results, and an array of symptoms, none of them necessarily conclusive."

Hernandez' jaw set in a firm line and he cleared his throat. Arnie sat back in his chair. Not good signs. He wished he were elsewhere. "Doctor Rogovin."

"Yes, Lou?" Saul was surprised at the formality.

"Is it because we're spics?"

"Huh?"

"I mean is it because we're spics that we won't understand the intricacies of a modern medical explanation? Now, I know that my mother is barely literate—never went to school much at all—but I'm a college graduate. And," his voice barely rising in volume but growing magnitudes in intensity, "I don't appreciate all this doctor-knows-best bullshit. So if you would please keep that in mind and give me an intelligent appraisal of what my mother has, I would be very grateful." The last word was a growl.

Rogovin flattened his palms on the desk and looked across at the finely chiseled features; there was just a breath of Indian in the slight slant of the eyes that were black with anger. Rogovin nodded. "If I had to make a bet—swelling of the glands in the armpits and the groin, and now the neck, weight loss, high white count," he shrugged, "I wouldn't guarantee it, but Hodgkin's Disease."

"Cancer?"

"Cancer of the lymphatic system, if you want it straight."

Hernandez drew in a slow breath, and exhaled. "Is it curable? How long?"

"You wanted a quick answer. That's all you're going to get because that's all I have to give you. Based on what I know, she might—I said might—have Hodgkin's Disease. If you're going to have it, you should get treatment here at Manhattan Jewish, or at Memorial because that's where the best Neoplastic Medicine in New York is being practiced. Cure rates? I don't know. Is it stage one? Is it stage four? That gives you a range from seventy or eighty percent recovery to a death sentence. The time, a week, twenty-seven years, two months."

Suddenly, Lou felt very foolish. "I'm sorry, Saul."

Rogovin shrugged. "We're in the same business, Louie. Chasing killers. Every once in a while a cop runs across some *putz* holding up a store and drops him in his tracks. Victory for the good guys. Mostly, it's walking, interviewing, mug shots, parole records, the whole mess. Boring. It's the same business. When I have more evidence, I'll let you know. And I promise to treat you like a grown-up."

Lou put out his hand. "Friends?"

Rogovin shook it and laughed. "Friends."

"Your turn, Saul," Arnie said.

"What can I say that you don't know? There is something very wrong here. Let's say we treat maybe 130,000 people every year. Out of that, about 30,000 are in-patients, and they spend about two weeks each on average in the hospital. That's about 400,000 days of care of in-patients. The rest, the other 100,000, is split between the Emergency Room and the Clinic. That's the operating base. There are also subtotals, pediatrics, surgical, like that. Every year about 500 people die. So and so many in this department, so and so many in that. There are reasons and justifications. Every death is looked upon, not as a happenstance, but as a combination of unique tragedy and scientific event. No, you mustn't think that because death is a permanent resident here we treat it casually. That's why, when we see a change in the mortality rate in a department, we fall on it like a ton of bricks. Gross Conference, Autopsy, Medical Board. We ask what the hell is going on here. Always there is a reason."

"What's the reason this time?"

"Nothing. Absolutely nothing. The incidence is random."

"Maybe you have a breakdown in policy. Maybe there is something that you are doing wrong as an institution."

"That," Rogovin admitted, "is the logical conclusion. There is something wrong with the management of this hospital. It is not keeping faith with the community because we are starting to see a rise in mortality and patient accident rates, not only above our own historical levels but, in addition, beyond the norms of the American Association of Hospital Management, and similar institutions in town."

Ross got up and paced a moment, then turned to the doctor. "Saul, have you ever thought that maybe—I mean really thought in your *guderim*—in your guts—that maybe you people are really fucking up? That it is your fault?"

Rogovin shrugged his shoulders and smiled sardonically. He pulled open the middle drawer of the desk and pulled an envelope out of a flat box. He flipped it across the desk. "Read it." Ross looked it over. It was addressed to James A. Beck, Chairman of the Board of Trustees of Manhattan Jewish Hospital. He opened the envelope, scanned the letter, then passed it to Hernandez.

"A resignation? From you?"

"Did you see the date, Arnie?"

"Yes, Saul it's six or seven months old. Why didn't you send it?"

"The randomness. A whole hospital can fall apart in Cochocton, Ohio. The pediatrics ward of a medium size city hospital can kill six kids, and sicken twenty-five others with an endemic staph infection. But each and every department of a hospital complex including a medical school that stretches over acres and acres in concrete buildings? And first here, then there, then over here again? Bullshit, gentlemen. That's what I say. That's not bad management. That's somebody trying to fuck up my hospital." Rogovin rose, his face colored with emotion. "And I don't like it one damn bit." He slammed the desk with his palm and went to the window to look out over the park. When he had calmed, he turned back to the policemen. "Certainly I had doubts. I was scared to death that it was me, or someone like me, who just wasn't doing a competent job. And that as a result, people were sicker than they should have been, and people died needlessly. But it's not that.

Whoever is trying to wreck this place has been so busy making it look like an accident, that it's obvious it's not. If I yell for help, we have a panic the city, and the hospital, can't afford. If I do nothing, I risk the continuation of a rising death rate, and a continuing increase in days of treatment per patient. In human terms that means people maimed or sickened and murdered. What happened in Neoplastic? That was an escalation. Do you know what that could have been?" Rogovin threw his hands up. "Anyway," he said more calmly, "that's why you're here."

"What do you want us to do, Saul," Arnie asked.

"First find out if there is something really wrong here, then find out who's doing it and stop them."

"And you want this done secretly—without notifying the Department or the Board of Trustees? Or my superiors?" Hernandez asked.

Rogovin looked at Arnie pleadingly. They had covered the same ground the previous evening.

It was Hernandez' turn to get up and pace. "Let's be practical. We want to minimize the damage around here. That comes first, right?" Rogovin nodded assent. "You described last night's business as an escalation. If these folks—and it sounds too big for just one looney—feel there are people crawling all over them, maybe they'll take even more drastic steps. Maybe they'll react to the pressure."

"I don't think so," Rogovin countered. "After all, we had a hell of a scare. They must know that we are concerned, and that we are going to tighten controls wherever we can."

"Okay. Let's accept that. Where are the softest points?"

Rogovin shrugged. "Everywhere. The place is full of sick people dependent on life-sustaining equipment and various dangerous substances to keep them alive. A hospital is a perfect place for a lunatic. His options are infinite."

Ross scratched at his scarred eyebrow. "Only lunatics generally go big, and leave trails."

"I don't know, Arnie. It took eleven years to catch George Metesky," Lou mused.

"Right. The Mad Bomber." Ross turned to face Rogovin. "A guy who used to work for Con Ed. He thought that they'd screwed him on a workmen's compensation beef. He had some kind of job-related injury. You remember him, Saul. He used to put pipe bombs in phone booths."

Rogovin sighed. "No soap. Too methodical. I'm not a hundred percent sure that I am aware of all of the incidents that this guy is responsible for. But there is no pattern, and there isn't any legitimate reason for a rise in the patient mortality and length-of-stay statistics."

Lou said, "So let it be a bunch of nuts."

"Then they have to be on staff," Rogovin said. "How else would it be possible?"

"Let's accept it," Ross said, "and figure out how to narrow it down."

Rogovin rubbed his eyes with the heels of his hands. "Ecchh! It's a snap. We only have 1,200 beds—1,300 if you want to count bassinettes—a couple of thousand staff and attendings, 500 students of one kind or another, 500 nurses, and two or three thousand nonprofessionals."

Lou patted Rogovin's shoulder. "Remember what you just told me about Mama's diagnosis? Physician, heal thyself! It's a process of elimination. We start with the files. We nose around gently. Like that, Saul. It takes time but get's results."

"All this without making it official," Rogovin said dubiously.

"Let's start small and see. Can I get in to see where the accident happened last night?" Lou asked.

"Certainly."

"And the lab, too. You didn't see the lab, did you, Arn?"

"Nope."

"You know where it is, Arn? I think the less we waltz around with Saul, the less likely that somebody's going to think we're on their backs."

Ross rose and headed toward the door. "He's right, Saul. For the time being, it's just a couple of fellows—old friends at that—with a sick mother on the premises. We'll be in touch. If you have anything to say, just call. And thanks for taking care of Mama."

Ross and Hernandez walked down the hall together, hands in their pockets, heads bowed in thought. Hernandez shuddered. "Let's just say we're right and there are a bunch of them. They must be entrenched and organized. And if everything here is a potential target, and they are going to escalate. . . ."

Rogovin had called ahead and Morris Nassiter and Melvin Farbstein were waiting for them at the door of the laboratory.

"Hello again, Sergeant Ross," the older man said. His skin was like parchment over a wide thin-lipped mouth and a prominent nose. Ross remembered the laughing eyes. He glanced at Farbstein and decided that he always looked upset. He introduced Lou and walked inside. "Where is the scene of the Great Escape."

"Hmmph," Farbstein offered, adding indignation to the narrow gamut of his emotions. He led the way to a glassed-in room further back in the lab. Sealed ducts and double doors immediately identified the room as a controlled environment.

"I guess we can't go in there, huh?" Ross asked.

"You can go in," Dr. Nassiter said. "But, if you should still be able to come out, you wouldn't feel so good."

Hernandez stifled a laugh. The old man talked like Myron Cohen. Farbstein looked shocked.

"How about it, Doc? I want to go in there." Ross pressed.

"So be it," Nassiter shrugged. "Step right this way."

It took twenty minutes to dress Arnie and Nassiter and Farbstein, and to brief Arnie on the drill for the contaminated room.

"The truth is," Nassiter said, "this week it wouldn't kill you. But you would waste a lot of Kaopectate. And if you were in close contact with people, especially if somehow they were in contact with your stool, you could pass it around pretty good." He admitted them first through one airtight door, then another. "This week it's coliform bacteria, and one little cage over there of hepatitic rats."

"Mice," Farbstein corrected.

Nassiter closed his eyes for a moment. "Mice. Of course. We are dealing with diseases which can be spread in an urban environment through the failure of sanitary equipment. That happens a lot in broken down tenements. You get a nice blockage in the main soil stack, some of the stuff these rat . . ." he looked at Farbstein, "these rodents are carrying, and you have yourself a colossal crabapple bellyache."

Farbstein pointed at the empty cage with an accusatory forefinger. "He was in there."

Ross, breathing through a micro-pore mask, looked

closely at the latch, and poked gingerly with a rubber-gloved hand. He shook his head, and turned to Farbstein. "You think this was deliberately opened?"

"Certainly."

Ross shook his head again. "I wouldn't testify to it."

"You're not a doctor," Farbstein said.

Ross squinted. "And eighteen years as a cop means that I still can't qualify to tell if a lock is broken? Here, look." He gently moved the lock horizontally. "Just enough give to open the latch. The rat jumps—boom!—it's open. Then it swings back on the hinges and closes again." Ross let the door swing back by itself. It clicked into place. "Now," he said with some satisfaction, "the rat's on the floor. You come in, he goes out. It's easy."

"I beg your pardon? Are you trying to blame this on me?" Farbstein bristled with indignation.

"Certainly not, Doctor," Ross smiled behind his mask. "Just providing you with an alternate diagnosis."

It was three-thirty by the time Ross and Hernandez walked out of the hospital on their way to the Twenty-third Precinct. Hernandez asked, "You were serious with that schmuck? It could have been an accident?"

"The odds are certainly against it. But I can tell you that whoever fixed that lock—if that's what it was—was very good. I can't tell whether it was done on purpose or the lock is just weak. That part I meant."

"Could this all be coincidence?"

Ross shoved his hands deeper into his pockets. "Aw shit, Roach, if you don't know, how the hell am I supposed to know?"

# 16

At the lunch counter in the cafeteria, which lies between the soaring tower of the Rosenstein building and the squat, older Hartz, a male nurse named Hesperes told Rosario Gonzalez that there had been a disturbance on the Neoplastics Floor in Morgenstern, but had no further details. Rosario nodded, then walked away to be alone with his thoughts. When his shift was finished he walked to Third Avenue, took the bus home, stopping at a little *bodega* to buy a few needed groceries, then mounted the steps to his apartment.

He sat in a deep chair in need of new springs and looked out of the window, not moving, until the sun fell. He drank a glass of milk and ate a few crackers with a piece of cheese. He cleaned up after himself, and went into the bedroom. He looked at the family picture as he did every night, as though by concentrating he could resurrect its subjects, all dead save one—himself.

The oddly weathered hills in the photograph had not much changed in eons. The karst country of Puerto Rico was marked by cone-shaped protuberances and corresponding depressions reaching hundreds of feet above and below the natural median surface of the earth, where ground water had dissolved limestone over the millennia. The conical mounds and sinkholes are strung like grotesque sculptures across the island north of the Cordillera Central. They are covered with a rough, low vegetation and an uncompromising soil. From the time of the Indians, whose prehistoric ballpark lies not far away, through the conquistadors and the American conquest four hundred years later, the area was thinly populated. Of all of the island it is the least arable and least hospitable. Yet, over the centuries, a small population developed in little villages and on spare lonely farms. A few small streams and rivers made life bearable.

The Gonzalez family had lived in the same general vicinity, about twenty miles to the south of Arecibo on the country's north coast, since beyond recollection. They had been born in substantial numbers and had died young, but they had persisted. With the American defeat of the Spaniards in 1898, and the annexation of the island, modest changes began to take place. Among them was the development of Arecibo, and the growth of Ponce, Puerto Rico's second city, on the south coast. In due course, a road was cut through the mountains to join them.

The engineers concerned with the development of the island's economy recognized that Puerto Rico is without significant natural resources. All fuel and sources of energy must be imported. In an attempt to ameliorate this problem, already recognized as serious more than fifty years ago, the Army Corps of Engineers examined the potential of a home grown source of energy—hydroelectric power.

There were running streams and rivers at various points in the island's center. Also, the land mass of the Cordillera was a magnet for the heavy clouds produced by the tropical heat and the surrounding sea. In the mountains it often rained, even when the rest of the island was bone dry.

Unfortunately, the streams themselves were not large enough, nor were their currents either fast or steady enough to power falls-type dams. Using lessons that they had learned dredging the riverways of America, the Army Corps of Engineers began to talk about barrage dams and manmade lakes. If the area is sufficiently enclosed—either a deep pit or a valley surrounded on all sides by hills—and there is sufficient area to provide water for year-round operation, and a fall of sufficient height is available to turn a suitable turbine, hydroelectricity can be produced.

The winding valley between the tall karst hills covered some seven hundred acres, forking at half its length into two separate basins. At its western end, the valley sloped off sharply into a sinkhole. The river, only twenty feet across at its widest point at full flood, sometimes meandered, sometimes rushed along its floor.

Perhaps a dozen families lived in the valley, or on the hills just above its floor. Each eked out its existence in the traditional manner. There were a few yams, some manioc root and, for the lucky, a few pigs and chickens.

Utuado, a town constructed on the road to Ponce about ten miles from the valley, had a school and a store, bringing a modest measure of civilization to the area.

The Corps of Engineers, after due consideration, decided that it was in that valley that they would build their lake and their dam. The Gonzalez family was among the first to learn that their little plot was to be sacrificed for the general good. Rosario's father, a mild-mannered man, took the blow with peasant calm and resignation. The government men explained that he would have a new plot, high on the hill above the valley floor. When they pointed it out to him, he was incredulous. How would anyone be able to climb there? The engineers smiled and explained that the lake would rise up the hills. He would not only have a new plot to farm, but a waterfront location.

Despite the fact that the Gonzalez family included seven children, the number thankfully limited by a destructive miscarriage in Mrs. Gonzales' eighth pregnancy, they lived in a three-room hut—house was too grand a term—made of odd pieces of wood, with stone steps and paneless windows covered by ill-fitting and leaky shutters.

The oldest brother, Felipe, died of pneumonia when they lived in a makeshift one-room dwelling on a hillside while the dam was being built. He had been fifteen. The tarpaper shack with the tin roof leaked even more mercilessly than had the old house, since destroyed. Yolanda, who was four, caught measles and died on the way to Utuado, her brain destroyed by a raging fever.

When the dam was finished, and the water began to back up, the inhabitants of the valley were invited to choose their plots at the level recommended by the engineers. The dam, three hundred feet long and almost a hundred feet above the floor of the western end of the valley, into which its spillway flowed, backed the water of the small stream into the rugged valley to the point at which it branched. The water, rapidly rising, divided at the base of the brush-covered cone, inundating the two continuing arms. When the water finally found its level, the lake was in reality two separate basins joined at their base by the dam itself. They called it Lake Dos Bocas.

Laboriously, Fernando Gonzalez and his wife and remaining children rebuilt in a small cove of the lake, isolated as they had always been from their neighbors. The days were no cooler, the rains no less enervating, the meager crops no better or worse. On the other hand, the lake made life a bit easier. It took the strain off of limited sanitary facilities and, at the same time, provided a regular supply of potable water. For the children it was a new-found form of recreation. While they did not know how to swim, they could splash about at the shallow bank.

In accord with its stated purpose, Lake Dos Bocas provided a steady flow of water through the spillway and the gallery, turning the turbines and generating electricity for residences and businesses all the way to Arecibo. In short order, the base of the dam provided a haven for a variety of aquatic plants, including water lilies which quickly spread out into the lake itself, forming a carpet of palmated green pads from one shore to the other, covering a hundred yards from the concrete structure.

In turn, the lilies attracted assorted wildlife, including an inch-long snail called Planorbis. Physically, the snail has no special characteristics, spiral in shape, and brown, living on aquatic vegetation.

The importance of Planorbis is the part it plays in the life of *Schistosoma Mansoni*, the blood fluke. When the Corps of Engineers brought their materials and their plans up into the karst hills, they brought more than electricity to northwestern Puerto Rico. They brought laborers with them—such as were available. And those worked and ate and voided their bowels and bladders during the years that the dam was being built, first on the valley floor, and then in the slowly growing lake.

Rosario's father was the first of the family to feel the presence of the new life form. At first, it was just an irritation of the intestinal wall, which translated itself into a mild diarrhea. Papa Gonzalez ate a lot of rice, and skipped the beans for a few days, convinced that was all that was necessary. He developed a dry hacking cough, which over a period of months became increasingly frequent. When he developed a sharp pain and tenderness in his stomach, just below the diaphragm, he decided to see the pharmacist in Utuado. By then, everyone in the Gonzalez family had begun to show the same symptoms which he had already had.

*Schistosoma Mansoni* is a flat worm only ten to twenty-five millimeters long. It lives in the bloodstream—the veins and arteries—of its human host for up to twenty years, if the host should live that long. It breeds and lays eggs in the large intestine and the bowels, and when waste is evacuated, the eggs pass with it. They hatch on contact with fresh water and then seek a second host. For *S. Mansoni* the perfect intermediate host is the small snail that was drawn to the Gonzalez family's front door by the United States Army Corps of Engineers. After burrowing into the flesh of the little mollusk, the larva of *S. Mansoni* changes its form again, then leaves. The new creature, which swims about in water, enters the pores of any human who bathes in the water.

*S. Mansoni* is a rude and greedy guest. It lives on glycogen, or animal starch that it filters from the bloodstream of the host. It gathers in ever increasing numbers till it impacts the very blood vessels on which it is dependent for life. In its anxiety to reproduce itself, it damages the intestinal walls through which it passes. Its eggs, carried along in the bloodstream, are filtered out by the liver in a vain attempt by the host to cleanse itself. The resultant infestation of eggs causes hepatitic cirrhosis of the liver. In a matter of a year or two, the intestine of the host, laden with encysted eggs, is as rigid and inelastic as a length of old garden hose. And in the end, this parasite's greed is suicidal. With clogged blood vessels, hemorrhaging intestinal walls and a scarred liver, the host finally expires.

Rosario Gonzalez rose from the bed and stared out the window at the fetid, garbage-strewn gutters of 117th Street. He gnashed his teeth silently and pounded his fists rhythmically on the cracked sill. His head ached with the pain of memory, as it did every night. His flesh crawled with the guilt of his very existence. How is it, he asked himself for the thousandth time, that I alone was spared. For Rosario there could only be pain and revenge. Like some survivors of the Holocaust, his perception of his sin was his escape from death, his failure to share the ultimate punishment—and therefore to be unworthy even of death.

It had been more than forty years since the day the truck had come to take the Gonzalez family away. First, the doctor in Arecibo, where the pharmacist had sent Papa Gonzalez, had dosed him with salts and given him cough syrup. Then, on a second visit, he was taken to the small dispensary where an army doctor was visiting. The doctor had been alarmed. He took a stool sample and kept Papa Gonzalez overnight. The doctor had seen the same watery skin eruptions on the China Station, where the army had posted him before. Without even looking in the microscope, he knew that he would see the eggs, and possibly a few thrashing adult blood flukes which were choking the life out of Papa Gonzalez.

The headache passed. Rosario left the window and sat at the edge of the bed again. Whenever he became restive, he would reexamine the plans for the hospital, or enumerate the equipment he needed for his next operation. He permitted himself no diversions.

Rosario's vision of the truck, bumping along the dusty track that led to the blacktopped road, was conjured two or three times each day. He reviewed again each miniscule detail, to reassure himself that his perception had not changed.

He recalled the doctor's plastic smile and watching his mouth move as he spoke in unfamiliar English, a tongue unheard in the center of the island until the day of the tourists after World War II. The nurses spoke in Spanish, which was a comfort. But the smell of antiseptic and the array of instruments frightened him. One by one, his mother and his remaining brothers and sisters were taken from the waiting room, till he alone was left. He waited interminably. Then the nurse came to get him. They had to struggle with him, despite his small size, to make him lower his ragged shorts. Finally, a heavy-set army orderly held the upper part of his body firmly over the examining table, as the cursing doctor—red-faced with perspiration—put on a rubber finger cover, dipped it in vaseline and brutally probed his rectum. Rosario remembered screaming, first in fear, then in pain, and finally in shame. When the doctor was finished, the orderly let Rosario up. He tried to kick the doctor. The orderly slapped him across the ear and said something unintelligible. Rosario followed the nurse back to the waiting room with scalding tears on his cheeks.

The diagnosis was simple, schistosomiasis. Or bilharziasis, named for the Swiss scientist who identified the microorganism. Under whatever name, it is endemic in many countries—Brazil, Thailand, China, Egypt, Yemen, and Puerto Rico.

Schistosomiasis kills. There is only one cure. Various

compounds of the metallic element antimony. When the Gonzalez family fell ill, there was only one such compound—antimony treated with potassium nitrate—called tartar emetic. It kills the worms, the eggs, the larvae, and flushes them from the system. You vomit them, you shit them. You expel them. If it doesn't kill you first.

The higher the dosage, the more certain the cure, and the more dangerous. Anything over one-half percent is Russian Roulette. It is administered intravenously.

Papa Gonzalez died the first day. Olivia and Hernan the second. Ricardo lasted two weeks. Mama, Maria and Rosario were sent back to Dos Bocas the third week. They would have to be checked at intervals, but it seemed that they were cured. Maria, who was nine, lasted two more years. The treatments destroyed her a little at a time. When the doctors stopped the treatments, the symptoms would return. Finally, emaciated to a skeletal state, she joined her brothers and sisters in death. Mama fought to the end. When she realized that it was the *Yanqui* medicine that killed, she refused to take any more. She prayed that Rosario would persist; it was her duty to live to protect him. Not long after the end of the War, hemorrhaging profusely, with a liver the consistency of pumice, she wept and gave up the ghost. The tartar emetic worked on Rosario. The parasites were flushed from his system, and he lived.

He was shuffled off to an orphanage on the eastern side of the island, near the huge Roosevelt Roads Naval Base. It was a civil orphanage run by the commonwealth, with some help from the military. When he was twelve he was molested and finally raped by a male orderly who gave him his regular monthly medical checkup. The man was transferred a week later, and nothing more was ever said about the incident. Rosario went to a vocational school to learn the building trades. In time, he became a mechanic and an electrician. Then he emigrated to the *barrio* of New York.

Spanish Harlem was a fallow field for the seeds of hate that had been sown in Puerto Rico. Rosario quickly decided that even the rural poverty of the island's mountains was better than the squalor offered to poor Puerto Ricans in New York.

Rosario was over twenty before he had sex with a

woman. She was eighteen. They married and struggled together in New York.

As he sat at the edge of his bed, he put his hands over his ears, so that he could not hear her screaming. "More, more, more." How she would writhe against him, and plead for his love, and for his body. Sex dulled the pain and the memories drifted into the background. Though he was thin and wiry, he possessed great physical strength and stamina. When he found the degree to which his lovemaking pleased his bride, he extended himself. He practiced self-control so that he would outlast her, so that she would never go unsatisfied. In return, she was his abject slave and admirer. After two years of marriage, she got pregnant. They waited patiently and joyfully. She went into the Manhattan Jewish Hospital where she delivered a dead baby, strangled by the cord, and where she died of a massive hemorrhage without ever regaining consciousness.

Rosario Gonzalez turned over on the bed, pushed his face into the pillow, pulled another over his head, and screamed. He screamed until his voice cracked and his throat hurt. He screamed until the tears would no longer run. Then he rose and turned on the light to contemplate the blueprints of the Manhattan Jewish Hospital.

# 17

Eddie Biggs was tired. His hands hurt from the hitting and twisting and pinching of Emily Stolzfuss's muscular body. He had been careful not to touch her face, because he knew that the marks took a long time going away.

He had let her arm loose once, early in the day, to twist it and turn her over. She punched him savagely in the neck, knocking him to the floor again. He recovered quickly enough to keep her from pulling the gag out of her mouth and freeing her other arm. Then he punched her in the solar plexus twice at which point Emily fainted. Eddie untied her and turned her over so he could work on her back where the marks wouldn't show.

Eddie Biggs was annoyed at his lack of success with Emily. It was supposed to be easy. A runaway comes into town. Wants to get away from her folks. Maybe poverty. Maybe they beat her. Maybe they won't let her run around. Usually, she's already broken in by a boyfriend. Or maybe they're fuck-happy at fifteen, and have twenty boyfriends. Then, the mack—Eddie liked to think of himself as The Mack—picked her up, showed her how good it could really be. In exchange for protection from street hoodlums, for bailing her out when she got caught in a police vice drag, and for providing her with a person to depend on, and a real authority figure, she gratefully took on ten to twenty johns a day and happily turned most of the money over to the mack. That's how it was supposed to be.

Eddie'd had a girl work for him before. Charlene was her name. She was fourteen and fat and black, and from North Carolina. She'd done okay for a while, till she overdosed and died on him. A lot of the working girls did smack, or snorted coke.

Eddie flexed his arms. He felt a little better. Emily lay on the bed staring at the ceiling. She was breathing very shallowly, as though by staying absolutely still, she would be invisible to him. She began to tremble when she heard him get to his feet.

"Turn over, baby. Sit up on the edge of the bed."

She winced as she pushed herself to an upright position, the bruised muscles in her back knotting in protest. She put her feet on the floor gingerly. He had twisted the toes on her left foot almost to the breaking point, and her ankles as well.

He walked forward toward her and when he was inches away, arrogant, with his hands on his hips, he thrust his pelvis forward and said, contemptuously, "Make it hard, like I showed you."

Emily closed her eyes and rocked her head back and forth until he pushed her away. "Now you kneel on the bed. No, stupid," he gave her a slap on the shoulder that left a hot red patch, "face the wall. We gonna try it from behind."

After a while, Eddie Biggs got tired of abusing Emily Stolzfuss. And besides, he was hungry. He tied her securely to the bedposts and put a gag in her mouth. "Now don't you go noplace while I'm gone," he chuckled. "You mad at me now, but you gonna get to love me. I'll bring you back some food when I comes home. You gotta build your strength if you gonna work the street tomorrow."

She lay in the dark numbed by the brutality that she had endured. She had been beaten, violated in every possible manner, starved, and left cold and naked for a whole day.

For all her pain and fear, Emily looked upon her predicament almost philosophically. She had called down the judgment of the Lord on herself. For the first time in twenty-four hours she managed a smile. Surely, she had called it down by her wickedness and, as surely, it had arrived. She wondered idly if Eddie Biggs were really the Devil. Thoughts of the stern Old Testament God with whom she was so thoroughly acquainted brought other memories, and her smile dissolved into tears.

When she regained her composure, Emily reflected that there wasn't much more that could happen to her. Her violation was complete, and Biggs's brutality eliminated any further thoughts of resistance. She had nothing left to fear except her imprisonment. She would play along with Biggs, and at the first opportunity, she would escape.

# 18

Cookie Alonzo was very happy when she went to bed. She was five years old and her big sister Iris had made her a chocolate pudding and read her a story. She pushed herself snugly into the corner of the bed she shared with Juanita, her eight-year-old sister, and hugged her little blonde rubber doll. Juanita was a big girl, Cookie thought, as she fell asleep sucking her thumb, and she doesn't have to go to bed till nine o'clock.

In the living room of the Alonzo apartment, Iris sat with her parents and her four sisters. Her three brothers, who were the oldest of the children, were away in their own homes. Angelica, the oldest sister, was curled up with a book from City College, where she was a senior. Papa still wore his tie and jacket. He was the manager of the record department at Gimbel's on Eighty-sixth Street, and did well. Mama was laughing at some dumb joke on the TV.

Iris felt a little guilty. She had fooled around a bit with boys before, but Alex Klinger was the first real man she'd ever been to bed with. She had lied to her parents about sleeping at a friend's house the night before. It was the first time she had done so.

She tried to watch the television but, between her wandering thoughts, and her increasing intestinal discomfort, she was unable to concentrate. She got up quietly from her chair and headed toward the bathroom. Her mother raised an eyebrow and wondered what was the matter. That was the fourth time in an hour that Iris had gone.

Iris leaned against the door of the bathroom. She had no sooner risen than she was overwhelmed again by the urge to relieve herself. Her legs trembled and perspiration stood out on her forehead. Suddenly, she was nauseous. She was sick in the sink. Then she fell back again on the commode. After a few moments, she decided she felt well enough to get up. She turned on the water to run a bath, and cleaned up the sink. She stripped and eased herself into the warm water. It made her feel a bit better, but her head buzzed and she continued to be gripped with cramps.

After a while her mother went to see if she was all right. She found Iris unconscious in the tub.

# 19

Abner Stolzfuss sat stiffly in the seat on the plane to New York. He had never flown before, and his concern was not for his safety, but his offense to his God. Sly though he might be in adapting the ways of the world to the ways of the Lord, Abner was strict old-order Amish, and his battle with his conscience over this flight was a very real one.

Unhappily, more and more Amish children were giving up the strict community life and venturing into the outside world. Once broken, the covenant between the Plain People and God could not be mended. Those who left were never welcomed back. They were shunned and, in the words of a even older church, cast into the darkness—excommunicate and anathema. Abner Stolzfuss could not admit the possibility that one of his children should have taken on such ways.

It was possible, he thought, that Emily might have strayed to see the outside, but never that she could have done so to sin. A childish lark. It would certainly bring a shunning on her for some time, till the elders of the church felt that she had done her penance, and had indeed repented. But, eventually, she would be received among the righteous again. And despite her shame, she would surely be married to one of her own kind. Because, her father thought, looking out of the window of the Allegheny Airlines Twin Otter, she was a good girl, kind, with an open heart and an eagerness to please that charmed everyone that she met.

The woman in the fur stole next to him had stared on and off since the plane had taken off. She knew it was not the habit of her Amish neighbors to fly. She speculated on the problems that would bring this patriarch on his flight, and what indeed, despite a lot of loud nose-blowing and wiping with a large white handkerchief, would bring an intermittent stream of tears from his eyes.

In fact, Abner Stolzfuss was a frightened man. The sheriff in Lancaster had been none too gentle with him. He had made it plain that girls often ran off to Philadelphia or New York for adventures. And in short order, these children found themselves strolling the sidewalks for food and lodging. Not infrequently, such girls finished in serious trouble, badly hurt or, he had said ominously, worse. It was clear that the sheriff had little patience with Amish parents who sought to raise their children in an environment isolated from the modern world, refusing to consider the consequences.

Nonetheless, after an hour's discussion, it was decided that the most likely places to look were in the general vicinity of Lancaster and, if indeed she had run away, New York City. The sheriff asked if Abner Stolzfuss had a photograph of his daughter. There was an embarrassed pause. Of course, he would not. It was contrary to the Amish religion to have graven images in the household. And photographs were considered graven images. Abner Stolzfuss gave the sheriff a description that was broadcast as an all-points missing persons report throughout Lancaster and the adjoining counties. The sheriff then made a telephone call to New York. The information unit at Police Plaza directed him to the Street Crimes Unit on Randall's Island. If someone wanted to look for a missing child in New York, that was the place to go. Street Crimes and Vice worked together on runaways, who numbered tens of thousands in the city.

When the Otter landed at Newark Airport a little after eight in the morning, Stolzfuss took his small suitcase, borrowed from a non-Amish neighbor, and hailed a cab. The driver drove him directly to the Randall's Island police headquarters. The driver asked for fifty dollars. Wordlessly, Stolzfuss paid him and stepped down.

In the lobby, Abner was overwhelmed by the noise and bustle. Many officers, guns exposed, in plainclothes without jackets milled about in the hall, talking at the top of their lungs. A uniformed policeman on a raised platform was engrossed in paperwork. Stolzfuss winced as an officer in a corner near the desk drove his knee into the groin of a boy with his hands cuffed behind him, then pulled him by the hair and frog-marched him down the corridor and through an iron door.

A freckle-faced Irishman with a shock of red hair was

talking animatedly to another policeman when he spotted Stolzfuss out of the corner of his eye. "Hey, Leibowitz, is this one of yours?" There was general laughter as a short, heavy-set man with no visible neck turned to look at their visitor. "No *payess*. Not mine." He turned back to his conversation. Leibowitz's beat was the Crown Heights section in Brooklyn where Hasidic Jews, dressed in costumes carried over from a Poland and Lithuania dead three hundred years, with full beards and *payess*—long locks curled around the ears—played their Hebrew counterpart to the Amish of Lancaster County.

Abner Stolzfuss stepped forward to the desk and cleared his throat. He was used to being stared at. Well aware of his unusual appearance, he was wholly self-assured in it. It was the badge of his faith. On the other hand, he was a man of substantial wealth and power, and was not used to being ignored. "Excuse me," he said loudly, "I need some information."

The desk officer looked up and said. "What can I do for you, Rabbi?"

"My name is Stolzfuss, Abner Stolzfuss. I'm from Lancaster, Pennsylvania. The sheriff called. It's about my missing daughter."

The desk man looked down at him. The normal routine is to ask a bunch of questions, request photographs, get details of last appearance, then send it around. The ones that are found usually get picked up for some small crime. One of the papers the desk man was looking through was a bulletin announcing a big push on runaways, and demanding cooperation with out-of-town police forces looking for strays of their own. He looked down at the stern face and shrugged. "Lieutenant Policello is in charge of our new runaway investigation unit. I'll call him. You wait over there." He pointed to a long row of benches.

Arthur Policello belched, shook his head in resignation, and took a swig from his bottle of Gelusil. Forty-six years old, he thought, and a physical wreck. His brother Lou, the priest, had it better. He belched again. His desk was a ragged pile of letters and photographs of smiling, prim children posing with their dogs and their mothers in Duluth, or Minneapolis, or St. Louis, or wherever.

The phone rang. "Policello," he growled.

"Lieutenant, this is Gates at the desk. There's a man out

here from Lancaster, Pennsylvania. He said the Lancaster sheriff's office called the department. They sent him here. He's lost his daughter."

Policello closed his eyes. He slapped his hand on the same memo that had crossed the desk out front a few minutes before. "Send him in."

Policello put the Gelusil in the desk drawer, buttoned his shirt and adjusted his tie. He thought about putting on his jacket, but discarded the idea.

His eyes opened wide when the substantial figure of Abner Stolzfuss filled the door. "Please sit down." Stolzfuss did as he was asked. "You're Amish, aren't you?" Policello asked.

"Yes, I am," Stolzfuss replied, already feeling more at ease.

"I spent a week down your way with my wife and kids a couple of years ago. The Downingtown Inn. It was a lot of fun. Very interesting, I mean."

"We get a lot of tourists. It's curiosity about our ways, I suppose. And our cooking."

The lieutenant smiled. "I remember that part. I'm afraid I didn't really get to sample much of it." He patted his stomach. "It's the job. I got an ulcer. What can I do for you?"

Abner Stolzfuss told him about the disappearance of his daughter, his own efforts to find her, and his discussions with the Lancaster sheriff's office.

"Is there any reason, other than supposition, to think that she came to New York, Mr. Stolzfuss?"

Stolzfuss shook his head negatively. "It was just that the sheriff seemed to think that most runaways end up here."

Policello let out a deep breath. "He's right. Do you know that the Minneapolis Police Department has two officers who come here once a month trying to spot missing kids?" Policello nodded. "It's the Big Apple. I don't know what these kids expect to find here. But whatever it is, they sure as hell don't find it."

"Do you have children, Lieutenant?" He paused, "Oh, I'm sorry, you told me."

"I have a son and a daughter, Mr. Stolzfuss. And I worry about them all the time." Policello looked up into Stolzfuss's face. The eyes were deep set and ringed in black. The veins in his eyes stood out in red streaks. He's been crying and he hasn't been sleeping, Policello thought.

He wanted more Gelusil. "I don't know how much we can do to help you, Mr. Stolzfuss. Have you a photograph?"

"No. It's against our religion to be photographed."

Policello wiped his face with his hands, then clapped them together. Maybe it wouldn't be so hard to spot this one. Maybe she hadn't found herself a pimp yet. Maybe she was as pure as this poor old buzzard seems to think she is. Maybe she's still wearing one of those granny outfits they wear. But it's not bloody likely, Policello snorted to himself.

He clapped his hands together once lightly. He'd made up his mind.

"I'll tell you what we're going to do. First, you're going to give a description to a police artist and he's going to draw a picture. Is that all right with you?" Stolzfuss hesitated. "Mr. Stolzfuss, in the absence of a picture to recognize her, in a city with over seven million people in it . . . ." He shrugged.

"Yes, yes, of course." I have gone this far, Abner thought, surely the Lord will not ill-judge me.

"Then we'll get it out to every precinct in town. They'll pin it up on the board and give a handout to the beat cops. If she gets spotted, they'll pick her up. I'll need all kinds of details. But then you can pass that along to the officer that will be assigned to the case."

Policello looked at a roster on the desk. "I'll see that someone runs you over in a squad car. The man's name is Ruggles. Sergeant Albert Ruggles. He's in the Street Crime Unit at the Twenty-third Precinct." Lieutenant Policello led Abner Stolzfuss to the parking lot. A couple of blue and white patrol cars sat idly in the shade of the building. Another, its motor idling, waited by the entrance to the driveway. A young patrolman exited from the side door of the station sweeping his long hair under his peaked uniform cap, and headed toward the car.

"Hey, officer," Policello called.

The policeman turned and threw him a salute. "Yes, sir."

"You want to run this gentleman over to the Twenty-third, and see that he gets in to see Sergeant Ruggles. I'm going to call over now. I'd like him to get through with a minimum of flak, if you know what I mean."

"I'll deliver him personally, Lieutenant."

Policello shook hands with Stolzfuss and handed him his bag as he sat in the back of the car. "Good luck," he called out as the car pulled away. Fat fucking chance, he thought as he turned back to his office, belching.

# 20

Rosario had arisen at six in the morning and taken the subway at 116th Street north into the Bronx. He got off at Findlay Avenue and walked southwest toward a vast gutted plain. Great tracts of land covered with abandoned apartment buildings rose up from lots of crushed brick and the detritus of what had once been a thriving community. At the edge of one such group of buildings Rosario stopped in the shadows and waited. As the sun rose higher, a small figure appeared, perhaps a quarter of a mile away, at the edge of the field of debris. Rosario watched carefully as the figure picked its way through the tumbled stones, dirt and splintered planking. The figure, now plainly a man in blue jeans and a corduroy jacket, stooped, remained bent for several minutes, then straightened, and walked off in the same direction from whence he had come.

After five minutes, Rosario walked purposefully, but without hurrying, across the field. He stopped where the man had, moved two crossed boards marked with a splash of white paint and found a small wooden box. Within it was a roll of newspaper in a brown grocery bag. He took the bag, crumpled its top to make carrying it easier, then walked back across the open field to the shadow of the building. He waited five more minutes, scanning the field and the buildings with an eagle eye, trying to discern the slightest movement. When he was satisfied that he was entirely alone, and that he had neither been seen nor followed, he extracted the roll of newspaper from the bag and placed it in the lunch pail he had been carrying. He discarded the bag in a trash can at the entrance to the subway. He got off at Ninety-sixth Street. With the same steady pace, he walked to the hospital, entered at Leibner and went into the basement to punch in. "Hi, Rosie," the guard said. "Hi, Mac," he replied.

Rosario could see from the cards in the rack that he was the first of the day shift to have punched in. It was eight-thirty. But no one was surprised. Rosie always came in a little early. The foreman swore by him. "One of the best I've ever had."

The lead electrician of the night crew was always glad to see Rosie. He smiled and patted him on the shoulder. "Just got a new *Playboy*, Rosie, hot-cha-cha. I'll leave it for you. Keep your hands to yourself. Ha ha. None of that old five-on-one, right? Ha ha."

Rosario waited ten minutes, then, checking the wall clock, he went quickly back to his locker, carrying the convenient *Playboy*. He opened the lunch pail, removed the roll of newspapers and, carrying it under the magazine, hurried back down the corridor. When he got to his post at the emergency generator room, he slowed down. In the morning the halls were deserted. He took the corridor under the buildings from Leibner, through Green, and into the basement of Waldman. Once there, he left the main corridor and slipped through a door marked "Emergency-Maintenance Staff Only." Another corridor, lighted only by red emergency lights, stretched out before him. At the end of the hall was a standpipe leading up through the ceiling. Rosario put the bundle in his shirt and shinnied up the pipe to the first big fitting. He pulled himself up until he could stand on the big spoked wheel. A sign, "Emergency Cooling Water Supply" hung from a chain around the wheel stem and clinked eerily when Rosario's foot struck it.

Rosario moved aside a foot-square panel in the ceiling. Then he peeled the papers away from the bundle, and carefully put the dozen sticks of dynamite through the hole where they nested against about a hundred others that had been painstakingly acquired over the past year. He replaced the panel and dropped agilely to the floor. He slipped out and went to the elevator bank in the basement of Waldman where he dropped the newspapers into a large dumpster. Then he continued down the main corridor to his station under Leibner.

The pile of dynamite sticks that Rosario had placed in the inter-floor space vibrated slightly as the electrical generating equipment on the floor above spun into action. Power from the generators activated pumps and valves that operated lighting and cooling equipment in the Louis

Gluck Hyperbaric Chamber. The chamber, located at the north end of the Waldman Pavilion, is in a squat windowless building which gives much the impression of a brick blockhouse, impregnable and a little forbidding. Inside is a steel cylinder large enough to use as an operating room and capable of containing sixteen atmospheres of oxygen. Outside the single door that connects the hyperbaric building to the outside world, a sign embossed in metal also shivered slightly from the mechanical vibration. It read, "Absolutely NO Admission. No use of cigarettes, cigars, pipes or flame-producing devices. DANGER of fire or explosion. OXYGEN under pressure. DANGER."

# 21

Lieutenant Francis Xavier Flaherty, Commander of Homicide Zone Four, raised his eyebrows another notch. He sat behind his desk with the door closed. A pile of DD-5's teetered precariously before him. He put aside the sheet he had been reading, and cocked his ear. Though he was unable to distinguish the words, he could hear Detective Sergeant Arnold Ross bitching. He wrinkled his forehead. He also heard Sergeant Hernandez. He looked at his duty chart, then at his watch. It was noon. Hernandez was on four-to-eights, Ross on eight-to-fours. He leafed through his case outline sheet, a little extra form he'd developed over thirty years on the job.

The Job. Flaherty shook his head, and pushed a strand of his thinning white hair away from his forehead. No common cases for Ross and Hernandez. He'd had them under his command for four years. They were the best of the four detective sergeants assigned to H/Z 4. And the best he'd ever had. Hernandez was steady, thoughtful, and dependable. Ross? Well, Ross was something else.

"What's he cooking now?" Flaherty asked himself aloud. He pushed his chair away from the desk quietly, opened his door, and let himself out. He could see, through the frosted glass panel of the sergeants' office, that Ross was gesticulating extravagantly. Flaherty was not too proud to eavesdrop. "We could comb these fuckin' lists for twenty years, Roach. We'd still never find anything. Shit, is everybody in this place a P.R.?"

"The ones who aren't Hebes," Hernandez replied acidly.

Flaherty smiled triumphantly and opened the door. "Not interrupting, am I? Ross? Hernandez?"

He strode across the room and picked up the file from under Ross's nose. He leafed through it.

"You wouldn't mind letting me know how you're spending the taxpayers' money would you? I don't want to interrupt your busy schedule, but according to your reports, Ross, you're working on the hatchet job on that fag in the men's room. And you," he turned toward Hernandez, "are supposed to be working with Albert Ruggles on a pimp killing. Right?"

Deadpan, Hernandez said, "Backwards."

Flaherty looked at him, then put down the file, "Huh?"

"You got it backwards, Lieutenant. Arnie's doing pimps. I'm doing fags."

Flaherty's Irish face turned a rich red. "Smart ass." He banged the desk and pointed at the files. "What is this? You running your own private police department?"

"I'm not on duty, Lieutenant," Hernandez said.

"No, but you're in my office, and I want to know what it is you're cooking up this time. One of these days, you're going to end up writing books, and being consultants to the movies, and I'm going to lose my pension for failure to supervise."

Hernandez looked at Ross questioningly. Ross shrugged meekly. "Uh . . ."

"Uh . . . what," Flaherty demanded.

"Can this be . . . sort of unofficial?" Ross asked.

"No deal. That's my decision. I'll listen." Flaherty kicked the door shut and sat down. "Now, talk."

"Either there's something wrong with the management of Manhattan Jewish, or they have a killer or killers loose on the premises."

Flaherty closed his eyes slowly, then opened them again. "That's all?" he asked sarcastically.

"Look, Lieutenant," Ross leaned forward speaking in a low earnest voice. "You know Saul Rogovin. He's the one who called us in on this. He's the one who asked us to keep it quiet. He's afraid to panic the community. Get it in all the papers."

"Details." Flaherty said.

Ross gave him a quick rundown from his notes—the statistical variations, the accidents, the extended average length of stay, and the incident on the Neoplastic Floor. "What do you think, Lieutenant? If it goes on the books, we have a problem."

"If it doesn't go on the books, we have different kinds of problems. Can you imagine what the press will have to say—not to mention the Health and Hospitals Corporation, the Health Commissioner, and the dudes at City

Hall—if we cover up some lunatics operating at one of the city's biggest hospitals?"

Flaherty stood up and held his hand against his brow. "A fine can of worms this is." He paced back and forth across the small office, then stopped and turned to Hernandez. "You agree that this should stay off of the books?"

"For the time being. There are two sides. If we go on the record, it will eventually pop out in the open, and any chance of catching the perps from the inside, catching them all from the inside, goes down the drain. Maybe we turn them off, maybe we don't. Maybe they just stop and go away. That certainly hasn't been my experience. Maybe they go for broke and do something really crazy as a one-time goodbye. You know, break out in the open."

"And if we keep a low profile?" Flaherty asked.

"Maybe," Hernandez continued, "we get a shot at all of them. Maybe we keep their operations at a low level."

"So they only kill a few more people," Flaherty asked sourly.

"Yeah, I guess so." Hernandez replied. "But we prevent a crescendo."

"Maybe. Ross, what's your thought?"

"I say let us finish with these records. Let's strain them to see if there are any really outstanding possibilities." He pointed at a green folder on Hernandez' desk. "Those are the people who've been fired in the last five years, or just laid off. Lou's going to go through them to see if any are related to current employees—or if they've been rehired. We're also trying to find out if any of the employees have ever been patients, or have relatives who have been patients at the hospital. Or better yet, if they have relatives who died at the hospital. Somebody with a potential ax to grind."

"And if that's a dead end?"

"Meanwhile we're trying to track down who has access to the microbiology lab. That seems to be the most obvious lead. It's the only incident that is clearly identifiable, so far as I can tell."

"You don't have enough manpower, Ross. You're dealing with a massive problem here. What's the total number of possibles—four thousand?"

Ross started to object. Flaherty held up his palm to stop him. "I know. The probables are a much smaller group, and you can cut it down fairly quickly. I still think that your first chain of action is hopeless with only two people pursuing it. Even with a computer program, matching and mixing is a big job."

Flaherty paused a moment, then went on. "What we'll do is this. Forget the step-by-step stuff with the staff. Stick to cross connections from the file of people they've let go. Just do name matching. You might as well do the same with the list of people who have relatives who died in, say, the last two years. How long has this been going on?"

"About a year," Ross replied.

"Then go back two years. Cross-reference the names who died with those who worked at the hospital." Flaherty shook his head. "But between us girls, I think you're jerking off. The only place you're going to find anything is at the end of this dead rat. Otherwise . . ." He shrugged and stood up.

"What should I tell Saul?" Arnie asked.

"Tell him you told me. And tell him I gave you ten days to come up with something concrete. The next step, assuming there are any further incidents, or the ten days pass without some sign of progress, we go to the Commissioner and the Chief of Detectives and let them decide. Right?"

Ross and Hernandez looked at Flaherty, then each other, and said, in unison, "Right."

Flaherty started out of the door, when Ross called out to him. "Listen, Boss, what do we do about the stuff we're working on?"

Flaherty stopped at the door. "The fag case's a bummer, I guess. A quick pickup, the wrong guy, a nasty murder. What do you think, Lou?"

"I've had it three days, Lieutenant. I'm working it with Charlie. All we can do is one step at a time. Follow up neighbors. More questioning of patrons of the bar. Where does he hang out?"

"What'll Charlie say if you just back out?"

Hernandez smiled. Charlie Spinelli had been his partner for over three years, almost since he had arrived at H/Z 4. Short, fat, and permanently out of breath. Twenty-two years on the force. "Charlie doesn't ask questions. Charlie doesn't talk. He'll just pick up the loose ends."

"How about your new baby, Ross."

"I personally think he's too cool to ask a lot of questions. And besides, we're working this with Albert, down in Street Crimes." Ross frowned. "I guess I'd better talk to Albert. I was going to ask him about this hospital thing anyway—whether he'd heard any shit on the street."

"Fine. You tell Charlie to follow up on the—what's his name?—oh yeah, the Richard Woodley case. And you, Ross, you can tell your new partner . . ."

"Baxter, Superspade Marvin Baxter," Ross said.

"You be careful about that spade shit, Ross. I'd hate to see him bust that big Jew-beak of yours one more time. Anyway, you tell Wilt Chamberlain-Wyatt Earp to do what Albert tells him. And you handle Albert Ruggles as best you can. Ten days, boys." He shut the door behind him.

"Arnie, you think you can take Baxter?"

"Betcher ass I can," Ross replied, flexing a muscle and grinning.

"How about Albert Ruggles," Hernandez asked with an innocent smile.

Ross dropped his arm and folded his hands in front of him. "Now we're never going to try to find that out, are we?"

"I suppose not, you sheeny chicken. Back to work."

# 22

While Flaherty was on the third floor of the Twenty-third Precinct House, chewing out Ross and Hernandez, Abner Stolzfuss was led up to the second floor office of the Street Crimes Unit, which shared space with the plainclothes officers of the Precinct Investigation Unit. The young officer with Abner crossed the outer office—with its dozen desks and shirtsleeved detectives—to the office in the corner. He knocked, and entered, leaving Stolzfuss behind.

"Sergeant Ruggles?" the officer asked.

"That's me. Are you the man Policello sent?"

"Yes, Sergeant."

"Thanks. The guy with you?" Ruggles asked. The cop pointed over his shoulder with his thumb. "Okay, you can take off. Send him in."

The uniformed cop ushered Mr. Stolzfuss in, said "Good luck," and left.

Albert Ruggles rose from behind his desk. "Sit down please. Lieutenant Policello explained your problem. We're going to try to help you."

Abner Stolzfuss was at a loss for words. He was a big man, and he had big sons, but the black man in front of him was immense. He was six feet six inches at least and must weigh perhaps three hundred pounds. His head was round and a receding hairline gave way to a medium length Afro that made him seem even bigger. His features were big and broad, with thick lips and a blunt nose separated by a thick black moustache with some gray salted among its bristly hairs. When Ruggles sat again behind the desk, he folded his hands before him. The knuckles and edges were encrusted with calluses. A revolver dangled like a child's toy from a holster under a bulging arm.

"The easiest way for us to begin," Ruggles said in his rumbling voice, "is with your idea about why your daughter left, Mr. Stolzfuss. Tell me what she did the day before. Had you any reason to suspect that she was going to run away?"

Stolzfuss spent fifteen minutes answering questions about Emily's movements for the previous days. Haltingly, trying to face an unpleasant truth, he outlined what he believed to be Emily's motivation for her flight.

"I suppose that I have been inadequate as a father, else-wise she would have been stronger, and not have broken the Lord's law."

Ruggles shook his head sadly. "I understand the special . . ." he hunted for a word, ". . . rules of your religion, but this really isn't a special case."

He held up his hand to forestall a protest. "I don't mean that in the sense that Emily isn't special, or even that a girl from a background like hers isn't a rare case. The problem is that we have so many runaways—maybe fifty thousand a year we know about—that we see just about everything."

Ruggles stood and stuffed his hands into his pockets. "It's very discouraging for the parents and the police as well, but it's hardest of all on the kids. I'm going to call in our artist to take a description from you. It won't take but a few minutes." Ruggles went to the door and called out. "Manuel, could you come in here?"

Manuel Lopez, the police artist, was a thin, smiling Latin with large bright eyes and a droopy moustache. He was as thin as Ruggles was bulky, dressed in a pair of tan slacks and a turtleneck sweater. He sat next to Abner Stolzfuss with a large bound book. "Okay, Mr. Stolzfuss, this is how we start. This is a form book. It has all sorts of face and feature shapes. Lots of different noses and lips, and so on. First, we mix and match till we get a general idea. Then, I take a sketch pad, copy that outline, and you tell me the little differences. I think you're going to be surprised at the outcome." Within fifteen minutes, choosing among a variety of black outlines on clear plastic sheets overlaid with first one, and then another of the features, Lopez had a reasonable outline of Emily Stolzfuss. He transferred his work to a pad, and skillfully changing and shading in counterpoint with Abner's voice, it took him five more minutes to render an accurate lifelike portrait.

"Thanks, Manuel," Ruggles said. "Get that run off and sent around, will you?"

Ruggles turned back to Stolzfuss, who sat expectantly at

the edge of his seat. "The picture will be printed and sent around as a hand circular to all of the stationhouses in New York. In addition, with your okay, we'll send it out to some other departments. Philly, Trenton, Newark." She could be anywhere, he thought. Stolzfuss remained perched at the edge of the chair, as though awaiting the results.

Ruggles eyed the pile of paper work on his desk and chewed at his lip. He walked out into the room. Stolzfuss followed him with his eyes but did not move. "It's done by Qwip. Sends the picture over the phone." Ruggles stood silent for a moment, hoping that Stolzfuss would get up of his own accord. "There isn't anything else we can do now," Ruggles said. The old man's eyes brimmed with pain and resignation.

"If it is the Lord's will that we be so punished. . . ." He rose to leave.

Ruggles glanced at the papers again, then shrugged. "Wait a minute, Mr. Stolzfuss. You got some time to spare?"

The gaunt gray man raised his head and looked at Ruggles questioningly. "I will have the rest of my life to ponder my failings."

Ruggles's voice rose in anger, at whom he was not sure. "Well, all right. We're gonna go looking. But it isn't gonna do any good." He pulled his jacket from a hook by the door while securing the shoulder holster with the other. He struggled into the coat, and was two steps out of the office before he realized that Stolzfuss was not beside him. He turned. "Well, come on, Mr. Stolzfuss."

Bewildered, Abner followed as Ruggles wove his way among the desks in the outer office and stuck his head in a room. "Manny, gi'me two, three copies of that drawing." He hesitated a moment. There was a whirring noise as the copier made a couple of passes, then he withdrew from the doorway. He glanced down at the copies and grunted. "See, pretty clean," he said, showing them to Stolzfuss. Emily's name and description had been typed in at the bottom of the sketch.

Ruggles walked rapidly out of the front door with his odd companion in tow, oblivious to the stares of the various officers, complainants, and perps milling around the front desk.

"My car is over here," Ruggles said, pointing to a non-

descript ten-year-old Ford sedan with faded blue paint,
marked with the dents and scratches that are the service
stripes of New York City automobiles.

The interior of the car was in worse condition than
many a pickup truck that Abner had seen hauling prov-
ender and grain to and from the farms in Lancaster
County. He registered great surprise when Ruggles turned
the key and the car roared to life. Ruggles caught the look
on his face.

"Oh yeah. On the outside she's just a heap. Inside she's
all heavy duty police machine."

He pulled away from the curb and began to talk. For a
moment, Stolzfuss had trouble adjusting to his new tone of
voice. How many persons were hiding inside this giant
black man? The solicitous and gentle man who had
greeted him at the door of the office, the angry man who
had, without being asked, agreed to take him who-knew-
where, and this calm professional type, who described the
maelstrom of the city as Abner himself instructed his sons
in the mysteries of birthing a cow.

"To someone from the outside, it looks very complex.
Some ways it is. It's big. There are seven million people
who live here all the time, and we pick up another three
or four million any given day." Ruggles guided the car
across 101st toward Fifth past seedy tenements. "There
used to be a million more permanent residents, but they
all beat it out to the suburbs. They figure to get the ad-
vantages without paying the price." He turned down the
avenue toward the Ninety-sixth Street transverse that
would take them to the west side.

"There seem to be a lot of places where a kid who runs
away could go. Statistically, there are. Five boroughs. God
knows where you could end up. But," he ground to a halt
at a red light and turned to Stolzfuss, "they don't. The pattern's always the same. There are a couple of dozen main
spots where kids who run either start off or end up."

He stepped on the gas and moved westward uninterrupt-
ed for a couple of blocks, then turned downtown again.

"This is Broadway, the longest street in town. It runs
from the Battery at the south end of Manhattan Island all
the way up to the city line where the Bronx meets Yon-
kers. If your Emily was a different kind of kid, I might
have gone right back there. About a mile behind us is
Columbia University. Some kids are culture bugs—sort of

intellectual groupies. They dig the college scene. Sometimes they'll attach themselves to some guy that lives in his own apartment, or even pad in a dorm." Stolzfuss winced. Without clearly understanding the words, the inference was clear.

"But those are the lucky ones. And almost always, they get picked up, or just get bored and come home." At Fifty-ninth they caught another light, and Ruggles turned and asked, "Does Emily listen much to pop music?" The reply was a blank stare. "I mean rock and roll, that kind of thing?"

"Not, not in my home," Stolzfuss answered thickly. "We don't have the facilities. We don't believe . . ." He ran out of words. How to describe another century—not only in morality, but in time?

Ruggles stretched his neck uncomfortably in his collar. Shit, he thought, how can she listen to music if they don't believe in electricity? Dumb, Albert, dumb. "Anyway," he plowed ahead, "anyway, some kids come here because of music. They're the real groupies. They try to attach themselves to some musician, or band." He shrugged his massive shoulders. "Some catch on. Others just get kicked around a little by the hangers-on in the show business scene. Then they go home, mostly."

Ruggles guided the car down Ninth Avenue past the produce stores that lined the street below Fifty-seventh, hawking the spices and smells of all the world. Below Forty-second, Stolzfuss was aware of a grimy winding concrete structure that formed a clumsy vault above the traffic and attached itself, lamprey-like, to a large building on the west side of the street.

"The gate to Gomorrah, Mr. Stolzfuss. The Port Authority Bus Terminal. This is where they all come in. We'll just cruise a while. Then we'll go in and see a friend of mine."

Ruggles worked his way through the traffic and turned east a few blocks below the terminal, then he turned left again. "This," he said, "is Eighth Avenue." The roadway in front of Stolzfuss was jammed with cars of every description, radiating fumes and noise, and ill will. The buildings were rundown and filthy, deprived even of what tinseled allure darkness and the contrasting glitter of a few neon lights might provide: porno theaters, crummy restau-

rants whose appearance beggared the name, smut stores
with seedy people milling at their doorways.

"Look out your window," Ruggles said. "See her," he
indicated the east side of the street with a nod of his head.
"A long-time resident." The black whore stood at the side
of a building, its windows boarded save for a sleazy candy
store with a fly-blown plate glass window marred by a
taped-over crack. Fat thighs bulged between imitation
black patent leather shorts and the tops of knee-high boots
with stiletto heels and four-inch platforms. Grotesque pen-
dulous breasts cantilevered into points erupting from a
fuzzy pink sweater. The entire creation was topped by eyes
orientalized with mascara outlines, gaudy red lips and a
blond fright-wig.

"How could a man . . . ?" Stolzfuss could not finish the
question.

"I don't know. I couldn't." At Fifty-seventh, Ruggles
wheeled around again, back to Ninth Avenue. "That was
what we call the Minnesota Strip. And that's the starting
point and the end of the line for a lot of our runaways."

Ruggles reached under the dashboard and pulled out a
radio mike and thumbed the button. "SCU 141 for Tenth
Precinct Communications. Over." After a moment's
squawking there was a reply. He asked for the location of
two officers, and after a brief delay was told, "Between
Thirty-sixth and Thirty-seventh on Eighth. They'll hold for
you."

Ruggles drove to the appointed place and pulled to the
curb. A heavyset uniformed policeman with a large nose
and a moustache walked over to the car and looked in.
"Sorry, sir. There's no stopping here."

"How about over by Vinnie's," Ruggles said.

The cop nodded, "All right, all right, let's go." He
pointed his nightstick menacingly, then swept it in the
direction of the traffic. Ruggles pulled away and turned
west on Thirty-ninth, crossed Ninth Avenue, and parked
on the side street just past the side entrance of Vinnie's
Fruit and Vegetable Store. He killed the engine and waited
in silence. Stolzfuss watched the cars go by on their way
into the Lincoln Tunnel two blocks beyond, and then
away from the city. He regretted his lack of courage at
wanting desperately to join them.

In a few moments, the uniformed policeman who had
rudely ordered them on appeared at the side of the car

with his partner, who seemed to be a duplicate, save for a smaller nose and a slightly lighter frame.

The heavier man bent over and touched the bill of his cap. "Afternoon, Sergeant Ruggles." Stolzfuss read his nameplate, Rodriguez, and assumed his slight accent to be Spanish.

"Rodriguez," Ruggles acknowledged. Then looking beyond him. "Constanza. You learning anything? How long you been with Rod now?"

"Almost six months, Sergeant. I'm getting the hang of it."

Ruggles smiled broadly. "I'll just bet." He pointed to his passenger and said, "This is Mr. Stolzfuss. He's missing a blonde fifteen-year-old daughter." He reached down on the seat next to him and handed one of the sketches out of the window.

Rodriguez looked at the picture hard for a moment then passed it to Constanza. After a pause he shook his head. "I haven't seen her. When do you think she arrived?"

"Two, three days ago," Ruggles replied. "Green as grass. She's from a family of . . ." he searched for the word.

"Amish, we are," Stolzfuss intoned. "Old order Amish. And if she were properly dressed she would be all in gray with a bonnet."

"Then for sure we haven't seen her," Constanza said. "We'll ask the night shift."

"I put out a missing bulletin. It'll be down at Tenth Precinct by now, sketch and all. Do me a favor. I'm personally interested. Keep an eye out." Ruggles started the car again. "I'm going over to see Mancuso. You know if he's there?"

Rodriguez leaned forward over the window again, "He was there half an hour ago. And don't worry—we'll look out for her." He touched his cap again.

Rodriguez and Constanza looked at Ruggles's car as it pulled away. "Poor fucker," Rodriguez said, "Got a better chance of being struck with lightning in the subway." They walked off swinging their nightsticks in unison.

Ruggles talked into the mike again, circled a few blocks, then pulled into an open spot next to a meter. He emerged from the car, popped in a quarter, and turned the handle.

"Mr. Stolzfuss, you see the terminal up there, two blocks. You go in the door on the side of the street, and walk up the steps. At the top you turn to the right and walk down a hall till you come to the security office. It'll be on your right. They'll be expecting you. I'll meet you in a few minutes.'

Ruggles gave Stolzfuss a headstart of almost a block then ambled after him. Just as Stolzfuss reached for the handle of the door, a young black woman with a large kerchief wrapped around a beehive of hair emerged briskly, bumping into him. He excused himself and entered. Ruggles sauntered up the block. When he drew even with a well dressed slender black in a conservative suit and tie, he reached out his arm and grabbed him by the testicles and forced him against the exterior wall of the terminal. He shielded the man from passers-by with his bulk. He tightened his grip. The man drew in a rasping breath.

"The wallet from the man in the beard and hat. Put it in my pocket, or I'm gonna put your eggs in my pocket," he squeezed again, "scrambled!"

The pickpocket's eyes rolled up into his head. "Hurry up, motherfucker," Ruggles said, "I ain't got all day." The man put the wallet in his pocket. "You stay away from around here for a while, or you gonna be singing soprano in the jailhouse choir." He gave the man an extra squeeze, and left him huddled against the wall.

Ruggles followed the directions that he had given to Stolzfuss. When he entered the security office he found him sitting stiffly on a chair watching Jim Mancuso light a cigarette.

"Albert, how you is, ma man?" Mancuso looked as though he hadn't shaved in a week.

"Chasin' haws an' chicken thieves, as usual." Albert shook his hand. "Have you met Mr. Stolzfuss, Jim?"

"We just introduced ourselves, Albert."

"I'm afraid I have a small lesson for him." Albert shook his head and sighed. Then he extended the leather wallet to Mr. Stolzfuss. "Your pocket was picked when that girl bumped into you. She was what we call the stall. I got this from the hook, the man who actually picked your pocket."

Mancuso kicked at the floor angrily. "Did you make them?"

Ruggles shook his head. "Never saw him. Gave him a little squeezin' and invited him out after he offered the wallet back."

Mancuso ran his hand through his hair and took a deep

drag on his cigarette. "It used to be a hell of a lot worse than it is now. It was just unsafe to be in this building. But we've added more men from Street Crimes in these scuzzy outfits," he pointed deprecatingly at his ragged clothes. "It's worked. They're not really sure anymore that what looks like an easy-to-roll drunk isn't going to stand them on end and put cuffs on them. Or that some push-over Minnesota sixteen-year-old isn't really a pretty—and very tough—twenty-four-year-old policewoman with a two-hundred-pound partner six feet away. The statistics are better, but we're far from perfect."

Ruggles gave the last of the sketches to Mancuso, who promised to see that they got around the security staff and regular Street Crimes men who worked the terminal. He'd let him know if he heard anything. Ruggles thanked him, and asked Mr. Stolzfuss to go out before him, and wait at the car.

When Ruggles got to him, it was ten after five. They got in the car and sat looking at each other for a moment. "You think you're up to doing something really tough, Mr. Stolzfuss?"

"I can try."

"This is the hour. In a way, it's not much different from looking for a needle in a haystack, but it's a possibility. Rush hour, the girls come out. It's one of their best times. The johns—their customers, that is—are out of the office and on the way home. If they make a quick stop, well, no one is the wiser. 'I had to stay late at the office.' Or, 'My train was delayed.' So between say five-fifteen and six-thirty is one of the best times for the working girls." He looked the old man in the eye and measured his words. "If your Emily is on the street, and we cruise slow, we might just see her."

Ruggles drove slowly enough so that Stolzfuss's country sharp eyes might pick out his daughter displaying herself in a doorway, but at the same time, with enough speed to keep the word from going out that the Man was on the prowl, and clearing the street. At Fifty-third Street, Ruggles heard the older man draw in his breath sharply. He drove on nonetheless. "Did you see her," he asked.

"I don't know. It's possible. A blonde girl. Young. A strong look to her. We were moving fast. The face was un-clear."

"I'll pull around," Ruggles said. "We'll double check."

The traffic had not thinned at all, and it took an eternity to cross Fifty-fourth to Seventh and circle back. Ruggles made certain to stay to the right. Stolzfuss leaned forward anxiously, straining to see. The girl had not moved. Ruggles spotted her and stopped the car. She looked at them uncertainly. Ruggles could read her mind: A freak in a beard and a big spade. Forget it. She walked off rapidly.

Ruggles looked at Stolzfuss. "Not her, huh?"

"No, but it could have been. She was the same size, the same age. . . ." His voice drifted off.

Ruggles nodded. "That's the problem, of course. They're all young, and many are blonde and healthy. You want to look some more?"

"Just up to the end of the street." It was more a question than a statement.

"Sure. Sure. You just tell me if you want me to stop again."

After a silent moment, Stolzfuss said, "I can't believe that my Emily would show her legs like that, or her breasts."

They came to Fifty-seventh Street and Ruggles pulled to the curb. "You see how it is, Mr. Stolzfuss. Walking back and forth and looking never does any good. Especially with you being so easy to spot. If she was there, well, it would be like ringing a bell. We'd never catch her."

"But we wouldn't have to catch her," Stolzfuss said in protest.

Ruggles looked at him with pity. "Mr. Stolzfuss, don't you think if she wanted to come home she'd get in touch with you, or at least with the police?"

The old man's mouth became a grim straight line. "Not if she thought she would be shunned." The word had the knell of death.

"I think you should go back to Pennsylvania. We'll let you know if there is anything that you can do."

Stolzfuss shook his head deliberately. "Please. I must stay here. I have considered what I am doing. I, in my way," he swallowed hard, "am violating my covenant with God. I must stay at least until you have exhausted the first . . . possibilities. But I don't know where to stay."

The first possibilities, Albert thought, are in the morgue. "Would you like to go to a hotel?"

"I have never been in one," he said plaintively. "I

would prefer to stay among my people. But of course, they are not here."

"Stay put for a minute, Mr. Stolzfuss." Ruggles turned off the ignition and left the car, walking into a small cafeteria up the block. When he returned after a few moments, he had a satisfied smile on his face. "Mr. Stolzfuss, you and I are going for a short ride. This is a big city, Mr. Stolzfuss, and it takes all kinds."

Stolzfuss watched in silence as Ruggles guided the car through the crowded streets in the darkening spring evening. Eventually, they crossed the Madison Avenue Bridge into the Bronx. Lengthening shadows and the absence of life gave the impression that the empty blocks were a war zone, or a memorial to a lost race. Lifelessness gave way to dilapidated but inhabited blocks which, by reason of their light and life, seemed pretty in comparison. At the corner of Grand Avenue, Ruggles turned, continued a few blocks then came to a halt. Stolzfuss looked out at a sturdy brick and stone building plainly marked, The Mennonite Church.

Ruggles came around the car and opened the door. "I called them on the phone. They're expecting you."

A door in the small brick house adjoining the church opened, and a small, gray-bearded man, dressed like Stolzfuss, stepped down the sidewalk to meet them. He extended a hand. "Will you share our bread, Brother."

In a few minutes, Ruggles was headed downtown. It was settled that he would call Mr. Hagenzeiker, for such was the man's name, as soon as he had something to report. He didn't expect to have much. As an afterthought, he got on the radio to make sure that somebody had bothered to check the hospitals and the morgues.

# 23

The Filipino doctor who checked Iris Alonzo into Municipal Hospital on Ninety-seventh Street and First Avenue was not sure that she was going to live. *In my country, we lose babies from this all the time,* he thought. *The bug gets into the system and gives them diarrhea and vomiting. They can't keep anything down, or in. No fluids. They die of dehydration as surely as though they'd been left to die in a desert.*

Iris's temperature was elevated to the point where brain damage was a distinct possibility. On the other hand, Dr. Malapang thought, she was young and in otherwise good health. He slapped a dextrose intravenous set into the large vein in her right arm and yelled for cold packs. The nurse stripped her down and covered her with refrigerated towels.

She heaved a little, and spittle ran down her chin. "Hey," the doctor said to another nurse, "get a culture on her saliva, and a stool sample." The nurse looked at him blankly. "Take it off the end of a rectal thermometer if you have to. Come on, wake up!"

The next morning, Iris was still incoherent but alive, when they brought in her youngest sister, Cookie. Fortunately, the Alonzos had spotted the symptoms and reacted immediately. The child was in no danger, since she was treated at an earlier stage of the condition than Iris had been.

The laboratory report was confusing as hell. It was some form of *E. Coli* bacteria, but nothing that the technicians or the Chief Pathologist had ever seen. It took all of Malapang's persuasive powers to convince the man, who after all had his pride, that he might check it out with their prestigious colleagues a half dozen blocks, and yet half a world away, from their city-run charity hospital. The Chief Pathologist considered the matter, and decided to call up someone who really knew microbiology—his classmate at Bellevue more than thirty years ago—Morris Nassiter.

While the pathologist at Municipal tried to get through to Nassiter, a slim Puerto Rican girl in a pink uniform and crepe-soled white shoes glanced furtively about the hall of the Green Pavilion at Manhattan Jewish then slipped into the stairwell and trotted down to the basement. A film of perspiration covered her upper lip, glistening on a shadow of down. A short walk through the subterranean corridor to a door marked: "No Access/Maintenance Personnel Only—DANGER—High Voltage." She slowed as she approached the door, checked over her shoulder and ducked in. When her eyes became accustomed to the dim light, she walked purposefully toward a jumble of dials and switches marked "Emergency Control Panel." She looked behind it expectantly.

Rosario Gonzalez sat quietly reading by the light of a small lamp. When he heard her footsteps he raised his head slowly. She thrilled as he lowered the book and reached his hand out gently to cup her breast. "What is it?" he asked, flexing his fingers softly.

She shivered and stuttered out the words. "It's . . . it's Alex."

Rosario stood and put his book on the chair. "What about Alex?"

He had removed his hand from her body, but she was overcome enough by his nearness to be slow in answering. "What about Alex," he repeated.

"He's not in again today."

"Did someone try to contact him at home?"

"Rafaela did. She called him a lot, she said. He doesn't answer."

Rosario blinked in the half gloom. "Have her go to his house. She goes there often, doesn't she?"

"Yes, they go out."

"Tell her to go this afternoon after work."

The girl nodded but stood still, as though waiting to be dismissed. "Goodbye, *muchacha*," Rosario said. Leaning forward, he kissed her lightly on the lips. "Be careful leaving."

She opened the door a crack. An orderly was passing,

humming tunelessly. When he was gone, she dodged outside and closed the door behind her, moving swiftly down the hallway in the same direction from which she had come.

# 24

Albert Ruggles leaned wearily against the corner of Arnie Ross's desk and rubbed at bleary eyes. "So," he said, "as you gentlemen can see, while I am real interested in your problem, I am too fuckin' tired to take an immediate active role."

"I'll make you a deal, Albert," Arnie said. "If you listen to my tale of woe, I'll maybe pitch in on yours."

"Just like a sheeny," Albert commented to Lou. "Hey, Ross, you ever read about Shylock?"

"Yeah, you coulda paid him off three hundred times with the amount of flesh you're carrying."

Albert managed a smile, then wiped his eyes again. "No shit. It was grim. After I took the old man to that church, I went down to the youth center on Eighth Avenue where that priest . . ."

"Father Carbano," Lou added.

". . . Father Carbano and those social workers try to turn runaways around. I spoke to this chick who's the psychologist. A very bad scene." Albert shrugged. "She says for sure that the kid hasn't passed through their hands, or tried to get in contact with them—either in the kind of clothes the old man described, or any other kind. Maybe she hasn't been here long enough."

"Maybe she likes the street," Ross said. "You know there are some that really dig the life, or really go for their old man."

Albert shook his head. "Like the lady said, they only get about ten percent of the kids to go home. Most of the time home means child abuse, or incest."

"So it's better to end up giving head to ten, maybe fifteen guys you don't know every day," Ross asked.

"I guess some think so," Albert said, rising and stretching. "Anyway, I got to get some sack. What time is it?" Ross told him. "Okay then, I'll go home and clean up and grab some shuteye. I'll be back in six hours. Four o'clock. Okay?"

"Just keep in mind what I said, Albert," Lou stood and looked at him. "This is strictly quiet. Don't hassle anybody. But if you hear . . ."

"Anything about some nut with a hard-on for Manhattan Jewish, let you know."

"That's the one."

"I ain't deaf, man. See you."

Ross sat down again behind his desk which was littered with three-by-five-inch cards that had been taken from the hospital's personnel records department. "Come on, Roach, let's finish this batch. Then we can go get some coffee."

Hernandez' desk was neatly organized. Four small piles of cards were stacked against the edge nearest him. He sighed. "Where the hell are we?"

"Dubermann, Elsie. The last of the D's."

"How many cards you figure we got left?"

"We been through about nine hundred. That leaves maybe three thousand more to go. We've pulled maybe twenty."

Hernandez flipped through the stacks. "Twenty-three. If the ratio holds up, we'd have about a hundred individuals to check."

Ross made a face. "And that assumes that our freak is in here someplace. Well here's our first E. Gainsborough Easterling."

"You're shitting me."

# 25

Morris Nassiter was late getting to the hospital. He had been lecturing at University Medical Center on Thirty-second Street and had been caught up in traffic. He enjoyed student contact, and was often a guest lecturer at faculties other than Manhattan Jewish. On this day he was annoyed by the delay in his schedule. The interruption caused by the loss of Farbstein's mouse, and the ensuing embroilment with Rogovin and his two odd friends had been stimulating as a change from routine. But at the same time, it had slowed his progress in the development of his paper on the mortality potential of foreign intestinal bacteria. He expected to read the paper before the Royal Medical College in London in the fall.

Nassiter grumbled to himself as he left the car in the lot on Madison Avenue. He stuffed papers into his briefcase and walked carelessly across the avenue, heedless of a near collision with an automobile, or the imprecations of its startled driver.

Once in the lab, he took off his jacket and drew on a newly starched white coat and sat at his desk. He ran through the day's mail quickly; a number of advertisements, a request for a donation, a brief personal note from a friend. He was about to open his notebook when his eye strayed to his in-box. An eight-by-ten brown envelope had been dropped into the box face down. He pulled it out to find that it had been stamped "URGENT BY HAND" in several places, and bore the return address of the Municipal Hospital. It had evidently been delivered either the previous evening or earlier in the morning. He cursed and called the information services of the hospital. "Have I had any calls? This is Morris Nassiter."

After a pause, the operator replied, "Yes, Doctor. From Municipal, a Dr. Jack Feingold. Three times."

"When?"

"Last night, sir."

*"Vey is mir."*

"What, sir?"

"Never mind." He hung up. Why is it that they think if you aren't a surgeon or a cardiologist, it doesn't matter if your messages come by carrier pigeon? He opened the envelope with a scalpel he kept on his desk for the purpose. His eyes flicked rapidly over the pages. He adjusted his glasses and looked at them again, more slowly, then reached out for the phone. He dialed a number. A frosty voice answered, "This is Dr. Rogovin's office."

"It's Nassiter. Let me talk to him."

"I'm sorry, Doctor, he has people with him. May I have him return the call?" The voice was prim and efficient.

"Lady, go inside his office and put a piece of paper under his nose that he should come outside and talk to me immediately on an urgent matter." As an afterthought, he said. "Don't make me repeat myself." She had already gone.

Rogovin sounded breathless when he came to the phone. "Yes, Morris?"

"You should take better care, Saul. You're making Type A sounds. Like a business executive on his way to his first infarct."

"Jesus, Morris," he hissed into the receiver, "I've got two trustees in my office."

"Good. Put them on intercom so they can hear that Jack Feingold, the Chief Pathologist at Municipal, has found a case of gastro-enteric fauna he's never seen before, and that it's almost killed two Puerto Rican girls. Would I like to look at some samples? Tell me, Saul, would you like to bet which dead mouse the samples resemble?"

Rogovin straightened up from the desk, drew the silk handkerchief from the breast pocket of his coat and wiped his forehead.

"Hey, Saul, are you there?"

Rogovin put the receiver back to his ear. "Yes, Morris. Let's skip the bet. Go find out what Feingold has. Tell me as soon as you know. I'll be here all day. And for God's sake, play it down if you can."

"You're right, Saul, we don't want to tell anybody about the epidemic." He hung up while Rogovin spluttered at the other end.

Nassiter shed his white coat and put on his jacket again. Glancing out of the window, he decided that he would walk the few blocks to Municipal. He picked up the phone again and called Feingold. "Jack, I got your envelope. I'd love to take a look. Thank you for the opportunity. We haven't had a chance to talk over anything interesting in a long time." Nassiter applauded himself for his tact, and headed for the elevator.

When he got to Municipal he marveled again at his good fortune in being appointed to Manhattan Jewish. Though the hospital plant itself was fairly new, Municipal showed the strain of its service as a city hospital, and the deleterious effects of budget cuts which the Health and Hospital Corporation had endured for the crisis years since someone had finally admitted that the city's piggy-bank was empty. He walked through the front doors, glancing toward the Emergency Room which carried out the same process of triage as at his own hospital. He didn't pause, but went directly to the office of the Chief Pathologist.

Feingold was a short stocky man who had seemed out of breath in medical school thirty years before. He was still out of breath. "So, Jack, how are you?"

Feingold breathed in deeply, then shrugged. "It could be worse. You? Cushy over there, huh?"

Nassiter shrugged back. "I'm never satisfied."

"Coffee, Morris?"

Nassiter shook his head. "No. I'd like to look in a mike though."

Feingold led him through a series of doors and cramped rooms to a small laboratory with a single microscope set up with a series of slides and a chair at the end of an otherwise bare table. When Nassiter sat down, Feingold provided him with a pencil and a yellow pad. Nassiter flicked on the microscope light and adjusted the lens barrel. The blurred image clarified and a series of slender rods capered across the field. Nassiter counted them under his breath, observed their progress for a few minutes, then made a note on the paper.

Feingold passed him another slide. "Stool from patient one."

Nassiter nodded and looked. The ritual was followed through a half dozen additional slides, some bearing live cultures in sputum or stool, others dead and stained, still others in a growth medium.

Finally, Nassiter stood up. "Could I look at the charts? How about some background?"

"Come." Feingold motioned him to a sink at the back of the lab where Nassiter washed thoroughly.

"Jack, you're watching how that material is handled?"

Feingold looked offended. "Like the plague, how else?"

"Tell me about the patients?"

Feingold lifted his shoulders expressively. "What can I say? Two Puerto Rican sisters, one sixteen, the other six. Sick as dogs. Malapang, the Filipino resident who brought in the first girl—the older one—saved her. Total dehydration. She's still comatose. The little girl came in later, not quite so bad. Did a lavage, straight onto IV. They—the parents—are pretty sharp people. The minute she showed any signs of illness they brought her in. It was the morning after the big girl was brought in. The little one is punchy but awake. She knows nothing. Tell me, Morris, what is it you see? It's a bacteria. Not one I ever saw in a book even."

Nassiter smiled. "Why should you have ever seen this? It's a . . ." he paused, remembering to watch his mouth, ". . . an unusual strain." He tore the notes off his pad and stuffed them in his pocket. "Uh, say, Jack, you wouldn't mind if I pocketed a couple of your slides, would you?"

Feingold hesitated, then said, "Not if you intend to do something besides look sheepish, and let me know what comes out of this."

Nassiter laughed. "If I had something to say, I would. Listen, I promise. When I have something, you'll know. In the meantime, I wouldn't let just anybody handle those girls, and I'd be tempted to treat their bed linens and such with epidemic care."

Feingold nodded agreement and bid him goodbye. Nassiter took the carefully packed slide case, slipped it into his pocket, and walked back to Manhattan Jewish.

# 26

Saul Rogovin had had a hard day. It wasn't over yet. He checked the time. It was three-thirty, and he was on his way from his office to the fourth floor of Morgenstern Pavilion. Under his arm was a patient file with a little red tab affixed to the top. The tab indicated the special interest of the Medical Board, and the need to refer to Dr. Rogovin. He was both professionally and personally concerned and dismayed. Carmelita Hernandez was showing no signs of improvement. Her white count was sky high. Tenderness of the pancreas—inflammation. Nodal edema. Permanent exhaustion. The stepping stones of Hodgkin's Disease. Her discomfort seemed to extend to the lymph nodes in the groin and knee. Phase three. The recovery rate is poor when Hodgkin's gets below the rib cage. There are chemotherapy techniques that are new and promising. And there's radiation. But she's no kid, Saul thought. And she's weak. Who knows?

Waiting for him in Mama's room, Ross and Hernandez made aimless, cheery conversation with the patient who was too tired to respond.

"Mama, it's fascinating. Instead of just sitting here doing nothing, you should help us to sort cards," Lou said.

She smiled weakly. "It's a . . ." she hunted for a word, ". . . *una verguenza* . . . a shame . . . that you should spend your time with little cards."

Ross smiled at her and patted her hand. "At least it keeps us off the street and out of trouble."

"*Gracias a Dios.*"

"Look at it this way, Mama," Arnie continued. "We've been here for a half hour. So from ten to three we got from D to L. Already that's not bad. Who knows? By tomorrow, the day after, we could be finished."

"And like Arnie says, Mama, we've only collected about fifty cards. Maybe in the end we'll only have seventy-five."

"And then," Arnie said, rising from the bedside chair, "maybe we'll be finished interviewing in 1991."

Rogovin tapped at the door and walked in. "Well, Mrs. Hernandez, don't you ever run out of visitors? They're going to wear you out. Didn't your daughter-in-law just leave?"

Mama hitched herself up on her elbow. "Yes. But she's coming back. You leave my boys alone."

He shook hands with Lou and Arnie. "Relax, Mrs. Hernandez, you can keep your delinquents until it's time to go down for another set of X-rays." He checked his watch. "Which is supposed to be in about ten minutes."

She fell back on the pillow and closed her eyes. Lou looked at Rogovin. His face was frozen into a noncommittal professional smile. "Will you excuse us for a couple of minutes, Mrs. Hernandez," Rogovin said. "We'll be outside in the hall." He waited for a reply, then realized that she had dozed off. He motioned to Ross and Hernandez to follow him, and left the room.

Rogovin stood with his back to the wall in the broad corridor, holding the folder open in front of him.

"So, Saul," Ross asked.

"It's too soon . . ." he held up his hand to stem a torrent of words from both Lou and Arnie. "It's just too soon to make an absolute diagnosis." He paused, "However, I'm afraid that it is Hodgkin's Disease."

Lou swallowed. "Cancer of the lymphatic system!"

Rogovin sighed. "You'll drive yourself as crazy playing doctor as I would playing detective."

"But that's what you called it."

Rogovin nodded agreement. "Essentially. There's no point in going into clinical details. We really don't know for sure." Again he had to motion them for silence. "We simply don't know yet. There are many things to test. There are many false symptoms that indicate one condition and either mask or misrepresent another."

"When do we find out where Mama stands," Arnie said.

"When we find out. And then there are a variety of chemotherapeutic treatments and radiation to deal with the disease—if indeed that's what she has."

"How long, Saul? I mean . . ." Ross faltered.

"A month. Twenty years. It depends on many things. When we are surer of the diagnosis, we'll know more."

"Twenty years?" Lou asked.

"Why not? If it is Hodgkin's and we get rid of it, she is otherwise healthy. She's tough, your mother."

An intercom box above their heads squawked. "Doctor Rogovin, Doctor Rogovin, please take the house phone," then repeated itself.

"Excuse me for a minute," he said over his shoulder as he walked toward the nursing station. He picked up the phone, identified himself, then waited a moment. Lou and Arnie could see a look of concern sweep over his face, drawing down the corners of his mouth and wrinkling his forehead, making him suddenly look older. He nodded as though his invisible caller could see him, then straightened and hung up the phone. He hesitated for a moment then returned to where Ross and Hernandez stood waiting.

"We have, uh, a little problem. Would you come up with me to see Morris Nassiter?"

"The pathologist?" Lou asked.

"Microbiologist, yes. You've met him."

"What about Mama," Ross asked, looking at Lou.

Lou opened the door a crack and glanced in. His mother, looking gray and tired, snored softly, her chin on her chest. He turned to Ross. "She won't know we're gone. And she has to go for X-rays anyway. Margarita's coming back. And we can stop by later."

Ross's face took on a stubborn set, then softened. "Okay. Okay. But I want to hear the rest of the diagnosis."

Rogovin talked as they walked toward the elevator. "There isn't any rest. As soon as I know more, so will you." He paused as they waited for the elevator, then said, "but there's no sense in kidding. Mama is sick."

They followed Rogovin silently through the halls to Nassiter's lab, each coping with the new reality of Mama's condition as best he could: Lou in sad contemplation, Arnie in fear and anger.

Nassiter stood at the door waiting for them. "Saul. Gentlemen. Please, come in." He closed the door behind them. A figure was huddled over a complicated looking microscope set into a bench from which a spaghetti of wires trailed. "You remember Farbstein? Say hello, Farbstein."

A muffled "Hello" came from the vicinity of the scope.

"It seems," Nassiter said, wiping his hands on his coat, "that our dead mouse has friends in town." He motioned the three men to his glass walled office and called over his shoulder. "Farbstein. When you're through ogling the fauna, you might step over here and talk to these gentlemen."

In a moment, Farbstein joined them, and in the absence of an extra chair sat on the corner of the desk. "No doubt about it," he said with obvious satisfaction. "If you add together the symptoms, well, we've certainly been on the right path."

There was a pause, then Nassiter said, "We're very pleased for you, Farbstein, being proven right and so forth, and of course, being reunited with your friends. But would you mind telling Detectives Ross and Hernandez what you mean?"

Farbstein sniffed. "The bacteria in the stool samples of the two girls are conclusively the same as those in the digestive tract of the experimental animal that we found in Neoplastics the other night."

Hernandez frowned and leaned forward. "What girls? Could this be an epidemic?"

Farbstein said primly, "Certainly not. Unless of course it became well established in a food handling atmosphere. And even then, there would have to be no interruption by sterilization or antisepsis."

Ross looked pleadingly from Nassiter to Rogovin and back.

Nassiter smiled. "What Farbstein means is that the chain can be broken fairly simply. If someone had the bacteria on his hands and handled a tomato, then gave you the tomato and you ate it raw, the possibility exists that you would get the same reaction as the two young ladies who are suffering over at Municipal. On the other hand. . . ."

"Hold on a second," Ross interrupted. "Are you telling me that the bug that mouse had has made somebody sick? You are sure it's from that mouse?"

"Yes to both," Nassiter answered. "To make a long story from my esteemed colleague short, two Puerto Rican girls, sisters, were brought into Municipal last night several hours apart sick as dogs. The older one, a kid of about sixteen, almost died, and still is in lousy shape. Their pathologist, who's an old friend, gave me a ring because he didn't recognize the specific form."

Farbstein piped up. "No doubt about it. That's our bacteria. All of the characteristics . . . ."

"Right," Nassiter said.

"But how did they catch it?" Ross asked.

"That's what I was trying to tell you when you interrupted, Sergeant Ross."

Arnie ducked his head. "I'll shut up."

"As I was saying," Nassiter went on, "If you washed that tomato I was talking about in a strong solution of iodoform, you would kill the bacteria, and you could eat the tomato without adverse effect. It's a matter of vectors. If somebody who had been playing with our mouse were a cook at a diner, and if he didn't wash his hands thoroughly, he could make enough people sick to fill half a dozen emergency wards. Of course, he would infect himself also. In countries where they use night soil as fertilizer . . . ."

"Huh," Arnie said.

"Shit. In countries where they use night soil, the chain doesn't break. It goes into the food, the bare feet, the hands, then the mouths."

"On the other hand," Farbstein interjected, "It doesn't always bother the people that have it."

"Oh yes," Nassiter agreed. "Revenge is a two-edged sword. We always complain about Montezuma's Revenge because we are not used to the forms of *E. Coli* that live in Mexican intestinal walls. I assure you that the entire population of Mexico doesn't run around with the shits all day. On the other hand, if they drank water in certain parts of our country, they might just get Uncle Sam's Revenge. Some strains are better, some worse."

"And this strain, Doctor," Lou asked.

Nassiter frowned. "It clearly has killer potential. A weak, or very young or old person, or even someone who went untreated, could very well die."

Rogovin said, "At least the cases didn't pop up here. That's a relief."

"Maybe they missed," Arnie said drily. "We'd better get over to Municipal and find out what that girl has to say. Maybe she ate in a restaurant, or had dinner at a friend's house. It had to come from somewhere. At least we have something to get our teeth into. Cheer up, Saul, if the contact turns out to be somebody who works here, we've got a leg up on your sabotage problem."

On the way out of the lab, Arnie patted at his pocket. "Shit, I left my note pad in Mama's room."

"C'mon, Arn," Lou said. "You can pick it up tomorrow."

"I'll meet you downstairs."

"Okay," Hernandez said in exasperation, "But make it snappy."

Ross threaded his way to Morgenstern Four and walked down the corridor to Mama Hernandez' room. He looked up and down the hall, and when he spotted what he was looking for, he ducked into the room.

When the red haired nurse was opposite the crack that Ross had left in the door, he opened it and bumped into her.

"Oh, excuse me."

"You, again."

"What else? Do you mind stepping in here for a moment?"

"I certainly do. I know you're a cop, but I work for a living."

He put his hand on her elbow and firmly guided her into Mama's room. "Do you know that I lied to a fellow officer to see you?"

"Should I be flattered?"

"No, but you should give me a date."

She slipped out of his grasp and headed to the hall. "Never trust a crooked cop."

"My dear," he said, in the voice of W. C. Fields, "the only pad I want to be on is yours."

He followed her out of the door and turned back toward the elevator. She was headed in the other direction, but he heard her chuckle. Before the elevator came he patted his pocket to make sure that the pad was really there.

# 27

Rafaela Arenas shuddered as she stepped inside the dingy tenement in the East Village. She was wearing slacks and a sweater under a light jacket. Her head was covered by a kerchief. She had been told to be careful and to avoid being recognized. A rat scurried across her path and she recoiled against the moldering plaster wall. The halls smelled fetid, and the stairs creaked as she mounted toward the second floor. Some of the apartment doors hung crazily from their hinges, some were missing entirely. A garbage bag stood in front of a closed door, some of its contents trailing on the floor.

Alex's apartment was at the end of the corridor. The bulb was out and the door was shrouded in darkness. Rafaela shuffled her feet, afraid to fall, and unwilling to touch the damp walls.

"Alex," she called softly. "Alex, are you in there?" When there was no reply, she knocked, and called again, raising her voice. She waited a moment, then reached for the handle. At first, it resisted, and she withdrew her hand. When she tried again, she felt the rusty mechanism begin to give. She slipped her bag over her arm and twisted with both hands till she heard a click. Pushing against the handle, she forced the door backward on creaking hinges.

The odor from the darkened room struck Rafaela with the force of a blow. She retreated momentarily into the hall, fighting a wave of nausea. She stepped inside the room again and closed the door behind her. Though her eyes had become accustomed to the relative darkness of the hall, she was still unable to see in the small front room, which was without windows. In a moment shapes became clear to her and she was able to wend her way to a corner table and a lamp. She flicked a switch and a single dim bulb came on, illuminating the small space. A chair was turned over, and the articles from a small table next to it were strewn across the floor. Rafaela was forced to take a deep breath as her stomach wrenched at the staggering odor of decay that filled her nostrils.

"Alex," she said, "Jesus, Alex, are you in here?" She looked at the door to the bedroom, hesitated a moment, then with determination, crossed and pushed it open.

Rafaela reeled away from the door vomiting. The violent spasm wrenched the muscles of her diaphragm, bringing tears to her eyes. She heaved for a full minute till there was nothing left for her stomach to expel, then stood shaking, still bent over at the waist.

She raised her head and looked back into the bedroom shaking. A ray of light fell across the stiffened form of Alex Klinger, twisted in the rictus of pain and death, his head thrown back and his eyes and mouth agape, in a pool of filth where he had shitted himself out of existence. A rat scurried across a naked abdomen already chewed raw. Rafaela began to hyperventilate, and stumbled against the wall. Her heart was a trip hammer in her breast, and she lost momentary control of her bladder. "Jesus, Maria, Nombre de Cristo."

She rested against the wall till a scampering sound made her bolt with fear to the door. More by reflex than design, she shut it behind her as she ran into the hall.

Despite her desire for anonymity, she ran down the dark corridor and negotiated the steps two at a time until she reached the lower landing. She stood panting at the front door of the decrepit building, trying to compose herself. A door opened on the floor above and she fled into the street.

Rafaela looked in both directions. The subway was to the west, but there were too many people on that street. She turned toward the East River and walked briskly away, her heart still pounding, her mouth sour with the taste of vomit. At the next corner two teenage Hispanic boys fell in behind her and muttered vulgarities for a block, then peeled off in another direction. She walked to the river and turned north on the walk that parallels the F.D.R. Drive.

As she walked, her arms clutched to her stomach, she gained more self-control, and was able to fight off the intermittent bouts of trembling that had gripped her since she had seen Alex Klinger's gnawed corpse. Her wet panties slipped into the crevasse of her labia, causing a painful burning sensation. She looked up to locate herself. She was nearly at Fourteenth Street.

Suddenly, she was very sore and tired, and felt unable to go on. She waved frantically as an empty cab turned west from the southbound service road. The driver saw her and slid to a halt a hundred feet up the block. She ran to the car and jumped in, gratefully leaning against the seat with her head back and her eyes closed. She was startled when, after a moment, the driver turned and asked, "Well, lady, where'll it be?"

She hesitated, then looked at her watch. It was nearly five. She hoped that he had not left. "Manhattan Jewish Hospital, please. The Morgenstern Clinic, Lexington and Ninety-sixth."

# 28

Despite her high resolve, Emily Stolzfuss was grateful when Eddie Biggs returned to the dark room. She was stiff from being spreadeagled on the bed, though Biggs had loosened the bonds considerably, allowing her more movement. And she was hungry and thirsty.

"Well, look what your old man brought his chick. See. I got you some good food." Biggs unwrapped the contents of the bag on top of the bureau. "Cheeseburgers and a malted. And some coffee, too. Who says I don't love you?"

Emily salivated at the smell of food, at the same time wondering how one word could encompass Eddie's thoughts about love and her own.

Biggs untied her hands and feet. Nonetheless, she remained still for a moment in fear, trying to anticipate his next thought, to avoid another beating. He stepped back across the room with a twinkle in his eye. He had understood. She sat up stiffly and rubbed her wrists and ankles until the circulation returned. She swung about and put her feet on the floor, then stood shakily. When she was sure of her footing, she walked to the bathroom and sat on the commode. Biggs followed her and stood brazenly at the door. She shrugged and relieved herself as he watched grinning.

When she was done she walked to the doorway but he blocked her way. "Is baby gonna sing for her supper?" With another shrug, Emily knelt on the dirty floor, unzipped his fly and blew him.

"You ready," Eddie Biggs commented as Emily sat on the bed chewing into her second cheeseburger. "No question about it. You ready. That was fine head you give me. Tonight, you gonna be a professional. Wait till you see what I got you." He triumphantly produced another package and unwrapped it. "Look at this dress." She continued to eat noisily, ignoring him. "Look, I said," his voice took on a nasty edge. She stopped in midbite and turned her eyes toward him. He was holding a flimsy electric blue dress and a pair of very high-heeled black pumps. "You gonna look terrific." She turned back to the cheeseburger.

When she had dressed, Biggs stepped back and regarded her with the critical eye of an artist. He was well satisfied. She stood somewhat shakily on four-inch stiletto heels. The dress, which was immodestly translucent, was hemmed midway between crotch and knee. The décolleté plunged toward Emily's navel, barely concealing the edges of her nipples. Beneath, a black garter belt of synthetic lace held black stockings against her firm legs. "Remember, lessen they gives you extra, you just opens the top button to let yo' titties out, and spreads yo' legs. That's why you don't need no pants. Everything is extra in this business. All they is entitled to for their twenty-five is either a blow job or a fuck. That's how come you don't need no panties. You got that?"

She nodded. She followed him unsteadily into the hall and watched as he locked the door behind them. Just being outside of the room gave Emily a feeling of elation. She was close to freedom.

As Eddie Biggs passed in front of her to go down the stairs, he jabbed her in the solar plexus with his elbow. The air hissed out of her like a punctured balloon. "Just in case you gets any ideas, baby, I'm gonna watch you like a hawk. You opens your mouth for anything besides to suck a dick or ask for money, and I'm gonna fix you up. You got *that*?"

She gritted her teeth and straightened up, then followed him down the stairs holding back her tears. How had he known? she wondered. How could he have known?

Eddie had plans. He sat in the subway as it rocked back and forth, squealing its way around corners from station to station on its way to Fifty-first Street. He was thinking about the disposition of the expected evening's take. Let's see, he thought, if she does ten johns—and that ain't so many—we ought to net two hundred, maybe two-fifty. I can rent a decent car for tomorrow night and stop ridin' with all these house niggers. He looked about him at the tired faces and sniffed audibly.

Emily sat slackly beside him, unconscious of the fresh stares she drew at every stop. Once a uniformed cop passed by. She could see his blue pants through her downcast eyes. She toyed with the idea of yelling for his help, or throwing herself at his knees and begging for mercy, but Eddie casually slipped his hand over her knee and squeezed tightly. He had read her mind again. And besides, the cop, after leering at her breasts, sauntered to the end of the car and sat in an empty seat, reading a newspaper. Eddie relaxed his grip and continued to contemplate his rosy future. A week to a nice apartment. A month and he'd have a Caddie. The subway jolted to a halt and shook him from his reverie. "Let's go."

Eddie and Emily walked to Fifty-third Street and Eighth Avenue. She wobbled on each step, and only the strength of her grip on the banister prevented her from toppling backward. She paused as they reached the sidewalk, panting, her calves cramped.

Eddie casually eyed the block across the street. A short Puerto Rican girl with a red shirt patrolled the far corner, eyes flashing, pocketbook swinging, her mouth busily at work on a wad of gum. At the opposite corner a black girl huddled in a doorway. Eddie checked her over and laughed. Six feet tall and skinny. He nudged Emily. "Some chick," he said. He led Emily across the street past the doorway, and mimicked in a squeaky voice, "Hullo, baby, how they hanging?"

Emily was startled when a baritone voice replied, "Fuck off, asshole."

"C'mon, baby," he said to Emily, "we gonna find a spot for you to work." He continued down the street, leading her by the arm, between her and the gutter, occasionally commenting about this or that. To Emily, his words were indistinguishable from the droning background noises that assailed her. She walked as steadily as she could manage, her eyes fixed ahead.

A small man in a faded blue suit with a shirt and no tie stepped into her field of vision. He stopped in front of Emily, blocking her way. She looked down at his wizened face. He was in his sixties, and short enough to be a dwarf. His teeth were bad. He made clutching motions with dirty clawlike hands. "Nice tits, kid," he said in a raspy metallic voice. "What'll you do for ten bucks?"

Eddie Biggs reached out and pushed the man in the chest. He stumbled backward, away from Emily. "You gonna stick it in her nose, little man? She don't do nothin' for ten dollars." Eddie slipped his arm around her waist and guided her haughtily past the dwarf, who crouched against the building, his face a twisted mask of silent hate.

Halfway down the block Eddie turned to Emily and said, "See how your old man take care of you? Now if he'd said fifty dollars. . . ." Eddie laughed and pushed her forward ahead of him. She fought the bile down her throat as she imagined the grimy claws invading her body.

At Fifty-fifth he pulled her to a halt and looked around. He nodded in appreciation. "This is prime." He tugged at her arm and she followed him around the corner toward Ninth Avenue. About fifty feet up the block he led her up a flight of stairs above which a neon sign—of which only the "G" and "T" remained lighted—proclaimed the existence of the Gulf Hotel.

"Charlie," Eddie said, "this is Amanda. Say hello, Amanda." He squeezed her arm.

"Hello."

The man behind the counter grunted. "Y'unerstan', we keep what the johns gives us—plus you give us five. Y'unerstan'?"

Emily nodded indecisively, not altogether sure of what the man had said. The pressure on her elbow grew again. "What he mean is," Eddie explained, "that yo' customer gonna pay nine dollars for the room to him. Then you gonna let the customer leave first. Then when you leaves, you gonna give Charlie five dollars more. Okay?"

He squeezed. "Okay."

"Let's go, Amanda." Eddie preceded her down the stairs. When she arrived, he took her face in his hands and kissed her lightly on the mouth. "Off you go, baby. You just stand there on the corner and I'll watch how you cut it. You're on your own. Just keep 'em happy." He faded away into the pedestrian traffic.

Emily was tempted simply to run down the street screaming for help. She looked at the hostile, self-concerned faces of the Eighth Avenue crowd and decided that she might as well be alone. Eddie would come after her and catch her and. . . . She squeezed her eyes shut on a vision of a dozen old dwarfs and transvestites and whores laughing as Eddie Biggs beat her naked body on the sidewalk, while the cop on the subway stood by applauding.

Emily walked to the corner and looked bleakly across the stream of traffic, then edged back toward a doorway to keep from being knocked from her awkward pedestal. A man in his mid-thirties in a glen plaid business suit and snap brim fedora approached her nervously. His eyes shifted from side to side as though he were afraid of being watched. He was almost touching Emily when he managed to stammer, "Y . . . Y . . . You working?" His voice was high and squeaky with tension. He waited for a moment, and when she failed to reply, he turned to leave. Emily spotted Eddie from the corner of her eye. The man in the suit smelled faintly of cologne.

"Yes," she blurted. "You want to go out?"

"Shh," the man said. "You want to tell the world. How much?" He nearly whispered.

"Twenty-five dollars, and nine more for the room," Emily replied.

"Okay . . . okay." The man fidgeted. "Well, are you going to take me or not?" he added urgently in the same stage whisper. Emily turned the corner to the hotel, the john following warily, half a dozen steps behind. He increased his pace as they climbed the stairs, looking over his shoulder. They stood together at the front desk for a moment till Charlie, sitting in a decrepit armchair watching a ball game, noticed that they were there. He struggled to his feet and said, "Nine bucks. Here, fill this out."

The john took the three-by-five card. Curious, Emily watched. Mr. and Mrs. John Smith, 1 Main Street, Pleasant Valley, N.J. The john gave Charlie the card and a ten dollar bill. Charlie held the bill up to a fly-specked light bulb, then pulled a wad from his pocket. He added the ten, peeled off a single and said, "Room 26, up one flight." He dropped a rusty iron key and the dollar on the cracked glass counter top and plopped back into the chair.

Emily took the key and mounted the next flight uncertainly with the john close behind. She jumped a little when she felt him put his hand on her buttocks as she climbed. The next landing gave onto a corridor of peeling paint and rickety wooden doors. Number 26 was the first door to the right.

"Hurry," the john said.

Emily fumbled with the key, and after a moment managed to open the door. She saw a string dangling from the ceiling in the slim ray of light from the hall and tugged it. The lone ceiling bulb shed a tawdry illumination on a lumpy double bed covered with a single sheet. A stained sink projected from the wall opposite. Next to it a stringy towel hung from a bar. A wooden table and chair scarred with initials and cigarette burns leaned crazily in a corner.

"Oh, hurry up," the john said, "hurry up or it will be too late." She started at the sound of his voice and the slamming of the door behind him. She turned to find him struggling out of his jacket. "Hurry," he said panting, suddenly out of breath. "Hurry up." He had dropped his trousers and shorts to the ground in a ball, exposing a quivering erection. "Come on, you bitch, hurry it up," he gasped in a strangled voice. Emily tried to remember the steps that Eddie had told her. The john hopped from foot to foot like a little boy trying to keep from peeing in his pants. Suddenly, he pushed Emily on the bed, his face red from some effort she didn't understand. He yanked the flimsy material from her body and plunged forward. He had barely touched her when he uttered a squeaky animal cry. She felt his whole body shake through his hands, which were pressing her knees apart. She looked down. He had barely penetrated her.

"I did it." He thrust forward a little more, and sighed. "I made it." He looked at himself, as though to confirm his triumph. He stood straight, and cleared his throat. "A little problem you understand. I have . . . well . . . sometimes I can't wait. But I'm sure you see that all the time." He smiled nervously and pulled his shorts and then his slacks up around his waist. "Premature ejaculation." He giggled again. "I . . . uh . . . I can get it up, but I can't keep it up. Ha ha." He licked his lips. "Oh. yeah." He pulled a billfold from his hip pocket and threw a twenty and a five on the bed.

"Listen, sir," Emily started in her clear voice, just a tinge of the Dutch to it. "I have a problem. . . ."

"Oh, no," he said grabbing for his coat. "You said twenty-five. You're not going to hold me up." His face was pinched with sudden fear.

"I don't want money. I need help. Could you call a policeman."

"Are you crazy. You fucking whore bitch," he hissed.

"Please. I'm a prisoner. I. . . ."

The man rushed out of the door banging it so hard that it ricocheted from the jamb and swung back and forth eerily in the weak light. Emily sobbed once, drily, then got to her feet, sat on the sink and cleansed herself of the stickiness and dried herself with the towel. She sat on the edge of the bed for a moment and thought, then rose and went downstairs to the desk.

"Don't forget my fin, chickie," Charlie said from the depths of his chair. "Say what did you do to that john? Bite off his cock? He ran out of here like he was on fire." He pulled himself upright. Emily put the five dollars on the counter, and cleared her throat.

"Charlie. I don't like this. Can you help . . ."

He cut her off with a motion of his hand. "I ain't a psychiatrist, Blondie. You got a problem, you take it up with your pimp."

"But Charlie. . . ." She turned to the sound of footsteps on the lower stairs.

"But Charlie, what?" Eddie Biggs asked. "Where's the money?"

She held the bill out at arm's length. "Nothing. Nothing," she murmured fearfully. Biggs grabbed the bill from her hand and glanced at Charlie, who had resumed watching the game. He shrugged and turned back to her. "Okay, baby. One down, ninety-nine to go," he said, and pulled her down the stairs after him.

# 29

Rafaela had sat in the back seat of the cab throughout the long ride up the drive, trying not even to blink. Every time her eyes closed she saw Alex Klinger's corpse. She shuddered and looked dumbly out of the window as dusk fell on the city.

The cabbie dropped her on the Lexington Avenue side of the hospital as she had requested. She waited till a group of people, chattering in gutter Spanish, ambled down the street and turned into the hospital. She moved along with them into the lobby, and slipped off while they occupied the attention of the uniformed guard. It seemed to her that the clicking of her heels rang like cymbals as she hurried down the hall. She came to a door that led to the labyrinth beneath the hospital complex and dodged through it. She walked as quickly as she could to the area of the generators, and found the proper door. She hesitated for an instant. What if the night men were already on duty? Rosario had stressed to all of his people to stay away from him and each other at the hospital. They would be found out if they associated with one another. She shook her head in confusion. But he had told her to find out about Alex, and to tell him as fast as she could. She bit her lip and stifled a cry as the door swung open.

Rosario, thin and worn, but neatly dressed in his street clothes, looked at her and reached out for her cheek. "Don't be afraid, *muchacha*."

She stuttered, "Alex . . . Alex . . . he's . . . he's dead."

His expression did not change. His strange eyes did not flicker. He continued to stroke her cheek gently, and in a moment she ceased to tremble. Her breathing evened out, and she managed a small smile.

"We will go to my apartment, and you can tell me. Can you go alone, *muchacha*?"

She nodded and retraced her steps down the corridor. He watched her for a moment, then went in the opposite direction.

Rafaela was standing in the shadow of a stoop across the street from Rosario's flat when he arrived. She watched him enter, waited a minute, then followed.

The door of his apartment was open. Rosario sat on the window sill, the rays of the setting sun giving his skin a copper cast, and lengthening the shadows about his eyes, making him look almost Oriental.

He pointed to the hard-backed chair and said, "Bring it close to me. Tell me what you saw."

Sitting at his knee, looking up at him, she felt very calm. She described what she had seen.

"It is their vengeance," Rosario said simply. Rafaela looked up at him, into his hot eyes. "They have spread a sickness to kill Alex."

Rafaela's lips twitched as she stifled a thought. "What did you want to say, *muchacha*?" Rosario asked.

She cleared her throat once, then again. She feared that her bladder would fail her again.

"*Por favor*," he insisted.

"But Alex got sick from what he did, didn't he?" She paused. "I mean. He was doing . . . he was. . . ."

"He was in the struggle," Rosario intoned. "He was striking back at the monsters." His voice was an insistent low drone. "He was bringing the fight to their battleground. He is a casualty in the war against the enslavement of our souls and the destruction of our bodies."

As he spoke in his low monotone, Rafaela began to rock back and forth in the chair very slowly. "He struck out against them. He hurt them. But his sword . . . his sword of justice," his voice began to rise, "the hilt of the sword was poisoned. Even as he struck them, they lay in wait for him to strike him down."

He paused. "As they wait for us all. Do you understand that it was not Alex's hand that caused his sickness and his death? Do you understand that they lie in wait for us? Ready to strike us? To kill us, if we raise a hand against their tyranny?"

He put a thin hand on her arm. "Do you need to see again? Do you need to renew your faith?" Her arm quivered in his grasp. Her eyelids fluttered. "Tell me!"

Her voice cracked. "Show me." She rose from the chair,

guided by his hand like a puppet on a string. He led her toward the bedroom and through the door.

"How did they die," he asked gently, standing before the picture of his family.

"By the hand of the doctors."

"Why were they killed," he asked.

"Because they were good and they were weak."

"If we do not rise up, what shall they do?"

"They're going to kill us if we resist them, and make our children their slaves."

"And what shall we do?"

"Fight." It was a gust of air through clenched teeth. Her eyes were closed. He stood behind her where he could feel the shallow breaths. He undid her skirt and let it fall to the floor. "What," he underlined the word with a click of his tongue, "shall we do?" He stripped the still damp panties from her waist to below her knees in a single motion. They fell to the floor and she stepped out of them. "Fight." Her voice was guttural. "Fight."

He reached around her waist and began to stroke her gently as she would have had she been doing it herself. "Fight," she said. She leaned back against him. "Fight and hurt and win." There was a low moan in her throat. "Fight and kill."

Her body swayed back and forth against his. His hands moved in a rotating motion, just the tips of his fingers in strong but gentle contact, in twin orbits first apart and then together. "Fight and die," she cried, pulsing against him, her voice a sob. He held her to him as she thrust her pelvis into his hands, holding her, letting her surge against him as waves do against rocks.

When she was spent he turned her toward him and held her gently in his arms till she breathed evenly. She stooped to retrieve her clothes and on impulse, kneeling, grasped his hand and kissed it fervently. "Fight and die," she said.

He put his free hand on top of her head. "It is almost the time," he said. She looked up at him, her eyes wide. "They must be near. They will be near when they find Alex. There is no hope to hide him. It is almost time. I will call you."

"What shall I do?"

"Nothing, *muchacha*." He pulled her to her feet and watched as she dressed. "Do as you always do. I will tell you." He smiled gravely. "It is not today, and not tomorrow, but the day is near." She stood uncertainly before him. "Go home, *muchacha*."

When he heard the door close behind her, he sat at the edge of the bed and looked across the room. After a moment he walked to the wall where the schematic of Manhattan Jewish Hospital was pinned, and nodded to himself.

"It is time," he said aloud.

# 30

Arnie and Lou stopped into the station to check out their desks before heading to Municipal to see the Alonzo girls. Marvin Baxter, who had been on the phone when they'd walked into the H/Z4 office, walked across the bullpen and accosted them. "Excuse me, gentlemen. I just thought I'd let you know that Lieutenant Flaherty was very interested in your whereabouts before he went home."

Ross turned to him and smiled, "And I guess he told you to pass that along?"

"He did, indeed."

"Just like that?"

"More or less. He said tell that fuckin' Ross I want to know where he is. He should call me at home."

"Oops," Lou said.

Ross frowned. "Just a small piece of advice, Baxter. Flaherty, he's been on the job almost thirty years. He figures he's earned the right to work an eight hour day—nine to five. If he wants to be disturbed at home, that means you've done something. . . ."

"No, Sergeant Ross, it means that *you've* done something." Baxter tipped an imaginary hat, smiled, and returned to his desk.

Arnie looked at Lou for support. Lou shrugged and pointed at the telephone. Arnie sat at the desk and dialed the number, reading from a typed list scotch-taped to the cracked glass top. He listened as it rang twice. Then the familiar raspy voice croaked, "Flaherty."

"It's Arnie Ross, Lieutenant."

There was a silence. Then, "Ross, do you know who's here in my living room?"

"No, sir."

"My wife, my oldest daughter, and three of my grandchildren. I want you to know that, Ross, so that you don't have any delusions about the tone of this conversation. Sergeant Ross, you haven't been holding up your end of our bargain. You haven't been keeping me informed. What is happening at Manhattan Jewish?"

"No new problems. Not there, Lieutenant."

There was another pause. "Hey, Ross, I know you a long time. If there are no problems there, Ross, where are there problems?"

Ross told Flaherty about the Alonzo girls.

"When I come in tomorrow, I want a report on my desk. I want it short, and full of facts. When I read it, I'll make up my mind whether we go to Police Plaza with it or not. Is that clear?"

"Yes, sir."

Lou pursed his lips and let out a little whistle as Ross hung up the receiver and turned toward him. "You look gray, Arnie. Rough?"

"Short and to the point. He wants something concrete. He's nervous."

"He doesn't want to lose his pension. I guess his covering for us, and not telling headquarters or City Hall, is withholding evidence."

"Covering for us?" Arnie straightened his tie and closed his jacket.

Lou shook his head. "Sometimes you're dumb, man. That's what he's doing. We're taking a big chance for Saul, and Flaherty's covering. It's his ass, too."

They walked out together looking dejected. Baxter looked up from his desk and said, "I see you spoke to the Lieutenant." Ross lifted an eyebrow at him, and Baxter ducked his head in embarrassment. "Hey, listen, can I do anything to help?"

"Yeah, Baxter," Arnie said. "Just keep taking messages."

In the car, as they drove down Second toward Municipal, Lou said, "You know, you ought to give him a chance. He isn't going to be worth much to you if you don't give him a break."

"Fuck 'im."

"Arnie, you're a turd."

Ross was still all scowls when they walked into the hospital, leaving the car at the bus stop on the corner. They marked time wordlessly waiting for the elevator, and entered as the occupants streamed by. Lou had to pull Arnie's sleeve to get his attention when they reached the fourth floor where the Alonzo girls were sequestered. They walked down the corridor past a waiting room filled with anxious relatives. At the end of the hall a security guard held up his hand. "That's as far as you can go."

Ross and Hernandez flashed their badges and walked on. The guard ran after them and stepped in their way. "Hey, I'm sorry, but I have strict instructions."

"Okay, okay," Ross said impatiently. "Call Feingold. Tell him that Ross and Hernandez are here. We want to talk to the Alonzo girl."

The guard looked at them uncertainly, then said, "Dr. Feingold is down there." He pointed over his shoulder to the end of the corridor, "In that room."

"So go get him," Ross said.

"I can't. I'm not supposed to."

Ross pushed past the guard impatiently. "I'll take the responsibility." The guard stood stunned and watched Ross and Hernandez stride down the hall. The last door was marked with a yellow triangle and a sign, "Contagious Disease—Danger—Do Not Enter." Ross pushed the door aside.

Feingold stood at the edge of the room where two doctors and three nurses worked frantically, communicating in monosyllables at the side of the bed.

"Shit," the doctor at the center of the group, anonymous like the others in his mask, swore and glanced up at a screen. "Adrenalin-coronary needle." A nurse clapped a syringe into his hand. He felt for a moment for an intercostal space, slipped the needle home and injected. He reacted to a momentary change in the movement on the cathode tube, standing erect and wiping his brow.

Ross could see, between the doctor and the nurse, that the object of their attention was a naked girl. She had a pretty body which lay inert on soaked sheets. Her skin was a pale yellow, her face slack, lips crusted and dry. Tubes dangled from a urinary catheter, and from suction to her nose. Her right arm was affixed to a tape-covered board to immobilize it for the intravenous infusion dripping from a bottle in a rack above her head.

Suddenly, the cathode tube began to whine insistently, feeding life signs information through the thin wires attached to electrodes on the girl's chest.

The doctor reached out to a table at the bedside. "Everybody out of the way." He pulled out two stimulators shaped like potato mashers and attached by insulated cables to the cart. The nurse nearest him automatically dabbed them with jelly and stepped away. "Bang," the doctor said. The nurse hit a switch on the crash cart. A jolt of electricity surged through the stimulators into the girl's chest where the doctor held them. He glanced up at the tube, which continued to whine. "Bang," he said again. The body jerked like a rag doll. "Bang, hit her again." There was another jerk. The whine persisted. After two more jolts the doctor shook his head. "Shit." He replaced the electrodes. "Shit."

Dr. Feingold's head dropped a little on his chest. The doctor nearest the cart turned to him. "Couldn't do it."

"Scrub," Feingold said. "Scrub and disposal for everything you're wearing. Shoe packs—everything. I'll deal with disposal. We'll just have to leave her here." He turned and saw Ross and Hernandez, transfixed at the door. "What are you doing here?" His voice started to rise. "Are you crazy to come in here? I'm going to call the police."

"We are the police, we're here to see Dr. Feingold. Dr. Nassiter sent us." Ross spoke very quickly to forestall the man who was advancing on them, his eyes seething in anger above the cotton mask. "I'm Detective Sergeant Ross. This is Detective Sergeant Hernandez."

"And I'm Dr. Feingold. And you have some fucking nerve. Are you nuts? Why do you suppose we have a security guard standing out there? For decoration?"

Ross backed up and started to leave. "Oh, no, Detective whatever your name is," Feingold said in a slightly lower voice. "You stay right where you are. Right there. Don't you move a muscle. I'll see that you spend the rest of your life walking in Van Cortland Park. You're just what we need. Additional vectors." The doctor looked over his shoulder. "What do you think, Frank?"

The doctor, who had stood aside watching, said, "I don't really see how they could be vectored from over there. It's strictly contact. Just back them out."

Feingold turned to Ross. "You wait for me in the hall. I'm going to change. And don't talk to anyone about what you saw in here, either."

Ross and Hernandez fidgeted outside till Feingold reappeared in a few minutes. He looked small and old in a cheap suit. His face was seamed and tired.

"That was disgusting," he said. "She was all of sixteen years old. Sixteen."

"Was that the Alonzo girl?" Hernandez asked.

"Yes, that was Iris. Cookie is across the hall," he pointed. "God, I'm glad I'm a pathologist. I'm going to walk with you down the hall past the people in the waiting room, and I'm not even going to look at them. I don't want to see their faces."

Ross looked at him uncomprehending. "But Nassiter said we could come over here and talk to her."

"You mean she wasn't supposed to die, young man? You're right. But when there was no more moisture left in her body, when she lost water faster than we could put it back, and the body temperature got out of hand, she probably suffered brain damage anyway, so she wouldn't have done you much good. Well, she spoiled your chat by dying. She died of dehydration."

"I thought it was a bacteria," Hernandez said.

Feingold nodded wearily. "All right, Sergeant, she died of dehydration brought on by traumatic diarrhea caused by bacillus *E. Coli.*, form unknown, origin unknown except to her. But she can't tell you. Good night, gentlemen." He picked up his pace and disappeared down the hall and around a corner, leaving Ross and Hernandez standing in front of the waiting room and the milling relatives who waited, unknowing, in vain.

The two detectives drifted away from the group toward the bank of elevators. Ross said, "Maybe they know something."

Lou shook his head. "Not likely. They would have said what they know to the doctors." He looked up. "Let's ask for the file."

"Okay." Arnie paused. "Listen, why don't we wait until the doctor tells them she's dead, then ask them what they know?"

Lou shuddered. "Arnie, for Christ's sake."

"You want somebody else to die like that kid, Lou? Come on." Ross turned down the hall from whence they had come, Hernandez trailing behind him. They met the doctor who had been in Iris Alonzo's room as he carried his message of despair to the family. "Doctor," Arnie blocked his way. "We need to talk to you for a minute."

He stopped and said wearily, "Okay. What can I do for you?"

"You're going to tell the Alonzos now?" Arnie asked.

"Yes."

"I need to know where she got sick."

"We'd all like to know that, Sergeant. . . ."

"Ross. Arnie Ross. This is Lou Hernandez. I know you want to know, Doctor," he continued. "But have you got a place to start?"

"We've combed the other hospitals, both in the city itself and in the surrounding area. We've tried all five boroughs, both public and voluntary hospitals. And Nassau and Suffolk counties on Long Island, and Bergen and Essex in New Jersey. Nothing. Westchester as far as White Plains. Nothing there, either."

"Can you draw a conclusion," Lou interposed.

"Yes. This is an isolated incident. Some person who has limited contact with other people—or at least has since he or she contacted this bug."

"So there's no chance of a big epidemic," Arnie asked.

"It's not that kind of malady. If it were vectored in the kitchen of a food chain—okay, big problems. But then, of course, we would have had it all over the place, and every hospital within fifty miles would be screaming bloody murder, and the Department of Health and even, maybe, Disease Control in Atlanta would be in every corner, poking and trying to pin down the provenance. As it is, this poor kid got in contact, somehow, with someone who has this form of *E. Coli.*"

Ross pondered for a moment, then said, "And she passed it on to her sister."

"Probably. It could have been the other way around, of course. The little girl—her name is Cookie—could have picked it up somewhere, too. But the older girl was stricken hours before Cookie. It seems likely that it was Iris who passed it along."

"How's Cookie?" Hernandez asked. "Could we talk to her if we had to?"

"I suppose. She's quite a bit better. The minute she showed signs of illness, her parents brought her in. Once we saw her, we knew where to start because of Iris. She's sleeping. She is as dry as a bone, but her temperature never got unmanageable. No brain damage. And she's on intravenous with no problems. She's even been able to suck a little ice, and take some water by mouth. She'll be okay." He looked bleakly down the hall. "I'd better go and get this over with."

Ross put his hand on the doctor's arm. "Just one last thing. If this was just a one-on-one contact, is it possible that the person who gave it to Iris is still alive?"

"Certainly. This bacteria may be native to his habitat. It may be native to his digestive system for all we know. He may feel lousy when he doesn't have it."

Arnie took away his hand. "Listen, Doc, when you get through telling them the bad news, see if you can get across to them that we need to talk to them. Tell them that if we can find the person that she got this from, then maybe we can save some lives. Tell them we need to talk to them now."

The doctor nodded agreement and started down the hall.

"Oh, hey, Doc." He stopped and turned. "Was she a virgin?"

"I don't know."

"Who would?"

"Feingold." He looked at Arnie with distaste and turned away again.

"Listen, Lou, you go talk to them. You can do it in Spanish. They'll feel much better about it. I'm going to talk to Feingold. See what you can find out—lovers, friends, whatever."

Hernandez said, "Okay. But don't expect miracles. It will be a big deal if they can remember their own names right now." There was a shriek of pain from the direction of the waiting room. "See. I don't think we'll get much. If he was a steady, he'd be here. If he wasn't they might not know about him. She might not have wanted them to know."

"Give it a try, anyway." Ross trotted back to the stairway and disappeared through the door. He found Feingold in his office moping at a beat-up desk, his glasses almost down to the end of his nose. "Am I interrupting," Ross asked.

"Not particularly. I was just pretending to myself that I was looking at these papers. I was just looking over some regulations on the disposal of dangerous cadavers. We can't hand Iris Alonzo over to the undertaker in the usual fashion. The risk is too great. We'll have to ask for a

sealed bag. No embalming. Sealed coffin. Then crema-
tion." He looked up. "Some end to a sixteen-year life." He
cleared his throat. "Pathology is much easier when it
maintains the proper distance from its subjects."

"Huh?"

"It's easier to talk about dead tissue and gross organ
conference when the subject of the discussion is a collec-
tion of lifeless bits and pieces. To me she was a person.
And, of course, the cause of her death is particularly unusual."

"Was she a virgin?"

Feingold looked at Ross uncomprehending.

"Can you tell if she had intercourse recently?"

"Possibly. I can check."

"Now?"

Feingold looked at his watch. "Shit. I have to decon-
taminate again. I have to deal with some other people. Do
slides. . . ."

"I can make it an official request," Ross said.

"Don't bully me, young man," Feingold snapped. "I'm
in no fucking mood."

"Listen, Dr. Feingold, you want to stop anybody
else from getting this or not?" Feingold shook his head in
agreement, still bristling at Ross. "All right then," Arnie
continued. "Find out what I need to know."

Forty-five minutes later Arnie went back up the stairs to
look for Lou. He was sitting in the waiting room with a
notebook on his knee. The doctor was still with him, in a
chair opposite. The Alonzo family had thinned. Only the
parents and one older girl remained. The mother's face was
tear-stained but calm. The father sat rigid in grief, very
dignified, with a small moustache above the compressed
white line of his mouth.

Arnie stood at the entrance of the waiting area, reluc-
tant to disturb them, or to rupture the fragile rapport that
Lou had built with them through his gentle handling and
sympathy. He was speaking to them softly in Spanish, occasionally jotting a word or two in the pad on his knee.
Hernandez spotted Arnie out of the corner of his eye and
stood, switching to English, "This is my partner, Sergeant
Ross. Arnie, this is Mr. and Mrs. Alonzo, and their daughter Angelica."

Arnie extended his hand to Mr. Alonzo, who listlessly

accepted it. Arnie bowed his head in the direction of the two women. "I'm really sorry about this."

There was an awkward moment of silence. Mrs. Alonzo clenched her teeth in an effort to forestall another outburst of tears. "I know it doesn't make any difference," she said, her English clear, but marked with softly sibilant esses, "but it seems very unfair. She didn't live at all. She was so young."

Arnie glanced at Lou, who shook his head almost imperceptibly. They had given him nothing. Lou turned his attention back to the Alonzos. "I know that you're tired and that you want to go home. We appreciate your cooperation. We just want to do our best to see that no one else gets this sickness and dies." Mrs. Alonzo stifled a sob and clutched at her husband's sleeve. Lou continued. "It seems pretty sure that Cookie got this bug from Iris. Do you think—if the doctors say it's okay—that we might be able to talk to Cookie for a few minutes?"

Mrs. Alonzo raised her head to look at Lou, still clutching at her husband's arm. "But what can she know? She's only a baby. I always took her to school—or Iris did. . . ." She stopped in midthought, her forehead wrinkled. "You mean maybe they stopped somewhere? Or ate something?"

"Yes, Mrs. Alonzo," Arnie answered. "Something like that."

"Maybe she will be afraid to talk to you," Mrs. Alonzo said. "Maybe she will feel better if her mama is there."

The old man with the sad eyes and the little moustache reached out and patted her hand. "It will be much harder for them," he indicated the policemen with a thrust of his chin. "And it will mean starting all over again for you. They mean no harm. They only want to help." He paused for a moment, then said, "But perhaps Angelica could go." He questioned his daughter with his eyes. She nodded in agreement.

Lou rose from his chair. "Excuse me for a minute, please. I want to talk to Sergeant Ross. I'd like to make this as quick as possible, so that you can go home."

"Thank you," Mr. Alonzo said. "There are the arrangements, the priest . . . the arrangements."

"Of course," Lou said sympathetically, walking out into the corridor. When he and Arnie were out of earshot, he said, "Nothing. It's like listening to a broken record. My girl was a good girl. She never did anything wrong. No booze. No drugs. No boys. She was a regular church-goer."

"Cynical, Lou. Cynical."

Hernandez shrugged. "You're just mad cause I stole your act. Every time we interview the parents of some kid who's OD'd, or who's in the slam—it doesn't matter if she was the Whore of Babylon—they need to prove that their poor baby was the Blessed Virgin in person. Even when they're straight and sincere—like them," he jerked a thumb toward the Alonzos, "it gets on your nerves. And they don't help, so we learn nothing and the kid's death is even more meaningless. Did you get anything from Feingold?"

"The Virgin Mary wasn't a virgin anymore. Feingold says she'd had intercourse pretty regularly. Not that it was the Lincoln Tunnel or anything, but that somebody had been banging her. Also, there was evidence of recent activity—semen. He says she'd been screwing sometime during the last seventy-two hours at the most."

Hernandez frowned. "We'll never find out from them." He pointed at the Alonzos again. "If you showed them a picture they wouldn't believe it."

"Should we spring it on them?" Arnie asked.

"Ah, for what? They don't know. Take my word. Why be a prick for nothing?"

"How about the big sister?"

"Strictly one syllable. Yes and no. Not uncooperative. Just stunned and quiet."

Arnie turned back down the hall. "Who wouldn't be?" he said, "Maybe she'll loosen up a little if her parents aren't around."

Lou waited with the Alonzos while Arnie hunted down the floor nurse. She led the parents to the office to begin making the arrangements for their daughter's last journey.

Angelica Alonzo, stiff and grim, walked with the same kind of dignity as her father. She had the same long face and wide, thin-lipped mouth. Just the same, Arnie thought, she was pretty, with large liquid brown eyes and a good figure.

Lou, Arnie and Angelica stopped for a moment in the corridor outside Cookie's room. "Look," Arnie said, "I know how lousy this is. It was really hard on your folks. But is there anything that you know that you didn't say because they were there?" He fidgeted at her silence. "I mean was there something about where Iris might have been that you didn't want to say in front of them?"

Angelica looked squarely into Arnie's face as though searching for something. Her eyes played over the ragged features, the torn eyebrow, the scar on his cheek—a faint line from the corner of his left eye to the corner of his mouth. She appraised him, looking for some hint, and when she found no offence in his question, she took none.

"If there were any secret lovers, I didn't know about them. She wasn't on any dope. I guess the doctors told you that. Outside of a couple of beers, or an occasional rum and Coke, she didn't drink. I don't know much. I'm . . . I was. . . ," she shrugged, and a tear rolled down her cheek. "I'm four years older than she was. We were sisters. But I been going to school and working part-time for five years. I'm going to be a teacher. I didn't have much time to spend."

She stopped and took a tissue from her bag and wiped at her nose and eyes. "No, I don't have to spend the time, do I?" She struggled to keep control of herself. In a moment, she went on. "It's funny. Cookie was her buddy and her confidant. She would talk to her the way kids talk to a favorite doll or a stuffed animal. Cookie worshipped Iris. Iris played with her. She did all kinds of things. She baked cakes. She made her a pudding the night she got sick." She stopped in mid-thought, staring out across the hall.

Hernandez put his hand on her arm. "Did anyone else eat the pudding, Angelica? Anyone but Cookie? It's very important."

"No. Cookie ate it all. She said it was all hers. Iris made it for her."

Lou glanced at Arnie, then said, "You're sure?"

"Yes."

Arnie held the door open for her and Lou, and then followed them in. A nurse sat in an armchair near the bed, reading a magazine. She looked up and rose to meet them. "She's just dozing on and off. Her temp's lower. Are you the policemen?"

"Yes. Can you excuse us for a few minutes?" Hernandez asked.

"Okay. I could use a break." She stretched. "I'll be back in about ten minutes." She looked at the child who moved restlessly, pale and wan even against the pillow. An IV set dangled from a bottle into her fragile arm. "She's really a lot better than she was. If you see any change, ring for the floor nurse. Okay? But there shouldn't be any problem."

When the door closed behind the nurse, Cookie opened her eyes. They were sleepy and her gaze was vague. It took her a minute to focus on the group at the foot of her bed. When she spoke her voice was slurred with exhaustion and medication. "Hi, Angie. When's Iris coming to see me?"

Angelica Alonzo's mouth worked silently as she looked at her sister. She turned toward Ross and Hernandez for help.

Gently, Lou said, "She's busy now, Cookie, and she can't come. I have a little girl, too. Did you know that?"

"Nope. Who are you?"

"I'm Luis. This is Arnie. We're trying to help the doctors find out why you got sick."

Half an hour later, Ross and Hernandez dropped Angelica Alonzo back at her parents' home, and thanked her for her cooperation. After she left, they sat quietly in the car for a few minutes. Cookie had been tired and a little stubborn at the idea of sharing the secrets she'd had with Iris—even with Angelica. She finally gave in when she found out, to her delight, that Arnie and Lou were detectives. Just as the nurse had returned, and was about to eject them, Cookie relented. "She said that he was very nice. He told her stories and read to her. Just like she used to read to me. She said the stories were not like the stories in my books. She said I wouldn't understand his stories until I grow up. When am I going to grow up, Angie?"

"Soon, baby, soon."

"Do you know the name of Iris's prince, Cookie?" Arnie asked.

Cookie hesitated and looked at Angie, who nodded approval. "He was a very special friend," Cookie said. "Iris says he makes her really feel good." She saw that they were hanging on her words, so she dragged it out a little more. Then, finally, she said, "Alex. His name is Alex."

Ross and Hernandez sat in the car outside of the Alonzo home without talking. It had been a long and depressing day. And they were tired. Finally, Arnie turned and said, "What're you gonna do now, Roach?"

"I don't know, Arn. I'm so friggin' tired I could die. I haven't been home—not really—in a couple of days. I'd like to go see Mama, too."

Arnie looked at his watch. "Hey, man, it's eleven-thirty. She'll be fast asleep. I'll tell you what. You drop me off at Manhattan Jewish and I'll take a look in at Mama. Then you drive home. After, I can walk over to the precinct and get my car." He punched affectionately at Hernandez' arm. "If you don't go home and make a little deposit, Margarita's attention's gonna wander. You know how them hot-blooded *chollo* broads are."

Lou managed a weak smile. "Too true. You got a deal. If Mama's awake, you tell her I love her."

"I'll tell her."

# 31

Arnie got past the security guard in the lobby of the Morgenstern Pavilion and bluffed his way by the attendant on the fourth floor, waving his badge and making semi-official growling noises. He padded quietly down the hall to Mama Hernandez' room and slipped through the door. There was a faint glow from the small bulb in the corner opposite the bed. Mama lay still in the half dark, looking even smaller and more frail than when he had seen her last. Her breathing was even and shallow, and it seemed to Arnie that the thread of life had grown more fragile through the days of testing, as Saul Rogovin and his colleagues groped for a way to keep Mama from wasting away.

He sat next to her in a chair and reached out to touch the hand that had offered him kindness all of his life. He leaned back and, holding her hand, closed his eyes.

The touch was so gentle that he sensed rather than felt it. "Okay, Dick Tracy, you can't stay here all night."

He opened his eyes. "Little Red Rosenberg."

She straightened and looked at him with a combination of irritation and amusement. "Are you trying to reclaim your prisoner? The first time I saw you, you were going to arrest her. Next you came down to make a date with me. Now what? Are you going to tell me that you're holding on to her hand to keep her from escaping?"

Self-consciously, Arnie let go of Mama's hand. She didn't stir.

The red-haired nurse felt a twinge of contrition. "I guess that wasn't very funny."

Arnie shrugged. "Not really. Not much is, lately. How is she?"

Red hesitated. "Not my department, you know. I'm not allowed."

"Yeah, yeah, I know. She's 'resting comfortably.' Or her condition is 'guarded,' whatever the hell that means."

"That's the drill. More than that you get from the doctors."

Arnie got up and stretched. She was shorter by a full head than he was. He reached up toward the ceiling and felt the circulation returning to his cramped legs. "What time is it?"

"About one forty-five," she replied.

He chuckled. "I've been sleeping in here for almost two hours. How come you didn't notice me before?"

"I did," she said, "I've been in here ten times in those two hours."

"So why didn't you wake me?"

"You looked very tired. And besides, you weren't doing any harm. And if I made you let go of Mama's hand, you might have awakened her." The last was said defensively.

He looked down at her. Her eyes were green and bright. The flaming red hair, pulled into a bun at the back of her head under the tiny lace cap, and freckled upturned nose were as appealing to him now as they had been the first time he saw her. "Why did you wake me now?" Arnie asked.

"I'm going off in a few minutes. I didn't want any of us—me, or Mama Hernandez," she paused, "or you—to get into trouble."

"You call her mama, too?"

"Everybody does. She insists. A nice lady."

"How about a cup of coffee?"

Her teeth were bright in a broad smile. "At two in the morning?"

"A cup of champagne?"

She knitted her brows, looked into his eyes, then smiled again. "Why not?"

"In front of the building in ten minutes," he said. "It'll take me that long to walk over to the precinct and come back with the car."

"Okay, but if you don't mind, I'll wait in the lobby."

"Don't like the neighborhood, huh?"

"Nope. No faith in the police." She breezed out of the room, leaving Arnie to gather his wits and follow.

He walked through the dank, humid night, avoiding the garbage strewn in the streets. Only the screeches of fighting cats animated the slum surrounding the headquarters of H/Z 4. He pulled the car away from the curb in front of the antiquated building, and drove around to the entrance of the hospital. He pulled up to the door just as she emerged to look for him.

"Snazzy car for a cop," she commented, letting herself in.

"I'm on the pad—heavy. My specialty is shaking down pretty nurses. Are you gonna break my chops all night?"

She thought about it, and said, "I guess not. You know, we've never been introduced. Oh, I know who you are. You're the great Arnie Ross, the Jewish Robin Hood, the masked marvel of the bagel set. Mama made sure I heard all about that."

"You got a name?"

"Yeah. Rosenberg. Diane Rosenberg. You can call me Didi, or Red."

"My name is Detective Sergeant Arnold Ross," he said gravely. "And you can call me whatever turns you on."

"How about Sarge?" He winced. "Good," she said cheerily. "Then Sarge it is."

"You like the Twenty-one Club?" he asked.

"I've never been there, but I'll bet I'd like it, Sarge."

"Terrific. We're going to the State Diner." He pulled away from the curb.

"Great, Sarge. I've never been there either."

The State Diner suffers from excessive investment in bad Art Deco. Rounded repeating arches, the kind that abound at Radio City Music Hall, leap from every surface, in furniture, carved in the woodwork, etched on glass and mirrors where they are endlessly reflected. "On the other hand," Arnie pointed out, "they're open all night, even if it is on Tenth Avenue. The food is edible—if expensive—and the crowd is nouveau middle class. You like chili, Red?"

"Only if it's hot stuff."

"I'll spring for extra tabasco."

"Sarge, you're a prince."

By four-thirty that morning, they were much better acquainted and were back uptown nursing cups of coffee on the floor of Arnie's apartment.

"I would have loved to ask you back to my place, Sarge, but I wasn't sure how you'd react to four nurses with curlers, cold cream and flannel pajamas wielding frying pans and screaming rape."

"They should be so lucky. Frankly, I think that I could have handled everything but the flannel pajamas."

"You have to forgive them. Two are from Minnesota, one from Kansas, and the other one from a farm in Illinois."

"You got flannel pajamas?"

"I bring my pajamas with me everywhere."

"Even in the shower?"

"Girls from the Bronx," she said, studying her cup, "are notoriously shameless." She got up from the floor and stretched. "Show me your pad, Sarge."

They wandered around the apartment for a few minutes, the kitchen, the living room, and then the bedroom.

"What's that," she said, pointing to a bottle-shaped white canvas object standing in a corner. She gasped as in one continuous motion Arnie Ross spun across the room, leapt into the air almost to the height of his shoulders, and with an explosive exhalation of breath, snapped his legs out at the dummy, then landed nimbly on his feet. "It's my aggression release mechanism."

"You could kill somebody like that," she said, marveling.

"I should hope so." He smiled. "It would be a shame to have wasted all that effort for nothing."

She pulled the pins out of her hair and tossed them, with the white lace cap, to the top of the dresser. Her long tresses fell almost to her waist. "I have a super idea," she said.

The sun had already crept over the lip of the earth and was shining red on the East River when they lay back to have a cigarette. She brushed her hand aimlessly back and forth on the hair of Arnie's chest. He smiled faintly and stared out of the window. She had stripped him, stiffened him, drained him, and then done it again. He hadn't quite managed a third time, but he didn't mind. She had.

"Sarge, have you ever thought about keeping a pet?"

"You saw the sign in the lobby."

"Yes. But it said curb your dog, not your pussy." She poked him with her nails.

Arnie looked at his watch, balanced on its strap on the night table. "Ugh," he said. "In five hours I've got to be ready for work."

She smiled. "I don't have to be anywhere until eight o'clock tonight." She tugged at his hair. "I'm willing to stay if you let me."

"I'm willing to keep you, but I don't think that I can keep you and my job at the same time. And besides, won't your roommates miss you?"

"Hah," she pouted, "they can go find their own detectives."

"Okay. Okay. Then shut up and go to sleep or I won't be worth a damn all day."

"I doubt it," she said rolling over and pulling the sheets over her shoulder. "I doubt it."

Arnie got up and tugged the shade down, cutting out the morning light, crawled into the bed and was sound asleep in minutes.

The watch beeped softly, but with a piercing tone. By the tenth beep, Arnie was sitting up. It was eleven-thirty. Didi was sleeping. He laughed aloud. She smiled in her sleep. He'd have to remember that, he thought.

He walked into the living room, grabbing a pair of shorts and an athletic supporter on the way. He dressed quickly and began to run through a routine of brisk floor exercises. He cut his normal routine short after fifteen minutes, promising himself to complete the day's workout later.

For a moment, he stood absolutely still in the center of the room, gathering his concentration, physically relaxed, yet coiling his strength. In a split second he was transformed into a torrent of energy spinning about the room, a breath exploding with each karate blow aimed at an imaginary adversary, stopping short of a lamp, or a piece of furniture, or the wall. In a minute, the dance was over. He had tested each of his limbs, and the coordination of his body. He was ready to shower and dress.

When he turned to go to the bedroom, gleaming with perspiration, his breathing rate elevated by exertion, he saw Didi standing at the door. She was naked and the pinkness of her skin contrasted against the even paler walls. Her breasts were full, and fell a little from their weight. She was very quiet.

"Hi," he smiled. "You're up."

"You're a little scary. Did you know that, Sarge?"

"Because I exercise?"

"Because I think you could kill."

He stopped smiling and walked into the bathroom and stepped into the shower. She followed him and sat on the vanity with her feet on the closed cover of the commode.

"Do you kill people, Sarge?"

"Does it turn you on, or make you sick, if I say yes?" There was an edge of anger to his voice.

"Neither. I just never met anybody dangerous before."

"I'll tell you what, Red," Arnie said, lathering himself, "I'm a pussycat compared to some of the dudes you meet out there in the street. Just your ordinary garden variety pussycat."

He saw that she meant no harm, and he softened. "People who aren't on the job—with the police—or who don't get close to the work, don't get to see as much as they think. The world's full of kooks and fuck-ups. You see an occasional asshole push a kid off of a train platform. That Australian prints the most horrible picture on the front page of the *Post*, and you think that you've been exposed to the seamy side of life. I won't bore you with the statistics," he said stepping out and reaching for a towel, "but you take my word for it. I'm a regular pansy."

"Can't prove it by me, fella," she said, hugging her knees. She trailed him into the bedroom, sat and watched him dress. "I work in a place where suffering is perceived in a different way, I guess. Oh, we get our share of the victims. I worked the emergency room for a couple of months once. I wasn't the same for a year. Very scary. OR nursing is scary, too, though. When you see what nature does to people. Or even what they do to themselves from behind the wheel of a car. It's terrifying. But, I guess on the whole, it's a rewarding kind of feeling, and makes you think that the weight is on the side of the angels. Hospitals are mostly concerned with making things better. As the saying goes, part of the solution, not part of the problem."

Arnie adjusted the knot in his tie, took the snub-nosed Smith and Wesson .38 from the top of the dresser, and tucked it into the holster inside his waistband on the left side of his trousers. He pulled it once quickly to make sure it was where it ought to be, then pushed it back in and slipped on his jacket.

"You know, Red," he said, "one of the problems with civilians is they sometimes don't even realize how close they are to the creeps of the world. Even in a hospital."

She frowned for a moment, then mistaking his words,

said, "Aha, now it comes out. Mama Hernandez is a plant. There's some kind of drug ring operating in the hospital."

He patted her cheek and kissed her lightly on the lips. "I wish it were true."

Didi put her arms around his neck and kissed him back soundly. "I do, too. I'm sorry your favorite little old lady is sick."

He stood back a moment at arms' length. "Can you tell me how sick."

"I'm sorry, Arnie. Very. It looks like she has Hodgkin's Disease, and she's failing. Very sick." She took his hands in hers and squeezed. "I really didn't want to say anything."

"I knew, anyway," he sighed. "Saul told us, more or less. Is there any hope?"

She squeezed again. "I'm a twenty-five-year-old nurse. I'm good at my job. I like you a lot and I'll go to your bed even when you don't ask, but don't try to make a doctor out of me. We'll both end up unhappy, and you won't know a thing more than you knew before. It's a very complex disease. That's the real criminal in my world, disease. You're right," she said bouncing back to the bed. "You're a pussycat compared to disease."

Arnie smiled. "Well, that ain't all you got in there, toots."

"It's still better than your world, fella."

"See you later?" He headed for the door.

"Pick a time."

"Same time and place. You get off at two again?"

"Yup. Until next week. Then it's days."

"Great," he said in disgust. "In two weeks, I go back to nights." Arnie turned the door knob, then suddenly remembering, asked, "Hey, Didi, do you know anybody at the hospital named Alex?"

"Nope." She shook her head, then frowned. "I don't know." She paused then shrugged. "If it comes to me, I'll call you."

"Thanks a bunch."

# 32

Before Rosario Gonzalez went home, he stopped as he had done with some regularity over the preceding months to pass a few words with Jim Spencer, the technician who ran the Louis Gluck Hyperbaric Chamber. Spencer was a man of middle height, broad across the chest and shoulders. Though his work kept him in a windowless building during his working hours, his face was weathered and—with the slight graying of his crew-cut brown hair—gave the only clue to his age. Muscular arms roped with blue veins protruded from his short-sleeved white shirt, a sea serpent tattooed on each forearm.

"So, how's the old navy chief?"

"Dandy, Rosie, just dandy. And your good self?" There was a tang of the midwest in the dry masculine voice.

"I could complain. But who would pay attention?" Rosario's face shone with good humor. He sat down on the rail that surrounded the larger of the two cylindrical steel chambers that occupied most of the space in the vault-like room. Behind him, a short staircase dropped eight feet from the platform on which the chambers rested to the floor. This level contained the atmosphere metering equipment and the self-contained water, generating and pumping equipment. There was also a steel door that provided the only access from the chambers into the basement of the Waldman Pavilion next door. Rosario shifted his gaze to the fire exit in the corner opposite the cylinders, visualizing the two flights of diamond-etched steel steps behind it that led to a steel fire door exiting onto the street.

"Don't you ever get the urge for a smoke, Jim?"

Spencer smiled over his shoulder at Rosario as he rearranged the stack of books and papers that were spread over a metal desk between the two cylinders. "You gotta be kidding. With all this oxygen around? Boom." He finished with his books and walked over to Rosario, balancing a haunch on the rail next to him. "Thirty-two years in the navy, you get used to smoking when you can and forgetting about it when you can't."

"Were you always in submarines?"

"No, though I was always attached to the service. I had a rating as a diver. But after the war, I spent the bulk of my time training divers and submariners in pressure techniques and escape tactics."

"Ah, the decompression chamber?"

Spencer made a sour face. "Friggin' movies and friggin' amateurs. Recompression, not decompression, chamber. What you need when you come up too fast is more pressure, not less."

Rosie grinned. "That's not what Tyrone Power said."

"Fuck Tyrone Power." He got up and went back to the desk. "Let's see what the old man sent down for tomorrow."

As Spencer shuffled through his papers, mumbling to himself and making an occasional note, Rosario rose casually and walked over to the safety door in the corner. He leaned against the wall, and when he was sure that Spencer was occupied, he ran his hand along the steel frame of the door all the way to the top of the door buck. The copper wire, which had been so carefully molded into the edge of the frame, was intact and not readily visible.

Rosario glided back to his place at the railing unnoticed by his companion. "What's the tally?"

"I just show two here. The first one is the kid of some religious kook who won't let the kid have a transfusion. He's got what they call blood loss anemia. So instead of feeding the kid whole blood, which is the easiest thing to do, they give him fluids in an IV, give him shots of iron and then maybe four or five treatments of sixty or ninety minutes in the chamber at two ATA, and it reverses his symptoms as though he'd had a transfusion."

"ATA?"

"Atmospheres. Double the regular fifteen pounds per square inch. Two atmospheres." He flipped to the next page. "And then we have a kid who fell against an open oven door. Bad burns on his back. High pressure oxygen makes the burns heal faster and keeps the infections down."

Rosario got up and waved. "Well, have a nice evening, Jim. See you tomorrow."

"You too, Rosie. And see to it that the electricity doesn't go off in the morning and screw up my act."

Rosie waved as he headed toward the door. "As though you need anybody, with this backup system." He pointed to the green painted machinery under the chambers. "You could go to the moon and back in this dump if you wanted to. Good night, Jim."

Rosario walked down the hall into Waldman. The first door on the left was a utility closet. He ducked into it and turned on the light. There was a half-filled case of soap powder under the lowest shelf. Five pound boxes stacked two deep. Rosario pulled the last three from the top layer, and pulled out the ones from the bottom. They were noticeably heavier. He peeled back the tops where they had been taped shut and extracted the .45 caliber pistols that had been slipped into the powder in plastic bags. He checked each to make sure that they were loaded and in working condition, snapping the slides back and forth and letting the hammer fall on an empty chamber. Then, reloading and cocking each of the guns, he replaced them in the boxes, and then into the carton. He listened at the door, peeked, and then ducked out and down the hall.

Once out of the building, he turned the corner at Ninety-sixth Street and headed toward Lexington. A quarter of the way down the block, he checked to see if there was anyone in sight. He turned toward the fire door that led to the hyperbaric chamber. A slim wire led from the corner of the door jamb and down the metal frame to the street. He walked slowly, following it—with his eyes on the crack between the building and the sidewalk—to a point halfway to Lexington. There, a Luis Dominguez, who worked on the building maintenance crew, had been able to lead the wire, unobserved, into a space between two concrete sidewalk panels, and then into an asphalt patch that ran across the street to the opposite sidewalk. This had been done during street repairs almost a year earlier. In the same way, three months later, Luis had run the wire across the sidewalk into the lot behind the cyclone fence. It had been the first step in the complicated wiring system that they had installed under the noses of the administration throughout the northwest corner of Manhattan Jewish.

Rosario crossed the street and peered through the metal

cross hatching at the seventy-foot storage tower in the middle of the lot. This tower held the oxygen supply for the entire Manhattan Jewish Hospital complex. The box of wire rested unobtrusively against the corner of the fence. The only signs of the cache of dynamite painstakingly hidden stick by stick over a period of two years were a small stone here, another there, a rusted paint can, a stick pushed seemingly at random into the paper-littered dirt.

A source of life, Rosario observed, and a source of death. Oxygen, the staff of life, properly fused, could become a ball of fire. Heat and flame, accompanied by a hail of small metal particles, would form an avenging cloud to punish Manhattan Jewish Hospital and the sinners who guided it. The patients and the staff, in their thousands, were not part of Rosario's thoughts.

He strolled down the street casually with his hands in his pockets. It was a warm spring evening, and Lexington Avenue was crowded with strollers. Rosario faded into the milling mass of Latins, sitting on stoops, laughing and drinking beer, children running between their legs. At 103rd Street, Rosario caught the subway to 149th. He stood and exited from the car. He watched the train, splattered with paint and vain slogans, trundle up the tracks away from the center of the city. He was drawn away himself, and it wasn't until the train had faded from sight around a curve that he came fully awake and descended the stairs to the barren, litter-strewn roadway beneath the elevated train, and began his trek across the barrens of the South Bronx to his appointment.

Rosario sat in the doorway of a destroyed building for more than half an hour, fondling the envelope that he had taken from his lunch pail. Eight thousand dollars. In time there were a couple of flashes of light. He picked his way across the field and stuffed the envelope under a brick and left. He waited again in the doorway till the exchange was made. A white box from a flower store was left where the envelope had been. Rosario knelt in the shadows and untied the string. In the box, beneath a layer of old newspapers and wrapped in a bath towel, were five gleaming, black machine pistols. Their magazines, wrapped in a rubber band, lay beside them. As he carefully wrapped the parcel again, he calculated that there were ten thousand rounds of 9 mm ammunition for the guns stored with the dynamite under the floor of the Louis Gluck Hyperbaric Chamber. Finished, he hefted the box under his arm and walked off. On the train back to 116th Street he chatted amiably with the transit policeman sitting next to him.

# 33

The fly-specked clock behind the counter of the sleazy hotel indicated it was three o'clock when Emily Stolzfuss pulled herself up the flight of stairs for the seventh time. This john was a foreigner, tall and blond. He understood well enough about the money, but was otherwise slow in English. She sat listlessly at the foot of the bed, waiting for him to undress—as she had been taught, just in case he was a cop. Her face was slack, and her lower back felt bruised. The inside of her right bicep bore a blue mark from the thumb of an overzealous customer. The john took off his clothes and folded them neatly over the rickety chair. Through the wall she could hear the laughter of a black whore named Cheryl who patrolled the street not far from her own corner. They had chatted between tricks. She seemed to Emily to be twenty-five or so, though with a woman like Cheryl, Emily had no standards of comparison.

The john fished into his pocket and pulled out a small tube. Emily raised an eyebrow. Then he slipped off his shorts and turned to face her. She gasped, and he smiled. His organ was immense.

*"Gut, ja?"* he asked. "Tis Vaseline. Gut too."

It seemed to Emily that he took a very long time. Though he clearly meant to be gentle, he distended her to the point of real pain, and bumped savagely into her internal organs. As they were getting dressed, Emily was seized by a cramp in her abdomen. She fought it off silently and straightened up. God, she thought, I wish I'd sucked him off. She stopped in the midst of strapping her shoe and blinked back a tear. Could she really have thought that, she wondered. In only one night, could she have become so much a part of this.

"Here, girl," the man handed her a five-dollar bill. "Gut whore, t'anks." He closed the door behind him, and she

152

leaned against it, listening to his footsteps fade down the hall. She had to get away. In a moment, there were more footsteps. Cheryl's john was leaving. As soon as she was sure that the hall was empty, Emily ducked out into the hall and knocked on the next door. "Cheryl, it's me, Emil ..." she hesitated, "the girl from next door."

"So?"

"Can I come in?"

"Come on." Cheryl was still naked to the waist. Her breasts drooped and her nipples were wide and the same shade of black as the rest of her skin. Stretch marks of a lighter shade disfigured both her bosom and her stomach. Emily swallowed and tried not to stare as Cheryl dressed. There was a sweet cloying smell in the room from the crumpled little cigarette Cheryl was smoking.

"Want a drag," Cheryl asked.

"No. I want to get away."

"From what?" Cheryl took a drag and closed her eyes, holding it in.

"From Eddie Biggs."

"From your old man? You must be kidding. Prime little white pussy like you. They eat you alive out there alone. Everybody in the whole world would be sharin' your earnings, child. You just be grateful you got somebody to watch out for your little white ass."

The tears started to flow despite the fact that Emily tried to hold them back. "But I don't want to do this. I don't want to be a ... a ..." Emily couldn't find the word.

"Hooker, kid? Why not?" Cheryl laughed. "There's no better business in the world than the pussy business. Shit, you got it, you use it, you wash it, and it's like new again. Ain't no business in the world like that."

"But I hate it. He makes me do it. I want to go home." By now Emily was sobbing, her chest heaving with the effort. "I want to go home."

Cheryl looked at her with some sympathy and started to speak when the door opened. Eddie Biggs stood in the hall outside looking in. Cheryl picked up her bag.

"What you been doin', bitch? You been chewin' a little black pussy to change yo' luck? Or you been eatin' hers?" he glared at Cheryl. She walked toward the door. "You gonna answer me?" He blocked her way.

Cheryl slammed her bag into Eddie Biggs's groin. In addition to her wallet and a few articles of makeup, the purse contained a lead ball. Though it was a little smaller than a baseball, it weighed three pounds. Eddie sucked for air. "Now you listen to me," Cheryl said. "If you ever get in my way again, you handkerchief-head nigger asshole, I'm going to have my old man carve my initials on your cock, so you remember how to speak to a lady." She stepped past him. "And why don't you let this poor chick go? She don't want to trick no more." She looked at Emily. "And either way, honey, you'd best get yourself a real man if you gonna stick around, instead of this pussy," she looked at Eddie with contempt, "The word'll get out and everybody's goin' to steal your hard-earned money."

Emily looked at Biggs for a moment after Cheryl left, then decided to run. She stepped into the hall. Eddie straightened up quickly and thrust his hands into her open blouse, grabbing her nipples between his thumbs and forefingers and pinching sharply. Her head swam and her breath was taken away. Squeezing with all of his strength, he forced her to her knees. "You ain't goin' nowhere. When we gets home," he twisted his hands, "we gonna have a talk." Emily almost fainted. "Now get up, bitch." He wrenched her to her feet and slammed her against the moldy wall. "If you make one little move on the way, I'm gonna push you under the fuckin' subway. You got that, bitch?"

The train was a long time coming to the platform. Once a transit cop appeared, but Eddie was holding her hand. He held her pinky and twisted it. She wanted to scream but, instead, she stood petrified and trembling with pain and fear. They walked from the train station to the apartment, Emily barely able to control her bladder.

While they walked up the stairs to the filthy room, Eddie gave Emily little pushes at the base of her spine, not quite knocking her off balance. When they were inside, he gave her a resounding slap across the face. She spun to the bed and fell, her ears ringing. She lay there, shielding her head from another blow till it was obvious that he was doing something else. She looked up with relief to see that he was undressing. Maybe he wouldn't hurt her, she thought. Maybe he just wanted to get off. She stood up and, trying to smile, took off her clothes. "You want me, Eddie?" she asked. He smiled. "You want me to suck you?" The words came easier.

"Turn around, bitch, I want to fuck your ass." He lit a cigarette and took a drag. "Just bend over and hold that bed." She shuddered and obeyed him. She faced the wall, so she couldn't see him, but she could hear him walking around behind her. "Well, look what we got here. Five dollars. Last john give you a tip."

He pushed his hand down on the back of her neck, shoving her face into the mattress. "You tryin' to run away from me. You fuckin' me up. You ain't goin' no place till I say so. You hear me?" He stabbed the hot end of the cigarette against the bare skin of her buttock and held it there, listening to it crackle. Emily screamed into the bedding and struggled to get away. He pushed harder, and burned her other side. She pushed hard against his hand, making him exert all of his weight against her to hold her against the blanket. He took the cigarette away from the angry red burn, which like the first began to blister immediately. He dragged at the butt, reheating the coal. "Now y'ain't never gonna run away—or try—again."

He jabbed the cigarette between her buttocks against her rectum and the pain gave her a strength greater than his. She flung herself aside and her hand caught Eddie on the side of the head. Hysterical, she ran toward the door. He cut her off and punched her in the mouth. She was flung back, then rushed at the door again. Again she ran into Biggs's fist. Her head spinning, overwhelmed by pain, she screamed like a frightened animal, turned and plunged through the painted-over glass of the window. She hadn't even time to think as she cartwheeled through the air. There was a moment of explosive pain and impact, and then there was nothing.

Eddie Biggs stood for a moment in the middle of the room, which now was as silent as a tomb. He went gingerly to the window, as though afraid to step on something breakable. Emily was sprawled on her back. In the dim light of the airshaft he could see that she was spreadeagled on the piled debris at the bottom, her arms and legs akimbo. One leg seemed to be twisted in a funny way. He pulled away from the window and sat at the edge of the bed. If I run, they catch me, he thought. If I stay, they catch me. I can't leave her there. He started to cry softly to himself as he dressed. Damn honky pussy. There goes my Cadillac. He hesitated another moment, then went purposefully to the dresser and pulled a few items from the drawer.

Eddie looked at his Timex. A quarter to five. Another hour of darkness, maybe a little more in this late spring. He walked down the stairs like a cat. Instead of his good threads, he wore a pair of jeans and a dark tee shirt. His pointy shoes sat in the closet in favor of dark, worn sneakers. He stopped at the ground floor and looked around. The apartment that corresponded to his own was at the back of the hall. His eyes were accustomed to the dark and he stepped over the trash on the floor in front of him. Something scurried out of his way, but he paid no heed.

When he came to the door he rested for a moment to organize his thoughts. The occupant of the apartment was an old lady named Olivia Hunter. She eked out an existence on Social Security checks and food stamps. She was thin and seamed, with rheumy eyes. A life of washing other people's floors had brought her to a lonely, frightened end in a Harlem tenement among the rats and garbage. Eddie Biggs knew her because she would occasionally sit on the stoop during the warm noon hour when the penny-pitching young welfare clients were otherwise occupied, sharing a crust of bread with the pigeons, or talking to some of the little children in the neighborhood.

He would have to open the door, walk past her, get to the window and into the air shaft, pick Emily's body up and get it back across the apartment, then get out into the hall. All this without disturbing the old lady. He stopped and shook his head in despair. Never happen. She'd wake up and scream. Maybe he should run after all, he thought.

After a brief moment of panic, Eddie Biggs calmed and set his jaw. He tried the door knob. It turned a little, but was locked. He took out his knife, and fitted the blade between the edge of the battered door and the moldering old jamb. He pushed against the bolt and the weakened spring gave way.

Silently, Eddie pushed his way into the apartment. A glow shone through the window to the shaft. The old woman lay huddled on an old cot, partly covered by a nondescript blanket. Her stick-like arms protruded from a worn flannel nightgown. Eddie hesitated only a moment. He pulled on a pair of cheap imitation leather gloves that he had stuck in his back pocket and turned toward the window. The old lady sighed and moved restlessly. Eddie held still; he could hear his own pulse.

Eddie turned to the bed. It was easier than he had imagined. He simply wrapped his fingers around her neck and jammed his thumbs against her Adam's apple and squeezed hard. Still dull with sleep, and weak with age, hunger and ill use, Olivia Hunter succumbed as she had lived, with little fuss. Eddie hung on for some minutes after she was quite dead. To make sure, he shook her as a cat does a dead song bird. Her head flopped on her neck like a broken doll's.

Eddie Biggs went to the window. At first he was unable to open it. Fear and frustration made a bad taste in his mouth. He saw that the little catch at the top of the window was closed. Once undone, it opened with relative ease, and little noise.

Emily's naked body was strewn over a pile of refuse. Even in the dim light he could see that her right leg was bent at the calf in a forty-five degree angle. A splinter of broken bone protruded through the skin. Eddie was surprised that there was so little blood. There was a welling cut above her left eyebrow, crowning an enormous knot where she had hit her head. Her left hand was folded back on her wrist, badly fractured. He reached out for her and dragged her through the garbage and into the window of Olivia Hunter's apartment. She dropped onto the floor with a thud. He thought that she had stirred momentarily. He nudged her with his toe, but there was no response. He pulled the blanket away from Olivia Hunter's frail corpse and wrapped Emily in it. Then he dragged the bundle over to the door and pushed it against the wall. He checked his watch. Five-ten.

Leaving Emily behind, Eddie Biggs walked out into the street and looked around. As far as he could see, the streets were dotted with parked cars. Somewhere, he thought, he would find what he was looking for. Less than a block away, he found what he wanted—a blue Buick, a '68 or '69, faded, but in reasonable condition, with Alabama plates. He checked it over quickly for an alarm. There was none.

In his pocket he found a Z-shaped piece of metal bent from a screwdriver blade. He slipped it through the worn rubber at the edge of the window on the driver's side and worked it under the edge of the lock. With a quick flip the lock post popped up. He slid in behind the wheel and turned it to make sure there was no steering wheel lock. The wheel turned freely. He took a short length of wire that ended in alligator clips and slid along the seat till his head was under the dash. He cursed in the darkness, unable to see.

He struck a match and immediately blew it out, and lay frozen on the seat. In a moment the heavy footsteps subsided in the distance. He lit another match, located the two wires and scratched them bright with his knife point. He reached out and depressed the accelerator several times with his hand. Attaching one alligator clip he said a silent prayer, and touched the bare wire with the other. The motor coughed weakly a couple of times, then turned and caught.

The muffler was shot and the car needed a tune-up but it wasn't too bad. He let it warm up for a minute, then raising his head slowly and peering through all the windows, he sat up and drove away. He turned the corner once and then again, and parked in a space very near his building. He left the motor running and the back door open.

Fear propelled Eddie Biggs. He bounded up the stoop and down the hall, pushed open the door, grabbed the bundle and dragged it into the hall. He pulled the door shut till the latch clicked. He heard a noise and held his breath. Maybe he had imagined it. He lifted Emily's wrapped body and moved to the front door that was slightly ajar. He checked the block in both directions. The street was empty. He negotiated the steps with his awkward bundle balanced over his shoulder, threw Emily on the floor in the back of the car, made sure that she was covered by the blanket, and drove off.

Eddie sped west across town, trying to make the lights. He was torn between his desire for anonymity and his anxiety to get rid of his load. A young black man driving too fast in an old car has the same effect on New York policemen as a red flag to a bull. He made the Henry Hudson Parkway without incident and turned uptown to the George Washington Bridge. He breathed a sigh of relief. There are no tolls outbound from New York, only a double charge to enter the big city. He took the turn that headed south on I-95.

At a quarter to six, with dawn still some minutes away,

Eddie Biggs stopped at the side of the road and turned off the lights. To the west he could see the jumble of buildings that is Newark, and to the east—above the modest suburbs that line the west bank of the Hudson River—the angular upreaching skyline of Manhattan.

Eddie pulled Emily's body from the car and carted it over the berm and down to the edge of the swamp grass. The ground squished beneath his feet. He swung her back and forth four or five times to develop a rhythm and some leverage, and when he had enough momentum he let go. Her body, still covered in the blanket, went three or four feet through the air, and landed with a wet smack on the muddy ground. The tall reeds parted to admit her, then straightened and closed over her. Without waiting, Eddie Biggs returned to the car.

He drove back through the Lincoln Tunnel into the city, breaking Emily's five-dollar bill to pay the toll. He emerged from the tunnel at Fortieth Street and proceeded uptown. His luck held till the end. The parking space from which he had stolen the car was still empty. He replaced the machine, locked it and walked away. The sun was starting to climb over the East River when he slipped into Olivia Hunter's apartment again and, for good order's sake, ransacked it.

Now richer by six dollars and change, he emerged from the apartment and went up to his pad. He cleaned out all of the drawers, and stuffed their contents into the cheap suitcases that were the souvenirs of his travels and Emily's. When he was finished, he walked to the subway and took a train to the Port Authority Bus Terminal. For half a dollar he rented one of the cubicles in the men's room where he washed up and changed into his pimp suit and pointed-toed shoes. Then he rented a locker for the suitcases.

This done, Eddie Biggs walked over to the fast food counter and had a hearty breakfast with Emily's earnings. He bought himself a paper and sat on the bench in the center of the lobby, so that he would have a good view of the incoming traffic, just in case there was any good material around to start rebuilding his string.

# 34

Arnie Ross hummed to himself as he walked away from his car and headed toward the Twenty-third Precinct House. He bounded up the steps and threw a smile at the uniformed cop behind the desk. "Morning, Eddie," he said. The cop looked after him, surprised. Arnie continued up to the third floor, and pushed through the door of H/Z 4 still humming. Marvin Baxter, the new boy assigned to him, sat at his desk frowning over a pile of paperwork. "How you doing, hotshot?"

Baxter looked up and shrugged. "Very slowly. Very slowly."

Ross approached the end of the room and the choice between the two doors: one to the sergeants' office; the other to Lieutenant Flaherty. He picked the sergeants'. He sat down and scanned his desk. There was a note stuck to the end of a pencil in a jelly jar. "Call Didi." It was time-stamped five minutes ago. Curious, he called his apartment. The phone rang five times. He was about to hang up when she answered. "Hello."

"Is this Detective Sergeant Ross's apartment?"

"Yes," she said sweetly.

"What took you so long to answer, and what did you want?"

"I was trying to go back to sleep, and Alex."

"Alex what?"

"The second part of the question. You asked me if I knew anybody named Alex at Manhattan Jewish."

"So?"

"So it bothered me. And now I remember. Klinger's the guy's name. Very strange. Black guy with a light complexion. A mumbler."

Ross cradled the phone between his shoulder and his ear

and jotted notes on his pad. "What kind of guy is he, Didi? I mean, a doctor or what?"

"No. He's an attendant, a green coat. Mops floors, pushes wheelchairs."

"Good for him. Say, how do you know him? Did he push your bedpan?"

"Not my type, Sarge. No. He was on Morgenstern Four maybe six or seven months ago, for maybe a month or two. Oddball. He mumbled to himself a lot."

"Anything else?"

"Hey, it was a miracle I remembered him at all."

"True enough. Okay, toots. Get some beauty sleep. See you around." He hung up and headed toward Flaherty's office. Who knows? he thought. Every crummy little lead has possibilities. Now all I have to do is find how many other people named Alex have worked in Manhattan Jewish Hospital. He knocked at Flaherty's door.

"Come."

Arnie opened the door and presented himself. "Good morning, Lieutenant. How are you?" He stood in front of the desk beaming confidently.

Flaherty burped. He took the cigar from his mouth and looked at the end of it. Cursing mildly, he put it down in the ash tray. "What are you so fucking happy about? If you really care, I feel terrible. We had corned beef and cabbage last night, and I'm still eating it. I've eaten it six times." He popped a Gelusil into his mouth. "Let's talk about the hospital. Where is the written report that I asked for?"

"I haven't got it, but" Arnie hastened to add, "things have been quiet over there. And we might have a lead from the Alonzo kid."

"The one that's still alive, you mean."

Arnie lost a little of his glow. "Yeah. That's the one I mean. She mentioned the name of a guy who might have been a friend of her sister's."

"The one that died."

"Yeah." Flaherty was just a bundle of laughs this morning, Arnie decided. "The one who died. A nurse I, ah, know mentioned that there was a guy who worked in the hospital that had the same name."

Flaherty leaned forward. "That sounds like something."

Ross shrugged. "To be honest, I doubt it. One thing is, it was only the first name."

"The second name was different?"

"Nah. The kid didn't know the second name. Alex. Just Alex."

Flaherty sat back and burped into the back of his hand. "It's better than nothing." He looked up at Ross expectantly.

"All right. All right. I'll have the frigging report on your desk before you go home. I'll go chase down the lead first. You seen the Roach?"

Flaherty indicated the next office with his thumb. "He was here a little while ago. Been to see his mother." The last was said in a noncommittal voice. Ross peered at him, but the Lieutenant avoided his gaze. "Go ask him yourself. And have the report on my desk before I go home. Got it?"

"Yessir." Ross left the room, his mood dampened. He walked into the office where Hernandez sat, his head propped against his hands, leaning on his elbows, reading some papers on the desk before him. "Hey, Roach, wuz cookin', man?"

"Mama's not so hot, Arnie."

"She was all right last night when I went to see her. I mean, she was sleeping, and the nurse, Didi Rosenberg, the little red-haired one, she said she was okay."

"I dropped in to spend some time with her. She looks lousy. I talked to Saul. He wasn't too cheery. He said they're going to show her to one more guy. But they think that it is Hodgkin's Disease. She has all of the, what he called, exterior symptoms." He shook his head sadly. "It don't look so good for the spics."

"Hey, man," Arnie clapped his shoulder. "When does it ever look good for the spics? She's gonna be all right. Mama's tough, no? She got sick. She'll get well. They got another guy for her to see, right?"

"Okay. Okay. Enough pep talk. I saw you go inside. Get much flak?"

"No. He ate too much last night. He feels shitty enough to be in a rotten mood, but too shitty to be able to really do anything about it. Besides, I had a bone to throw him. You can stop going through that shit," he pointed at the pile of papers, "one at a time. I think we have a small lead." He told him about Rosenberg and Alex Klinger.

Lou looked puzzled for a moment, then broke into a

grin. "And I thought that you went to the hospital to visit my poor old mother. You lecherous bastard."

Arnie looked pained. "I gave my all for the department in the line of duty."

"My heart goes out to you. Klinger, did you say?" Arnie nodded acknowledgment. Lou fumbled through the pile of records until he came to a file with the proper name. He flipped it open, and scanned it. "He's a slavey. Union member. No comments of any kind. Social security number. Application shows. . . ." He stopped for a moment and looked up. "That's odd. He shows two years at City College. But that's it. He simply stopped. The rest of his employment record is just a bunch of idiot posts. Strictly unskilled manual labor. Ten years of it. And a dozen job changes."

Arnie craned his neck and looked over Lou's shoulder. "Funny. East Village address. You're right. It looks odd. Single, huh." Ross scratched his chin. "Just smells funny." He stood upright, reached for the phone, dialed a number and waited.

"Good morning, this is Sergeant Ross. Is Dr. Rogovin in? Okay, no, no, I don't need to talk to him now. I'm coming over. I'll be there in a few minutes. See if he can squeeze me in. I just need a moment of his time." He hung up, picked up the file from under Hernandez' nose and said, "Come on, greaseball, the game's afoot."

Hernandez snorted and followed him out of the room. "Sherlock Cohen, maybe? With that Jew beak."

"Bitter," Arnie said, trotting down the stairs. "Very bitter."

Lou folded himself into the passenger seat of Arnie's Porsche. "God. To pay all this money to be uncomfortable." He reached down and flipped the lever to push back the seat.

They left the car opposite the Morgenstern Pavilion entrance and entered the lobby, going straight to the reception desk. They waited while the nurse's aide phoned around to find Saul. He was in the Radiology Department and promised to come over in a few minutes. Ross and Hernandez toyed with the idea of a quick visit to Mama, but decided to wait.

Saul Rogovin emerged from the elevator, spotted Lou and Arnie, and motioned for them to follow him outside.

"What can I do for you, boys?"

"I think we have a small lead," Arnie said. "All it is is a maybe connection between that Alonzo case and a hospital employee."

"How maybe?" Saul asked.

Arnie shrugged. "That's what we're here to find out. Can I check if an employee of the hospital is at work?"

"Sure. We can check with his department and see if he's in. I can call his supervisor."

Arnie said, "Don't do that, Saul. You'll tip him off. If he doesn't find out himself, someone may tell him."

"Do you know anything but his name?" Rogovin asked. Arnie produced the personnel file. Rogovin looked through it quickly. "You want to trust me with this? I'll go up to personnel and ask where he's assigned. Then I can just walk over and see if he's punched in."

Lou looked at Arnie for confirmation, then said, "Why not? We'll wait upstairs in Mama's room."

Saul looked pained. "Listen, Lou, why don't you wait outside in the nice fresh air and leave your poor mother to get some rest. She's got a whole barrage of tests to deal with today."

Feeling glum again, the two detectives wandered across the street and sat on a bench next to the stone wall dividing the park from the sidewalk. Arnie, tired from his long night, dozed in the warm sun. Lou sat quietly and watched the passers-by. After about a half hour, Rogovin reappeared and crossed over to where they were sitting. Lou nudged Arnie in the ribs with his elbow. He sat up and rubbed his eyes.

"Very odd," Rogovin said. "The guy had a pretty good record. I spoke to his supervisor."

"What's odd," Arnie asked. "I thought you were just going to look at his time card."

"I did. But he hasn't been to work in close to a week. No call in. No nothing. And it's odd because he has had an exemplary record till now. His supervisor told me he'd even given him a call because he was concerned that something might be wrong with him. He's never taken off a day for any reason without calling in."

"Did you ask anything else," Lou added. "Did you ask if there was anything special about him?"

"I did, after we'd established that he'd sort of disappeared. The union's been notified and so has personnel. The supervisor said that Klinger was just very quiet, very intense." Rogovin paused. "He also said he was into politics."

Lou leaned forward, "How so and what kind?"

"When he talked, and it wasn't often, the guy said he was full of discontent, very angry."

"Violent?"

"Anything but. But angry at society, you might say."

"Looks like we have a clear shot at your adversary, Saul." Hernandez rose. "Come on, Arn. Let's go see if we can find him."

The address was on Second Street. Lou guessed that the number put it either just east or west of Second Avenue. "Right in the heart of the low rent district of the beautiful Ninth Precinct. Fourteenth Street junkies and whores to the north. Houston Street and the winos of the Bowery to the south. And the scenic East River, together with floating garbage and used rubbers to the east."

"Don't forget Broadway and the scenic loft district to the west. Very chic. Hey, Roach, remember when we used to call rubbers Hudson River whitefish?"

Ross pulled up to the curb on Second Avenue and glanced up at the number of the building on the corner. "Shit, the other side," he said. He wheeled the car around the block and parked in front of the stoop. A group of Hispanic teenagers first ambled forward to look at the sleek machine. When Ross and Hernandez emerged and stood on the sidewalk, the boys sensed cops and they faded away down the block.

Ross and Hernandez entered the tiny vestibule of the squalid building and checked the mailboxes. They found Klinger's name printed neatly on a little piece of paper and stuck in the slot above the corroded bell. Ross leaned on it. They waited and he pushed again. "Maybe he's not home," Ross offered. "Maybe we should come back later."

"Sure," said Lou with a sour smile. "Sure." He drew the short-barreled service revolver from the shoulder holster under his coat and checked to make sure that it was loaded. "We can always leave a card, like UPS or Con Edison."

Ross turned the handle on the door to the hallway. It creaked open. He reached around to his belt and pulled his gun, checking it as had Hernandez. "Yeah, Lou. We could get cards printed. We're sorry. We came to arrest you today at two forty-five in the afternoon. You were not home. We will call again tomorrow between nine and twelve. Signed your friendly homicide detective."

"Nice." Lou walked up the creaky stairs. On the landing of the second floor he stopped and looked at the number on the first door. "It's just down the hall," he said in a loud whisper. He wrinkled his nose. "Yecch."

Ross padded down the hall and said under his breath, "You can say that again."

They bracketed the door, Ross to the right, Hernandez to the left, against the walls. Ross nodded. Hernandez reached out with his revolver and tapped firmly at the door. "Mr. Klinger," he called. He tried two or three more times. Then he tapped harder and said, "Mr. Klinger, this is the police." A head stuck out of a door down the hall, took in the scene, and disappeared to the accompanying slam of a door.

Ross nodded again, pointing at himself with his free hand. Hernandez nodded acknowledgment. Ross spun away from the door, then kicked it sharply just below the knob. It flew open, and Ross spun through the door crouching, his revolver thrust before him. Hernandez, partly shielded by the door frame, stood erect, the barrel of his gun protruding into the room. Ross gagged, stood upright, and backed out of the room. His stomach heaved a half dozen times as he sought to control the bile that rushed to the back of his throat. Hernandez lowered his gun and holstered it. "Holy fuckin' shit."

Ross's stomach subsided and he straightened and stuffed his gun back into his waist band. "I guess we better call Morris Nassiter, or Rogovin. Holy fucking shit."

The remains of Alex Klinger had been reduced by a swarm of rats to a festering mass of bloated tissue. White bone showed in many places. The eye sockets stared emptily from the parody of a face. The abdomen had been chewed through and its contents spilled across the floor. Flies were everywhere. Ross shuddered and closed the door.

Hernandez looked at him. "Come on, Arn."

"Okay, okay." He opened the door again. He stepped across the room, avoiding the mess. One lone rat sat defiantly upright near the body. When Arnie flicked on the lamp, he scurried away to join the others in their holes. Arnie checked through the bits and pieces of Alex Klinger's life. A broken-down dresser contained a pile of shirts and underwear, and a few pairs of socks. The closet held two suits and two pairs of shoes, a couple of pairs of slacks and a ratty overcoat. Pushed to one side were three sets of hospital greens of the kind worn by nonprofessional personnel. Two pairs of rubber-soled white shoes were arrayed neatly on the floor.

While Arnie looked in the closet, Lou walked around the perimeter of the small room, looking at the spines of the books stacked against the wall. "Strange taste, Arnie. Into politics and black power." He stopped. "And every boy's primer, the two-volume edition of *The History of Guerilla Warfare.*"

Arnie was bent over in the closet. Without straightening, he stuck his arm out behind him, palm open. "Got your knife, Roach?" Lou slipped the six-inch steel and plastic object from his back pocket and pushed the button forward. The blade, rather than unfolding as in most switchblades, popped directly out from the handle at the end of a powerful spring. Lou turned it handle first and slapped it into Arnie's palm like a nurse in surgery. "What you got, Arn?"

"Minute," he grunted in reply. He squatted to avoid soiling his clothes on the filthy floor. He had spotted a patch in the farthest corner of the closet where the dust hadn't settled. The boards were as stained and old, but his trained eye spotted the difference in texture. In a matter of minutes, he stood up again.

"Is our dead warrior a user or a war profiteer? Or is he just a collector of odd samples of rare drug boxes?" Arnie said, stepping out of the closet and brushing off his hands. He pushed the button on the knife and the blade snapped back into the handle with a satisfying click.

Lou stepped in to check out the floor. A couple of boards had been cut through to make a rectangular opening about a foot and a half square. There was a cardboard box in the hole into which a variety of vials, ampules, and boxes of assorted pills had been stuffed. Lou leaned over and pulled loose a plastic bag, unrolled the top and sniffed the ragged brown, leafy material within. "Ganja. First class Jamaican weed." He rolled it up again and dropped it back into the box. "Gives me a headache."

"So don't smoke it," Arnie said. "Is it possible that what Saul thinks is a war against his hospital is just another little drug-related problem, as they say in the papers?

Lou shrugged. "Beats me, Arn. You think somebody wasted our friend?" He pointed toward the other room.

"He probably died of the crud he got from the mice. The crud he gave to that poor Alonzo kid." He hesitated. "But, you never know. What'll we do now?"

"If we report a homicide, or a possible, then it all comes out at once. And we can't dick around, either. No falsifying DD-5's and homicide reports for Mama Hernandez' little boys."

"So if we call Rogovin, and the Medical Examiner, and report it as a natural?"

Hernandez hesitated. "What if we were right the first time? What if somebody wasted the gentleman?"

"So the ME says it was homicide, and we go from there. The truth is, that if this is a drug war, and we didn't know it, we probably should've handled it quietly anyway. The ME says murder. Then we've got a leg up because if we don't know who, maybe we have some idea of why."

"Okay, Let's compromise. We'll call Rogovin first and see what he thinks."

There was an ancient metal phone unit on the floor in a corner next to the bed. Ross looked at it carefully. Not a sign of prints. "Too bad. It's the best place to find them."

"Well at least you don't have to go outside to make your call."

Arnie picked up the phone, fumbled with a little book and dialed Rogovin's direct extension. "Saul, we have something for you. A guy named Alex Klinger. Used to be one of your orderlies. Dead as a doornail. Chewed up and decomposing. Not your greatest fun-filled feature." He paused for a moment listening.

"No, we haven't gone near the damn corpse. It's a real disgusting mess." He waited again. "Our normal procedure would be to notify the precinct. This is the Ninth. If it was me, and I was a regular and I'd stumbled over this stiff, if it wasn't a follow-up on something I'd started myself, I'd probably call H/Z 1. They handle the Ninth. They're over at Manhattan Detective Headquarters on Twenty-first Street. I know Lieutenant Velasco pretty well."

Rogovin interrupted him with another question. "We were talking about that. We can't obstruct justice, but if you want, Nassiter can come down here. Yeah, Saul, we can give him a little head start. We'll wait ten minutes and then call the morgue on Twenty-ninth. Is that enough? Okay. Then we'll call the precinct."

Arnie called Marvin Baxter and had him pick up Nassiter and run him down under the siren. They arrived a minute after Arnie had called the ME. Nassiter, panting a little from his trot up the stairs, took one look at the mess on the floor and said, "Only the stomach contents and the stool are contaminated. He died of dehydration from acute diarrhea."

"You can tell from that mess?" Arnie asked.

"Strictly speaking, no. But I know what I'm looking for. The ME can do what he wants. But that's what he's going to find. Unless someone shot him while he was busy shitting his life away. Tell the ME what it is. They know about our cases, of course. Routine report."

Arnie glanced at Lou, who said, "Listen, Baxter, why don't you take Dr. Nassiter back to the hospital. Thanks, Doc."

"In the way, am I?" Nassiter beamed.

When he left, Arnie put in a call to the Ninth. It took him an hour to explain that he and Lou were following up on a case from their precinct, and to wait around for the identification and tagging of possessions. An extra twenty minutes went to the narcotics boys from the Ninth, who explained that, in their neighborhood, drugs were the big problem. They laid out the contents of the box on the floor and catalogued every item.

"Do you think that he was dealing," Arnie asked casually.

"Maybe," said the narc. "But it don't look like shit you could handle in big lots. You say he was a hospital employee?" Arnie nodded. "Well, you could say that maybe he felt that he was underpaid. And he considered the ripped-off drugs a tip for his hard work." The narc grinned. "Hey man, everybody's entitled in this town, right."

He flipped through the boxes and the bag. "The ganja's bought." He sniffed. "From the Rastars, man. Shit's straight from the home island its own bad self." He fumbled some more. "All right," the narc conceded. "Either he was a pack rat, or he was doing some light dealing. Maybe he's big and his stash was down, but I doubt it. Small time. Just a minor outlet."

Lou looked out of the window pensively as Arnie drove

uptown. "You got to figure," Arnie said, "that this is a drug scene."

Lou shook his head in disagreement. "Why should they push up the death rate at the hospital? Why should this Klinger use those sick mice to try to kill people in the cancer ward? Crazy. For drugs? Don't make sense."

"How about if one group is trying to play off against another?"

"You're wasting your breath," Lou said with finality.

"Okay, professor, so what is it?"

"The books interest me more than the drugs. I think instead of a drug dealer with a taste in politics, what you got here is a political freak, a Castro-ite or something. Maybe like FALN—the Puerto nationalists. And maybe, instead of being into bang-bang type violence, they're into slow, big-time violence. Instead of making the papers on the front page with mostly bullshit escapades, these guys are more interested in broadening the obituaries."

"Just racking up a score? Success in numbers?"

"Why not? Fuckin' city's full of crazy assholes."

"Well, one thing's for sure. It's getting past time to go legit on this. We got to start finding out who Klinger's friends and associates were. I hate to blow the whistle on Saul, but Flaherty's right. You can't sit on this kind of shit forever."

"So let's go to the hospital and start talking."

"Right. Then we'll call Flaherty."

# 35

John Krasnowski felt just terrible. His head throbbed like a heartbeat. His eyes, bloodshot and teary, stung with the breeze that blew in to the cab of his truck. His mouth was cotton dry, and his belly couldn't decide between nausea and cramps. His giant, rough, red hands gripped the steering wheel of the eighteen wheeler as though he were afraid that if he let go, he would fall off the seat. The heat from the big Jimmy diesel shimmered before his eyes making the Jersey Meadowlands look like a mirage.

Still, Krasnowski thought, there had been compensations. He had fucked his brains out while killing a quart of Booth's Gin with a waitress from that little diner on the Post Road near White Plains. He had dragged the big rig off the Thruway on his way down from Montreal with a load of machine parts. Good trip. Night. No bears. Good weather. He smiled weakly. Great pussy, he thought.

Suddenly, his head started to pound till he could hear the rushing in his ears, and his stomach rebelled at its contents. He looked in his mirrors and pulled over, first from the middle lane to the right, and then onto the side of the road. He shut her down and got out. He had hoped that the fresh air would help, but it didn't. His stomach convulsed and heaved up its largely liquid burden. "Yecchh," Krasnowski said aloud. The price of sin, he thought, leaning his back against the truck body. When he felt a little better, he lit up a Camel, pushed his limp blond hair out of his eyes, and walked back and forth on the dirt bank beside the road, trying to build back his circulation. He wiped his eyes for the hundredth time with a red bandana handkerchief.

Krasnowski hesitated for a moment, then wiped his eyes again. There seemed to be something in the reeds a dozen feet from where he stood. It looked like a human foot.

At first gingerly, trying to avoid immersing his cowboy

boots in the slime, Krasnowski peered into the tangle of green fronds. It was a body. He was tempted to get back into his truck and take off. He didn't need the hassle. Then curiosity got the best of him, and cursing the mud, he stepped forward into the shallow water and pushed the reeds aside. "Oh my sweet Jesus," he said. He reached over to pick up the girl's head. It had been resting against a stone, and where he moved it, there was a patch of blood from her scalp. He held her head up and bent over so his ear was next to her mouth. She must be dead he thought, suddenly frightened. Then he heard a faint whistle of air. Jesus, he thought, she's alive. He laid her back gently, turned, and forgetting his own physical woes, charged up the bank to the truck. He jumped into the cab and started the engine. The moment she was roaring, he flipped on his CB radio and turned to Channel 9 where the smokies always listened for emergency messages. "Breaker, nine, breaker, nine, this is the Ramblin Reck. I have found a girl badly hurt in the swamp on the north arm of the turnpike at mile marker," he peered out the window at the white post with the slender green sign, "seven-point-five. Send an ambulance. Over."

A state trooper was at his side in less than two minutes.

"I had a tough night. I got sick so I stopped the rig."

The cop looked at him impassively through his aviator rimmed green glasses, his campaign hat straight on his crew cut head. "Where is she?" he asked.

"I lost my cookies. I was walking back and forth," he led the officer along, "and then I saw her." As they arrived at Emily's resting place, an ambulance from County General Hospital in Hackensack, five minutes to the north, roared up with its siren blaring. The intern jumped down and joined Krasnowski and the trooper at the bottom of the bank. He took a stethoscope from the bag and asked the cop to hold it. He pulled aside the flimsy blanket that partly covered Emily Stolzfuss and, closing his eyes in concentration, with his fingers searched for a pulse of life.

"I heard her breath," Krasnowski said. "I'm sure I did."

The doctor looked up. "She's still with us, but not by much. God what a mess." He stepped back and looked at her. "Whoever did this must have been some shit." He hurried back to the ambulance.

The officer turned to Krasnowski with a hard stare. "Oh

no," Krasnowski said, "don't look at me. I just found her. I didn't have anything to do with this."

"If you didn't, mister, you got nothing to worry about. In the meantime, would you mind just coming over here and sitting in my car for a while. And may I have your license and registration."

The cop walked back to the car and pulled loose the mike. "Central, this is 73. I think we have an attempted murder here. Possible suspect in custody." Krasnowski shrank against the seat. That's what you get for sticking your nose in, he thought.

Dennis Vogel, M.D., was on his fourth day of emergency ambulance duty at Bergen County General. It was nearly the end of his first year of internship, and he still felt a swelling pride when he heard the word doctor used in his presence, and he realized that it referred to him.

The cop had put Vogel's bag, which together with its contents had cost his Aunt Marguerite almost $1,500 as a med school graduation present, onto the firm grass of the berm. His stethoscope dangled from his neck as he bent over the prostrate form of Emily Stolzfuss. He was enough of a doctor to know that he should leave this one sit for a while. He straightened up for a moment to relieve a crick in his back. Then, deciding to sacrifice the whites he was wearing, he kneeled in the mud and took stock.

He did the head first. Bruises and contusions of the face. All over the face, in fact. Possible broken nose. Both lips split, but all teeth seemingly intact. Two severe lacerations of the scalp, where tiny vessels always cause more bleeding than the seriousness of wounds would indicate. One wound on the side of the head caused by striking the rock on the ground. Superficial. The other? He palpated gingerly. Big edema. Deep cut. He gently lifted her eye lids. Pin pricks. Bloodshot. Serious concussion. Possible skull fracture.

He rocked back and took a breath, then wrinkled his nose. He shrugged off the putrid smell. That, he thought, is what you get for hanging around a swamp in New Jersey. He focused his attention on his patient again. Right arm broken above the elbow. Possible fracture of the right clavicle, though he couldn't tell without feeling around and risking further injury. Left arm okay. He wrinkled his nose again. Phew! He pulled aside the shreds of the blanket. Very nice. Very young. No broken ribs. Maybe.

He licked his lips, which had gone dry. At first he thought that he had made some kind of mistake. He turned Emily's right leg ever so gingerly. It was smashed like the limb of a discarded doll, broken between the hip and thigh. The knee was bent inward toward the crotch, and from the side of the thigh a large portion of the femur, splintered and sharp as a spear, protruded through a ragged and blackened wound. The source of the sweet sick smell was the putrefaction of that wound. The edges of the opening had blackened, and the telltale streaks of red—advertising the presence of blood poisoning—ran upward toward the torso.

By some miracle, the fracture had failed to sever the femoral artery which would have leaked Emily's life into the ground in thirty seconds. He was good enough a doctor to have the right instinct. It was too much for him and he should call for help. But kneeling here in the slimy mud of a late spring morning in New Jersey, there was no one to call. He could go back to the hospital and try to pick up another doctor. Or he could call in. Finally, he threw his hands in the air and said, "Sorry, little lady. You're just going to have to put your faith in old sure-hands Vogel."

He turned and yelled for the driver. "Hey, Jackson, Bring that rolling stretcher down here, foot end first." Please God, Dennis Vogel thought, it's my first tough one. For her sake and mine, don't let me fuck it up.

# 36

The ugliness of poverty and the hard dirty surface of the big city is relieved by small rays of light for the inhabitants at the lower end of the social spectrum.

And so it had been even for poor, old doddering Olivia Hunter. Now, her gentleman caller didn't show up every day, and he certainly wasn't regular in his habits. But she could count on him two or three times a week.

Herman White was well over six feet tall and weighed over two hundred. At twenty-five, he was a physical force to be reckoned with. Fortunately for him, and for his parents, he was as gentle as he was large. His father, a mortician, had been hard pressed at first to sympathize with the problems of his third son. But together with his wife, a kind and understanding woman of great patience and dedication, they had come to grips with Herman's condition. For all of his size and strength, Herman White had the mentality of a six-year-old child. Even in the ugliness of the environment that Harlem provides at times, even for its middle class citizens, they had been fortunate. Special schooling under a state program, and the fundamental decency of their neighbors had prevented worse problems. In any case, the Whites had decided to keep Herman at home rather than send him to an institution, and they had never regretted the decision.

One of the things that Herman did was to take a package of food from the kitchen every two or three days. A little meat, some crackers, some cheese, and occasionally butter or milk, put it in a brown paper bag, and wander off for three or four hours. At first the trips had been shorter, and even then Mrs. White had worried. But after a while, she realized that he was in no danger. One of his brothers had followed him over to Olivia Hunter's. He had met her on the stoop of the crumbling slum. A harmless old lady. No problem there.

Herman sat on the steps of Olivia's house for an hour. Then slowly it occurred to him that she was late. He was curious without being fearful. He stood and climbed the steps, then shambled down the hall to her apartment. The door swung open when he knocked on it. He wrinkled his brow as he tried to take in the scene. It was messy. Herman knew that messy was bad. Lord knows he had been told often enough.

"Owivia?" he asked. Herman wasn't very good with l's. "Owivia?" His voice was high and squeaky, and sounded odd coming from that big body. He spied the poor frail arm amidst the bedclothes and went over to touch it. It didn't move. He called her name three or four more times, then tugged at her arm. The small body slid forward easily in his grasp. Her tongue protruded from her mouth and her eyes stared vacantly. Herman dropped her hand as though it were red hot. Then he dropped his paper bag, and wet his pants. He screamed hysterically and ran down the hall to the door and out into the street. He ran along the sidewalk his arms flapping, his long legs flailing, knocking pedestrians aside. Screaming, he headed for home. Before he came to the corner, he ran headlong into Officer Arthur Miller of the Twenty-third Precinct. Twenty-seven years on the force, Miller knew every inch of his precinct, where he had served most of those years. "Whoa up, Herman. You know you're not supposed to run like that. You could hurt yourself, or somebody else. What would your mama say if she caught you running in the street like that?"

"Dead," he screamed. "Dead. Dead. Dead. Dead. Dead." Each time a crescendo. "Dead." Finally, he reached the peak of his vocal range and burst into uncontrollable sobs, trying to bury his head in the shoulder of the black policeman who was a half a head shorter than himself, knocking the uniform cap askew on the graying head.

Officer Miller put his arm supportively around Herman's shoulder and led him home. He trembled and shook like a leaf in the wind.

Good fortune continued for Herman and Officer Miller. Mrs. White was home. She spied the two of them coming up the block, and despite years of self-control and conditioning, felt her heart palpitate at the sight. Had Herman finally done something wrong? Would he finally have to be put away? She hurried to the door, and was standing before it when they came to the top of the stoop.

Mrs. White smiled bravely and said, "Now what have you got there, Officer Miller?"

He returned the smile, holding firmly to Herman's elbow. "I think we might just like to step inside for a few moments, Mrs. White." She stepped aside and let the officer steer her son through the door. Herman still had not reckoned with his surroundings. His eyes darted from side to side in panic and his breathing was irregular. His adam's apple bobbed as he swallowed repeatedly.

"He was running down the street, Mrs. White," the officer said. "He was running as though he were being chased by the hounds of hell."

Mrs. White walked to Herman's side and very gently took his hand in her own. "Herman, baby. You hear Mama?" He started to shake again. It finally dawned on him that he was with his mother. He squealed with relief and joy, squeezing her hand so hard that it was nearly broken. "Owivia." He repeated the old lady's name ten times. Mrs. White waited. Herman stopped.

"What about Olivia?" she asked.

"Dead." Herman replied, again in a rising crescendo of shouts, his unmodulated child's voice a threnody of despair. He stopped again, then recommenced shouting, "Messy."

Mrs. White was ashamed. Something had happened to the poor old lady that Herman went to visit. But with the conviction of motherhood and long experience, she felt relief. The officer may not know that Herman had nothing to do with it, but she did.

As much to hide her feelings as to care for Herman, Mrs. White turned her son away from the policeman and sat him down on the sofa. Spittle leaked a little at the corners of his mouth.

Composed again, Mrs. White turned back to Officer Miller and said, "I wish I could give you her address. My son Joe might have it. He's at work. Should I call him?" Miller agreed. In a moment, after a brief conversation filled with reassurances that there was nothing wrong with either Herman or herself, and protestations against Joe's rushing home from work, she jotted an address on a piece of paper, hung up the phone, and showed it to Officer Miller.

"That's where he was all right. He was about halfway down the block when I caught up with him." Miller looked at the shivering boy on the couch and thought a minute, then said, "Mrs. White, you do me a favor and keep Herman home for a while, till I call you. Will that be okay?"

She went to Herman's side and put her arm protectively around his head, cupping his chin in her hand. He closed his eyes and leaned against her warmth like a puppy. "He'll be here." Her voice was stronger than she felt. When Officer Miller closed the door behind him, she gently disengaged herself from her son and went to the phone. Her husband had rushed home from the office, just a few blocks away, at about the same time that Officer Miller was climbing Olivia Hunter's stoop.

Miller's anger was balanced by a world weariness born from years of confrontation with senseless cruelty and violence. Now, toward the end of his career, he felt that he was on the losing end of the fight.

"Now tell me, Charley," he asked the duty sergeant as he called it in, "who's gonna kill that harmless frail little thing? Shit. If he'd just sat there and waited a little while, she'd have croaked on her own. Not pretty, Charley, I'm telling you." He paused and listened. "Okay. I'll wait on the stoop."

A squad car arrived almost before he had returned from the corner call box. Windows started to fly open and heads began to appear as the blue and white car screeched to a halt with its bubble gum lights flashing. About a minute later, an unmarked car arrived and Marvin Baxter emerged, followed by the bear-like form of Albert Ruggles. Several windows were hastily shut and some heads disappeared.

The two detectives waited in the hall outside of Olivia's room until the forensics people arrived. Ruggles and Baxter listened as Officer Miller told his story in the spare, sure fashion of the thoroughly professional. Baxter took copious notes. Ruggles just nodded.

"Did you leave someone to watch White," Baxter asked.

"White?" Miller replied, confused.

"I mean, after all, he's certainly a suspect."

Miller looked to Ruggles for help. Ruggles rumbled, "You say 'White' like you were talking about a person. He" pointing to Miller, "has known this kid his whole life, he just told you. He's a retard, Baxter. I don't think his mother will let him get away from us." Baxter swallowed and looked at his note book.

Ruggles turned to Miller. "Look, you go over to that house and talk to the boy and his parents. Gently does it. If it looks like there's anything at all to go on, call me. We'll be here a while."

When Miller had left, Ruggles turned to Baxter and said, "Well, professor, what does your instinct tell you should be done next."

"My training and experience," Baxter answered frostily, "tells me that we should shake this building down."

"Right, professor." He patted his shoulder, then called for one of the uniformed cops. "Nobody leaves. We'll start from the bottom."

The process took much less time than Ruggles expected. More than three quarters of the filthy building's crumbling apartments were unoccupied. The remainder were tenanted by frightened people, most of them old, subsisting on social security. One or two were clever enough to find their way onto the welfare rolls that had been created for them, but which seemed so often to elude them while including many less deserving.

On the fifth floor, there was an exception to the rule, a weak-eyed junkie named Stanley O'Ree. "Did you know," he said in a daze, "that the first black player in the National Hockey League was named Willie O'Ree." He tapped the dusty mattress he was sitting on in emphasis.

Ruggles looked down from his great height with an unkindly eye.

"Tell me, citizen, would you kill a little old lady for a fix?"

O'Ree thought fuzzily, rocking back and forth on the bed. "Yeah, I guess so," he said.

"Would you fuck your sister for a fix," Ruggles continued. O'Ree nodded happily. "And your mother, too."

"Sure. Why not?" His eyelids fluttered.

"So much for that," Ruggles said to Baxter in disgust. Baxter looked at him quizzically. Ruggles went on, "This scum bag has been nodding for, oh maybe ten, twelve, hours at least." He grabbed O'Ree's shirt and shook him so his gaze focused on Ruggles's face. "Tell me, citizen, when did you score." There was no answer. "Confidentially, citizen, how'd you like me to start hurting your body? You see, you think you can't feel nothing inside that fog of good shit you pushed in your arm. But you are wrong." He emphasized the word with a jerk of his hand that snapped O'Ree's neck back hard. "And if you scream, nobody's gonna give shit."

He turned back to Baxter. "You see, he would have done it if he'd had the presence of mind. He would do all of those things I said to get his smack. But he's too weak. So he steals small things, or big ones when he can. He eats out of garbage cans to scrape for small doses. The old lady died five, six, hours ago they figure. This fuck hasn't been worth a shit for twelve. Right, citizen?" He pinched his cheeks together with his thumb and forefinger, eliciting a small yelp. "This is the kind of hero that you meet in the Street Crime Unit." Ruggles said, giving O'Ree another wrench, then letting him go and wiping his hand on his pants.

"Tough cop," O'Ree said vaguely. "You make the cunt yell from next door, too?" he asked dopily and in disgust. "You beat on her, too?"

Baxter interjected, "Maybe he means the old lady. . . ." Ruggles cut him off with a sweep of his hand.

Ruggles reached out for O'Ree's hair, which was an unkempt Afro. He grabbed a bunch of it and wrenched it nearly from the scalp. O'Ree screeched feebly and tried to pull away. "What screaming?" By the time it was over, about a minute, Baxter figured, Ruggles had gotten a story, more or less coherent, from O'Ree about a lot of screaming from down the hall. But he really hadn't heard it too well because, as Ruggles had said, he'd been nodding pretty good. The only other person that was on this floor was a small-timer named Giggs or Diggs or maybe Biggs. He'd occasionally beat up on O'Ree for some snort or anything he could get his hands on. He was gonna be a real Mack. A big man. He was lining up a string. Just three or four doors down the hall.

Ruggles and Baxter left O'Ree huddled on his mattress to contemplate how to replenish the good feeling when his fix wore off. They'd already been in the room down the hall. The door was still ajar. There were just two or three pieces of nondescript furniture. Even the window was broken. They'd just gone on.

Only three or four pieces of glass hung, wobbling in the old wooden frame. Ruggles looked at them with a practiced eye. The fragment of sunny blue sky provided enough light in the dank air shaft to see that there was blood on the glass.

"Go downstairs," Ruggles said to Baxter quietly, "and get the forensics guy up here. We'd like prints." He nodded. "We got something like a double here." He leaned out of the window and looked down at the trash heap. "Take a look in that mess of garbage at the bottom of this shaft. It leads right out of old Olivia Hunter's apartment."

"What am I looking for?"

"My best guess is a body. Or at least, the traces that a body's been there."

When Baxter came back up the stairs, he found Ruggles sitting on the edge of the bed. In his hands was the remains of a pair of white bikini panties. They'd been cut through to the waistband on both sides.

"I found them stuffed in a corner behind that rickety dresser," Ruggles said sadly, reading the label for the tenth time. "Lobel's, Lancaster, Pennsylvania." He folded the little scrap of cloth and put it into his pocket. "I may even know who it belongs to." He got up and said, "I really want to have this place done over—and I mean really."

# 37

The ambulance driver was taller than Dr. Vogel by half a head. His skin was a shiny black and contrasted sharply with the short white sleeves of his orderly's tunic. He dug in his heels to avoid sliding on the slippery grass bank that led to Emily Stolzfuss. The stretcher was a complicated trapezoid of aluminum tubing with rubber wheels. A white muslin sheet was wrapped tightly around the mattress. Broad linen straps ending in leather and metal buckles crossed at the level of the chest and ankles.

"Hey, listen," said Vogel, "this is a real mess. We have to be really careful or we'll. . . ."

"We'll kill her." The driver finished cheerfully. "I can see that, Doc." He sat on the ground and pulled off his shoes and socks. "No sense in fuckin' around, my man. Let's get to it. Shit. Look at that femur."

"How long you been doing this?" Dr. Vogel asked, shucking his own shoes.

"Eleven years. I've gone through maybe a hundred and fifty interns in emergency. Ain't lost one yet." The driver grinned, pulling up his pants legs and wading in the mud up to his calves.

"The important part, Doctor," he emphasized the word, "is not to move that leg. Shit, she should be dead already. A couple more inches and she's gonna pop that old femoral artery and spray us pink." He reached over and grabbed the edge of the stretcher and pulled it toward Emily. "Hey, listen, Doc, you want to drag this mother along. She don't go so good in the mud."

The driver stepped forward, the mud sucking against his legs. He looked at the broken shape and forgot his own discomfort. He motioned to the young doctor who was dragging the heavy cart behind him, and between them they arranged the heavy apparatus parallel to Emily. "Easy, now, Doc, together." They edged her up onto the mattress. She reacted not at all. "Hey, did you do a pulse?" Vogel nodded. "Better do another," the driver said.

"She's alive," Vogel said, his hand at the pulse in her throat, "absolutely."

"Now comes the hard part," the intern said, "we just gotta pick the mother up and move it to the hard ground."

They strained, trying not to upset the unwieldy machine. With a last push, Vogel fell on his face in the slime, but the front wheels of the stretcher caught on the grass, and the driver, pushing behind, forced the rest onto the bank. "Come on, Doc. Can't just lie there in that shit and wait for the world to roll by. Rise 'n' shine."

Pushing and pulling, they managed to get the stretcher up the bank and to the ambulance. The trooper and the truck driver, seeing their plight, trotted over from the patrol car and helped them lift the stretcher and push it in. The orderly hopped in and Vogel, kneeling next to Emily in the rear compartment, began to pray as the ambulance spun its wheels, caught, and hurtled forward on the highway, its siren blaring.

The driver started toward the southern exit, just above the entrance to the Lincoln Tunnel. Then, yelling over his shoulder, "Hang on," he changed his mind and spun the ambulance across the grassy divider and headed north toward the Teaneck exit. He took the curve on two wheels, cut north on Teaneck Road, and raced toward the hospital. After a near miss at the intersection with Route 4, he wheeled into the hospital's emergency parking lot.

Dr. Camillo Feruggina, the chief of medicine at Bergen County General, stood at the emergency entrance with his hands on his hips. Cleveland Jackson, the ambulance driver, had asked for him personally over the radiophone. Feruggina knew that Jackson was a reliable man. He had walked out on a board meeting to receive the patient. He brushed the driver and the intern, a kid named Vogel, out of the way in his haste to get to the injured girl. He noted both the speed and the care with which she had been delivered. He couldn't have done it better himself. Vogel's path would be a little smoother in the future.

"Sweet Christ," Feruggina said. He palpated the leg carefully. It was like clay. Bad break. Bad infection. Gangrene. He ran his hand gently along the curve of the thigh above the ugly wound where the bone had broken through the skin. Heat. Infection. All the way to the groin. "Take her up to OR 1—stat!"

Dr. Feruggina moved with the litheness of a tennis player, which he was six times a week. Despite his fifty-one years, he had managed to keep the fat off of his abdomen and the spring in his legs. He waltzed through the doors of the operating room and stood arms spread like an imitation of Christ to receive the garments of his trade. The OR nurse slipped the green robe around him and the cap on his head, then waited as he laved himself in the sink with Phisohex, using his elbows to turn the oversize faucet handles. When he was through, she slipped the rubber gloves onto his hands to the elbow. He stepped into the operating room and looked down at the patient, naked before him on the table.

"Clean her up," he snapped at the surgical resident at his side. "But stay off that leg." He saw to it that she had shots of adrenalin and penicillin, and that an IV was started. He checked the life signs again. The minor cuts and the open wound on her cheek were treated and, where necessary, sewn. Even without benefit of X-rays, he found that two of her ribs were broken.

The preliminary treatment, stitches included, took less then ten minutes. Then Feruggina took the scalpel and began to debride the moldering flesh around the break. In a minute, the perspiration began to appear on his forehead. He had reached his present position by merit alone. He knew quickly that the matter exceeded not his competence, but rather his equipment. "If we don't get this kid under some heavy oxygen, even an amputation at mid-thigh isn't going to help." He painted the area over with merthiolate, stripped off his gloves and ran out of the theater. He took the phone in the anteroom and dialed a familiar number.

"Sidney," he said, relieved at the sound of the stern and familiar voice, "I have a first class emergency. Drastic compound fracture of the femur. Six centimeter wound, open and suppurating. Obvious gangrene. Can you help me?"

"Wait one." There was a pause of thirty seconds. "I'll get you a police helicopter. Figure half an hour at the most. The big chamber is clear. What does the patient need?"

"At least, for openers, an hour or two under straight oxygen at two, or maybe three atmospheres. Then we have to think about debriding and rearranging the break and reducing the fracture. A lot of work. It's a kid. A girl about fifteen or sixteen. As strong as a horse, Julius, or she'd have been dead twice already. The fracture's bad enough, but the gangrene looks like one of your lectures at med school—a mess."

Relieved, Feruggina hung up the phone with the Director of Vascular Medicine at the Manhattan Jewish Hospital. Sidney Greenstein was a healer and teacher in the tradition of the old school. He had imagined, then demanded, then begged and cajoled the money to create the hyperbaric chamber. Now he ran it without regard to race, religion, or financial condition, to the benefit of the patients, formerly condemned to death, whose exposure to the high pressure oxygen atmosphere would cure them.

Feruggina went back into the operating chamber and checked once more that his chief resident had performed all of the menial tasks in a proper fashion. All of the bleeders had been tied off. She had been cleaned generally. They had done stitching. All that remained was the ugly black patch that was spreading across the golden thigh from the edges of the ragged wound. In a matter of moments, the thrashing of the helicopter's rotor could be heard throughout the hospital. Feruggina issued instructions and the surgical team ran the rolling cart out onto the parking lot, its load wrapped securely in blankets, a bottle of liquid nutrients dangled above from a metal frame. The helicopter came to rest and waited, with engine running, in the midst of the parking lot. The surgical team, led by Dr. Feruggina, pushed the cart out to the windy site and, helped by two policemen, they raised the prostrate form of Emily Stolzfuss into the flat bed of the Huey. The driver and Dr. Vogel joined Feruggina on the lot as the copter rose with increasing velocity into the sky, and veered off across the river toward Manhattan.

# 38

Saul Rogovin leaned forward in his chair with his elbows on his knees. His normally smooth, tanned face was wrinkled into a pained squint. He had been listening to Ross and Hernandez develop their theory for about ten minutes. He had already been briefed by Morris Nassiter about the death of Alex Klinger.

"So you see, Saul," Hernandez concluded, "we just have to go legitimate on this. You can't tell when it will explode again. These people could be looney freaks. You can't trust a looney." Lou shrugged. "We wish it was something simple, like a major drug ring."

"Yeah," Arnie added. "At least the lust for *gelt* has a predictable pattern. A social conscience? Well, hell, who knows?"

"Do you want to call Flaherty now?" Rogovin asked.

"It seems like the only reasonable thing to do, all risks considered," Lou replied.

Arnie saw the lines on Rogovin's face deepen as he winced. He cleared his throat. Lou and Saul turned to look at him. "Look, Lou, why don't we take a preliminary look around. We can talk to the people that worked with Klinger. We could see if he has any friends. Maybe he talked a lot about his politics." He paused and thought for a moment. "I might even be able to get a volunteer to sniff for us."

"But when do you want to do this?" Lou asked.

"Now, Roach. Right now." He looked at his watch. "It's eleven-fifteen," he said. He grinned. "I think my help might be a little sleepy, but I can try. Saul, may I use the phone?"

Rogovin nodded. Ross fumbled through his address book, located the number and dialed it. When a sleepy voice answered, he said, "Okay, Red, sleepy time's over. Off your butt and on your feet."

"Fuck you, Ross."

"Super. But later. I need you to do something for me. Can you meet me at Manhattan Jewish? Dr. Rogovin's office."

"When?"

"Now. Right now. About fifteen minutes."

"Come on, Sarge. Have a heart. I had a heavy date last night."

"So I'll go on a diet. Let's go."

She groaned, then said, "Half an hour. My best offer."

"I'll take it." He hung up. Ross stood. "Now. We have Klinger's personnel records. We know where he worked. We know who he worked with. Now we start talking to people."

"First," Lou said, putting a restraining hand on Arnie's arm, "we call Flaherty."

"Always thinking about your pension," Arnie grumbled, reaching again for the phone.

Flaherty listened patiently, then said, "You will report to me at three o'clock." There was a pause and a crunching sound as the lieutenant ground up a couple of Gelusil. "At that time, we will report this mess to the Chief of Detectives. If he is in a good mood—if he played golf well this weekend, he might just ignore the minor impropriety that you have been running your own detective agency inside of the New York City Police Department. If nothing horrible happens as a result, I may not be cashiered without rank, and I may be able to collect my pension."

There was another short pause. "By the way, what have you and Ruggles been doing to Baxter? He looked green this morning. I asked him why? This was just ten minutes ago. A corpse eaten by rats and a strangled old lady?" His voice started to rise. "Listen, you aren't holding out on me, Ross?"

"Christ, Lieutenant, would I do that?"

There was a sputtering noise on the other end of the phone. Then silence and more crunching noises. "Three o'clock, Ross."

Ross shook his head and put down the receiver. "He's thinking about his pension, too." He looked over to Hernandez. "I don't understand cops like you. Where's your dedication?" Before Hernandez could answer, Ross was halfway out of the room.

"Well come on. Let's go. Take the files. We haven't got all day."

# 39

From the moment that he awakened in the morning, Rosario Gonzalez had done nothing to indicate that this day would differ from any other. Perhaps he looked at the picture on the dresser a little longer than usual. Perhaps he lingered before the shrine of his martyred wife and child for an extra moment. He glanced at the blueprint of the hospital, but it was unnecessary. The plans were imprinted on his mind in flawless detail.

He put on a clean uniform and walked out of his apartment. Halfway down the hall, he paused, then returned to the apartment. When he emerged again, he had the pictures of his parents, his brothers and sisters, his wife, inside of his shirt. He would not let them fall into enemy hands. And besides, Rosario thought, he did not want to die alone. He went to work, taking his usual route at his regular pace. He entered at Waldman, waving to the woman on duty at the information desk, smiling at the guard. He descended the stairs to the basement and made his way along the corridor to the emergency generator station. The man he was to relieve was already in street clothes. He looked at his watch and beamed.

"Rosie," he said, "I can set my watch by you. See you tomorrow."

"See you," Rosario replied. "Where's Bill?"

"In the back between generator's one and two with a comic book. I guess in his own sweet way he's just as reliable as you are." The man waved and left.

Rosario walked behind the green metal cabinets that stretched from the cement floor to the ceiling, dotted with green and red lights and dials with flickering hands nervously darting between numbered lines. There was a low, numbing hum of machinery. Bill leaned back in a rickety wooden armchair, one foot propped against a control panel, intently reading about Superman. Rosie stepped up behind him and cut his throat.

He pulled the head back again to be absolutely sure. The gaping wound poured blood over the already soiled green uniform. The eyes remained open. Death had been so sudden and sure that the comic was still clutched in his hand. Rosario let him down gently. The foot slipped from the control panel. Rosario pushed the chair forward to prevent Bill's body from falling to the floor. No one else would be expected to come to the station until two in the afternoon, and by then, it wouldn't matter.

Rosario checked his watch and walked to the door. Two minutes to go. He made sure that the panels were all in order and that the main control room for the hospital's utilities, over in Rosenstein, would show no irregularities. There were three knocks at the door. He opened it about a foot. A pair of hands slipped the flower box containing the machine guns through the opening. Rosario took the box, and shut the door. He heard the cart rattle down the hall to deliver its load of stained linens. He carried the box behind the last panel and sat down in a chair. There were two clips for each gun. He loaded them carefully. Then, using two-inch wide surgical tape, he bound them together in pairs. Each bundle was slightly offset, so that there would be sufficient clearance between the end of the magazine and the chamber of the gun. The openings, through which the bullets were exposed, pointed in opposite directions. Rosario grunted in satisfaction. Each magazine held twenty-five rounds. When one was finished, the gunner had only to pull out the clip and turn it upside down to reload. He chambered one round into each gun and engaged the safety catches. Checking his watch again, he sat down to wait.

Across the street, a green van with "Plumbing" painted on its sides pulled to a stop at the gate in the fence around the oxygen tank. Alton Cheseborough, his partner in the truck, and the man who had been pushing the laundry cart, were the sum total of Rosario Gonzalez' male force. Alton whistled cheerfully as he removed a tool box from the bed of the van and shut the door again. The dark glass in the rear doors permitted his partner to see out, but no one could see in.

Cheseborough, an escapee from an Alabama road gang, waited until he heard three knocks from inside the van.

He himself was facing Lexington Avenue, and there was no one coming. The knocking meant that his partner, a Dominican called Egydio Martins, could see no one coming from Third Avenue. Alton knocked back.

Martins hopped out of the truck pulling a sign panel after him. It said "Men at Work." They set it up in front of the gate and took the keys—provided by the cleaning woman who worked on the administration floor—and opened the locks.

Martins, who had jumped ship illegally and hid out with his sister in Queens, checked a blueprint. Red dots indicated caches, blue dots placement areas. He took his shovel and quickly unearthed the buried boxes of dynamite. About a half hour after they arrived a policeman and a hospital security guard wandered by. They watched for a few minutes, talking about baseball, as Martins and Cheseborough placed the boxes under the stem and the metering system of the oxygen tank. The two spectators watched with interest as Martins, an inventive electrician, made sure that the connections were sufficiently complicated to prevent easy dismantling should their purpose be discovered.

The guard recognized Martins and smiled and waved. Martins waved back. The cops walked on. As he tied off the last connection Martins remembered the look on his brother's face when the Marines landed in the Dominican Republic in the mid-sixties to make peace. It must have hurt, where the Marine had shot him, just between his navel and his penis. He screamed for an hour before he became too weak. Then only his eyes screamed for three more hours, till he died. He was fifteen.

Martins stood up and motioned to Cheseborough. "Okay. If anybody touches those wires—bang! The whole enchilada goes straight up."

"You fixed it like he said, right?" Cheseborough asked.

"Yeah, it's booby-trapped. But he can set it off with this." He held up a small black box with a switch and two buttons. "You flip this to on." He indicated the switch. "Then this button arms it. And this one . . . whoosh!" He smiled in satisfaction. "And if that doesn't work, we've got the direct wiring."

He casually spread the dirt around in the spot where he had made the final connection between the explosives attached to the oxygen tank and the detonator terminals hid-

den in the tank room at the Louis Gluck Hyperbaric
Chamber. Satisfied with his work, Martins motioned to
Cheseborough and opened the gate. They locked it behind
them and returned to the van.

Cheseborough pulled the van to the side entrance of the
Gluck building and turned off the motor. He pulled out
the "Men at Work" sign and opened it on the sidewalk
about three feet from the door. With a hand sledge and a
chisel, he broke a sizeable chunk of cement out of the
sidewalk, and dug a hole about a foot deep, piling the dirt
in the gutter. He got into the back of the van and joined
Martins, who was eating a sandwich and setting up a
Chinese-made AK-47 assault rifle so that it pointed out of
the back door. When they were done, they checked their
watches, and sat down to wait.

Juanita Marques was usually solicitous of Mama Hernandez' well-being. This morning in particular she would
have been very concerned. Mama was about to undergo a
whole new series of tests that had been suggested by another doctor. Saul Rogovin had brought him in for consulta-
tion. A modest course of chemotherapeutic treatment for
Hodgkin's Disease had met with total failure. Mama had
suffered all of the nasty side effects, falling hair, nausea
and weakness, but without any of the benefits. Her white
count remained unaffected. Her weight, her very flesh,
seemed to melt away. So Rogovin had played this last card.

Despite her personal interest in Mama Hernandez'
health, Juanita Marques had a busy schedule before her.
She, with the orderly who had pushed the laundry cart
with the guns, was the main means for the transportation
of materials during the final vital phase of their operation.
She smiled. An operation blessed, consecrated, conceived
by Rosario Gonzalez.

Each of them, she suspected, had different views. But
she believed that Rosario was God, and that He instructed
her through the ecstasy of her orgasms. She shared them
with the others who watched. She felt them even when another woman was chosen. She felt a thrill in her loins and
hurried down the hall to the utility closet where her cart
was safely locked.

This morning, in addition to the usual cleaning products, the cart contained an electrical detonator, a wooden
box of hand grenades and several pistols. In her pocket
was a switchblade knife six inches long that she had taken

from her brother's drawer. With a fleeting last look down the hall in the direction of Mama Hernandez' room, she pushed the cart down the corridor and took the elevator to the basement.

Despite the advantage of the underground passageway system that linked the buildings in the Hospital Complex, the route from the basement of the Morgenstern Pavilion was a circuitous one. It meandered through the central courtyard across the full width of Rosenstein, into Leibner, then through Green and finally into Waldman.

Juanita was faced with a variety of problems. In the first instance, she must remain unnoticed, therefore, she had to travel at a reasonable speed, and without looking harassed. In the second, she had to make three trips before her part of the mission was accomplished. Third, she had to make the trips in such a fashion that the staff supervisor on Morgenstern Four would not become overly curious.

She moved through the halls daydreaming as she went. By the time she reached the basement corridor of Waldman, she was afraid that the moisture trickling between her legs would give her away. She hoped that Rosario might favor her with his body. She checked the hall and pushed the cart to the door, knocked tremulously, her heart in her throat. Immediately after the third knock, Rosario opened the door. He opened the door wide enough to admit the boxes and pulled them in. He looked up at her as she stood in the hall. He could see that her legs were shaking.

"Push the cart down the hall," he said quietly, "and come in here." She followed his directions. Once inside the door she stood quivering against the wall, spittle in the corners of her mouth and her eyes rolled so that almost only the whites showed.

"You want me to help you," he said comfortingly, his voice low and vibrant. "I know that. You must not fail me. You must do everything for me as I do it for you."

He opened the buttons of her uniform and lowered her panties to her knees. He pushed his hand against the rough hair of her pubis and penetrated her with his long slender fingers. In ten seconds the sympathetic vibrations of his movements back and forth brought her over the edge, and she thrust against him, biting her tongue till she tasted the salt of her blood in her effort not to cry out. When she had stopped shaking, he disengaged himself and arranged her clothes.

"Help me," he said.

She slipped out of the door, glancing back at him once, her eyes burning with fervor.

# 40

Didi Rosenberg appeared at Rogovin's office fifteen minutes ahead of schedule looking tired but neat in a blue skirt and blouse. Ross, Hernandez and Rogovin didn't show up for another ten minutes and when they did, they didn't look too happy.

"Aw, shit," Ross said.

"My sentiments exactly," Hernandez said, slumping his lank form into an armchair. Rogovin sat behind his desk and looked morose.

Didi cleared her throat. "Excuse me, Dr. Rogovin. Sergeant Ross asked me to come to your office." Rogovin nodded wearily in acknowledgment.

Ross looked across at her, then at Rogovin. Protocol problem, he thought. "Nurse," Arnie said in his most professional tone, "would you mind stepping outside and having a word with me?"

"Certainly, Sergeant," she said, batting her eyes demurely. He rose and she followed him into the corridor. When she stepped outside and closed the door behind her, he had slipped to the other side of the doorframe and pinched her backside. "Now that's a little more like it, Sarge."

He gave her a quick kiss and stepped back. "Listen, toots, we have a little problem here. We keep looking for strings to this Alex Klinger and we can't find any. He was kind of a loner. No relatives or anything like that. Here at the Hospital, less than nothing. According to his supervisor, the only person who was ever seen with him was an electrician named Martins, and it's his day off, and he's not home. We sent a patrol car. He lives alone and his pad is empty. Do you know anyone who ever talked to him?"

She frowned for a moment. "Gosh, Arnie, I really don't think so. Why?"

"I smell rats, toots. So does Lou. We think that maybe there's something going on right now, or soon anyway. Could you ask around?"

"I suppose. Now that I think about it, there's a cute chubby little Puerto Rican girl, a nurse's aide, who I think I've seen passing a few words with him."

"Can you remember her name?"

Didi shook her head. "Nope. But she's on duty days. I'll bet she's there right now. Are you coming with me?"

"No, I'll just spook her. But if you find out anything, let me know. Call me, I'll be in Rogovin's office. Call me either way."

"Okay. If she's not there, I'll call right away. If she is I'll try to find out if she knows about Klinger or was close to him. Maybe she doesn't know that he's dead."

"Could be. I'll be waiting. Don't let me down."

"Sarge, would I do that to you." She sashayed down the hall swinging her hips exaggeratedly. Ross grinned and ducked back inside.

Ross, Hernandez and Rogovin had been talking for less than two minutes when a tall imperious man in his late fifties burst into the room. He was elegant and thin with a large Roman nose set off by piercing blue eyes. An immaculate, starched white coat topped perfectly cut trousers. "Excuse me, Saul, but I haven't time to muck about. There's an emergency gangrene and multiple fracture on its way here from Bergen County General. They're using a police helicopter, and they'll be landing out there in the meadow. Can you make sure that I get maximum cooperation from Emergency and Administration?"

"Of course, Sidney." Rogovin seemed to be ready to continue, but was cut off by a curt nod, and the intruder's abrupt departure. He reached for the phone before the door closed. In a matter of a minute he had arranged the program to be followed by the departments who would handle such an admission so that there would be no red tape between a gravely ill patient and the services of the Hospital.

"What was that?" Arnie asked.

Rogovin smiled his first real smile of the day. "That was an honest to God physician, a true descendant of Aesculapius, Galen and Hippocrates. That was Sidney Greenstein, M.D., F.A.C.P., F.A.C.S., and so forth and so on.

The director of vascular surgery of the Manhattan Jewish Hospital."

"Is he always like that?" Lou asked.

"Only when he's in a good mood. Otherwise, he can be very difficult and abrupt."

"Some bedside manner," Arnie offered.

"Arnie," Rogovin said with feeling, "I'd let that man remove my entire insides if that was what he wanted to do."

Hernandez pointed at Ross and said, "Does he do brain transplants?"

Rogovin was peering out of his window. "Listen, let's just drop down there for a minute. If you'd really like to see when this hospital shines, you watch this. Follow me."

The three men walked down the hall and had the good fortune to catch one of the slow-moving elevators to the ground floor. By the time they had walked out of Leibner and through the courtyard, the personnel in the drama were already heading towards Central Park. Ross, Hernandez and Rogovin followed.

Inside the park, the large field had been empty before Greenstein's alert that the helicopter was coming. Once the word had been passed, a standard drill got under way. Lou and Arnie watched with amazement as a team of men in green opened a circle of white cloth that was meant to be the center of the helicopter's landing pad, and quickly staked it to the ground. An ambulance, which had been driven through the park entrance at Ninety-sixth Street and down the footpaths, was parked not far from the marker. A rolling stretcher had already been placed on the ground at waist height to facilitate the transfer of the patient from one conveyance to the other. A metal rod projected upward from the stretcher with an IV set in place and another spot for the one that surely would already be plugged into the patient's arm. Other monitoring and emergency equipment was lined up as if for an army inspection.

In a couple of minutes, the helicopter appeared out of the northwest, took one quick pass over the area to make sure of the landing conditions, and then settled with a roaring and clicking of the rotors. The medical team and support personnel rushed forward in a ballet of practiced movements, struggling against the wind from the spinning blades. Sure hands gripped the flat stretcher from the bed of the plane. A white-coated figure jumped out and handed over charts and X-rays, then remounted. In less than a minute, the stretcher had been placed on the cart and the cart in the ambulance, which rushed off through the park toward the hospital. Once it was clear, the helicopter rose. The people and equipment that had dotted the grass disappeared, and Ross, Hernandez, and Rogovin stood looking over a pastoral spring scene with no sound but the birds and an occasional auto horn.

"Some show, huh, fellas?" Rogovin asked.

Arnie and Lou nodded appreciation. "Like the landing on Iwo Jima," Arnie said. He looked at his watch. "Hey we've been here for fifteen minutes. What about Rosenberg? Maybe she found that girl. Let's go back." He turned and walked speedily across the street.

# 41

Didi Rosenberg wandered through the passageways below the Manhattan Jewish Hospital with the caution of a tourist reading a map in a foreign language. Though she was a member of the hospital staff, the largest part of her activities were confined to Morgenstern where she worked. Even when she wanted to go to another building, she usually went out of doors.

She stopped at a bend in the passageway to read one of the color-coded signs, and to check the color of the stripes on the wall that were supposed to serve as a guide. The key to the guide was printed in both Spanish and English, from which, she thought, one could determine that the administration was impartial in their desire to confuse. Cursing softly, she turned back, realizing that she had gone left into Rosenstein rather than right into Morgenstern.

Her miscalculation had permitted Juanita Marques to hurry down the same corridor with her cart emptied of its second load. Only one more trip and she would be free to join Rosario, and to bring their mission to a climax. She could barely restrain herself from shouting with glee when the elevator, with its door open, appeared before her in the basement. She loaded the cart, pushed number 4 and serenely waited while it stopped at each floor, adding and subtracting passengers as it went. She emerged on her floor and held her breath. Mrs. Welch, the tall heavy-set supervisor of the wing, was talking in an animated fashion to the floor nurse. Juanita swallowed, set her eyes straight ahead, and neither hurrying nor dawdling pushed the cart down the center of the hall. As she approached the talking women, Mrs. Welch patted her Afro, smiled, and looked at a chart in her hand. "I can't keep it all up here, honey. I got to use a system, too." She walked off, passing Juanita without ever seeing her.

Juanita recognized that the next part of the operation

would be the hardest. Despite the fact that in every large hospital there are minor, unaccounted-for drug losses, any loss is a cause for concern. Therefore, though Rosario determined that he would want some syringes, morphia and ether for his operation, he also decided that an attempt to stockpile a decent amount anywhere in the hospital ran an unnecessary risk of discovery. In addition, the systematic inventory of drugs in every hospital, on a shift by shift basis, makes the absence of even minor amounts a cause for immediate investigation.

Taking the key that had been provided by the woman in the janitorial service, Juanita waked down the hall with her cart and stopped in front of the room that held the drugs. It was almost noon, and the pink-uniformed food service personnel were running their stainless steel racks up and down the corridor feeding patients. In the confusion, with the floor nurses otherwise occupied, Juanita darted into the closet as she had a dozen times before in practice runs. She knew exactly what she needed and where it was kept. She dropped it into a laundry bag cushioned with towels, and then dropped a towel over the packages. She opened the door, stepped through it into the corridor and moved calmly down the hall. After going twenty feet, she knew that she was safe. If she had not been caught so far, she never would be.

"Hey. Hey, wait a second."

Juanita froze in her tracks. She fought back an urge to vomit, and struggled to control her bowels. Her tongue was thick with fear and she clutched the handle of the cart to keep from shaking. She decided to keep moving, to pretend that it could not possibly be her that the woman was calling. She recognized the voice. It was the young red-haired nurse from the floor. She must have seen her leave the storage room. She moved on toward the elevator till she felt the light touch of a hand restraining her. She stopped, looking dully ahead. The girl moved around in front of her, blocking her way, facing her. Juanita relaxed a little. The nurse was smiling and friendly, her small freckled nose wrinkled in a grin.

"Don't run away. I wanted to talk to you for a minute. You know," she said breathlessly, "I'm really embarrassed. I can't even remember your name."

"It's Juanita," she said.

"I'm Didi. I'm a nurse on this floor."

"I recognized you. Listen, I'm very busy right now. I got to go." She started to push the cart forward.

Didi put her hand on the cart and said, "I won't take much of your time. I just want to ask if you know somebody. There was a man who used to work here named Alex Klinger. I just wanted to know if you knew anything about him. I saw you talk to him a couple of times."

"What's it to you?" Juanita asked, her mind working wildly, glancing at the clock.

Didi had already thought out the answer to that one. "Oh, it's just that a mutual friend wanted to get together with him. They talk politics."

Juanita pushed the cart over to the wall, suddenly calm. "Come on into the ladies' lounge. I could use a cigarette."

They walked arm in arm to the lounge, chatting like old friends. "Do you know Klinger really well," she asked brightly.

"Yeah, I guess," Juanita answered, holding the door open for Didi. "He's a nice guy. Very quiet. Y'know what I mean."

Didi tried to scream when she felt the terrible searing pain, but nothing would come out of her mouth. She struggled feebly, but the feeling quickly went out of her arms and legs, and everything went black.

It had been easier than she could have imagined. Juanita had looked over Didi's shoulder to see if there was anyone in the ladies room, then slipped out her brother's knife, pressed the button, put her hand over the bitch's mouth and stuck the knife into her left side as hard as she could. It went in to the hilt. She opened the door to the broom closet, and dropped her in like a sack, with the knife still protruding, and quickly closed the door. She went to the sink and washed the blood from her hands. There was some on her uniform sleeve, and a trail on the floor. She took a few paper towels and wiped the floor, then threw them into the hamper. She put a couple of them over her arm and went outside to the cart where she removed a soiled towel from the bag and replaced the paper ones, hiding the stain of Didi's blood. Satisfied that she was undetected, she hurried toward the elevator. Once she had made it to the basement and the corridors, she knew that she was safe. She modulated her pace to one of determined efficiency. When she got to the door of the emergency control room and knocked, Rosario opened the door wide and pulled the cart in after her. He checked his watch. "Any problems?"

"A nurse asked me about Alex."

"What did you do?"

"I killed her and left her in the ladies room in Morgenstern Four."

Rosario's cheek twitched. "Will she be found?"

"Only if another cleaning woman goes in the closet. I cleaned up the mess."

Rosario looked at his watch. Three minutes. "All right. Take the cart to the place that I showed you in Waldman. Then wait." She did as she was told. The three minutes passed and the man with the laundry cart came to the door. Rosario loaded everything into it, save for one 9 mm pistol that he stuffed into his waistband beneath his shirt. He checked his watch again, and walked out of the control room for the last time.

# 42

The ambulance carrying the prostrate form of Emily Stolzfuss lurched through the park, went down to Lexington Avenue with its siren blaring, and stopped at the door of the Waldman Pavilion. Jim Spencer, the old sailor who ran the technical end of the hyperbaric chamber, stood at the curb as a part of the receiving team. Emily was rushed on her stretcher into the corridor heading toward Gluck at a dead run. Three doctors stood ready to perform surgery in the confines of the big chamber. The complete surgical team numbered an even dozen. Spencer manned the controls outside of the giant cylinder, guaranteeing the proper atmospheric pressure and percentage of oxygen.

It was expected that the operation itself, based on the information available from the Jersey hospital, would not take more than an hour or two. There would be debriding, reduction, clamping and stitching, and the setting and casting of the fracture. Perhaps a pin and traction would be required. All of the visible bleeders had been tied off. A quick reading of the skull was negative, but a tap was in order to check possible subdural pressure and the possibility of a fatal stroke. It was all handled with the brisk efficiency, commonplace in good hospitals.

It was pure luck that the cart which was whirling down the hall did not overturn the laundry basket that Luis Dominguez was pushing. The wheels and frame had been strengthened that very morning to accept the special load. Dominguez was concerned by the passage of the cart and the activity and crowding in Gluck. Nonetheless, with his absolute faith in Rosario's judgment, he followed his instructions to the letter.

Pushing the cart into the utility closet and quickly unloading its contents onto the floor, Dominguez stepped onto the pipes, pushed aside the ceiling panel, and began to load the material into the false ceiling. When he finished, he put the cart outside against the opposite wall, the signal that he had finished.

Dominguez stepped back into the closet, climbed up the pipes, slid through the opening and pushed the panel closed. When he was secure, he turned on the vapor lamp that he had brought with him, crawled along the dusty space, bumping himself here and there on ammunition crates or dynamite sticks wrapped in old newspapers, and began to unbolt a metal plate that led to the standpipe. This pipe provided water to the pumps in the hyperbaric chamber overhead.

He almost knocked his head against the plate when he heard the noise below. He drew and cocked the automatic pistol as Rosario had shown him, balanced it carefully in both hands and aimed it where a head would have to appear in the opening in the floor. There was a reassuring three taps. He still held the pistol at the ready. When he saw Rosario's face, he breathed a sigh of relief, and lowered the pistol. In hushed tones, he told Rosario about the unforeseen activity in Gluck.

Rosario shrugged, "It only means that there will be more death." He glanced at his watch. "Could we enter by this way yet?" Dominguez said only a single bolt needed to be undone. "When I tap from above three times, you release the bolt. Then . . ."

"Then I protect the hall with my life," Dominguez continued. Rosario kissed him on the forehead, and said, *"Vaya con Dios, amigo."* Then he let himself down into the utility closet and closed the trap after him.

The lady who took care of the keys slipped the set for the Louis Gluck Hyperbaric Chamber into Rafaela Arenas's pocket and went on her way down the hall. Rafaela clutched the keys. She had not been sure of herself since the day she had found the body of Alex Klinger. With a frozen smile on her face, she made her way through the hospital and out the front door. She felt much better once she saw the truck. She climbed into the cab and dropped the keys on the floor. She passed a few words with the men in the back huddled over their machine gun; then she slumped down in the seat and tried to sleep.

The lady who had delivered the keys to Rafaela walked to her locker and took out her hand bag. She went to the elevator in Leibner and rode to the executive floor where the Director of Medicine had his offices. She got off and walked down the hall past his office. She knew that he was making a speech at a convention in Baltimore that afternoon. Based on that information, it was decided to pass the message to his second in command, Dr. Rogovin. She walked into the anteroom where Rogovin's secretary sat and put down her bag. "I have something to deliver to the doctor," she said.

Rogovin's secretary looked up, somewhat irritated. "Just put it there. I'll see that he gets it."

"Listen," the key lady said with an edge to her voice, "that's a very important thing there. I have to be sure that he gets it personally. Is he in?"

"Yes he is," the secretary replied primly. "But he's got someone with him and you'll just have to count on me to . . ."

The words stuck in her throat when the bullet from the 9 mm. Browning entered her forehead and exploded her brain. The key lady kicked open the door of Rogovin's office without a pause and fired three times across the room.

The first shot hit Rogovin in the rib cage, tore up through his pectoral muscle and lodged in his left shoulder, breaking his collarbone on its way. The second nicked Lou Hernandez on the arm as he dove to push Rogovin out of the way. The third went harmlessly into the ceiling as the assassin pitched over backwards with no face. Ross peered through the gunsmoke into the doorway, then straightened up and stepped over the body. He saw that the secretary was dead, checked the hallway, then holstered his gun.

It took several minutes for help to come because they were in a nonmedical area of the hospital. Ross watched nervously as Rogovin writhed on the floor and, losing color, became ominously still. Hernandez had taken off his jacket and rolled up his shirt sleeve. His wound was just a scratch, to be treated with antiseptic and bandages.

In a moment, there was an hysterical burst of activity as the milling group in the hall was pushed aside by rushing emergency personnel and half a dozen security people who had responded to Ross's call. As soon as Rogovin was attended to, Ross picked up his private phone and called Flaherty.

"All hell's broken loose here, Lieutenant." He quickly outlined what had transpired.

"All right, Ross. I'll get some help. I've got," he leaned over his desk to get a clear view of the H/Z 4 squad room, "five people in here. I'll send four. How does half a dozen patrol cars sound?"

"Sounds okay to me, but I don't know what is going on here. Like I said, this broad blows away Rogovin's secretary, and while we're sitting there wondering what the loud noise was, she bangs open the door like John Wayne." He paused and watched the doctors working over Rogovin. "Shit, we're lucky to be alive."

"Nothing to go on?"

"I haven't even had a chance to look. I don't think that she was expecting to find us."

"You think maybe she had some kind of a bitch with Rogovin—strictly personal?"

Ross raised his scarred eyebrow. "I doubt it. Though anything is possible. I mean, she was a hospital employee—or was wearing the uniform anyway."

"Call me when you get something. Help is on the way."

Ross hung up and walked out of the inner office to the place where the secretary was sprawled and spotted the bag with the brown manila envelope perched on the edge of the desk. He was torn between his need to know and his desire not to disturb. Instinct told him to take the quick route. He pulled out the brown folder and read its bold-faced typed cover. "Non-Negotiable Demands and Statement of Policy of the Socialist Army of Redemption in the War Against Racist Murder by Medical Science."

"Oh shit," Arnie said aloud. "Fruitcakes." He was brusquely pushed aside by an orderly followed close behind by the trolley bearing Saul Rogovin, now covered with a sheet and plugged into two bottles that jangled together as the car was rolled to the operating room.

Hernandez was pulling his shirt sleeve down. A neat bandage had been tied around his arm. "I hope it leaves a scar," he said to Ross, looking at his seamed face. "I'm entitled to a cheap conversation piece, too. And besides, I lost a good shirt."

"You okay, Roach?"

"No sweat. So's Rogovin, really. The doctor that worked on him says he doesn't see any huge damage, other than a busted collar bone. No major organs. Anyway, they're taking care of him right now. What the hell happened? Do you know?"

Ross held up the envelope so that Lou could read it. "How's that?" he asked.

"Crazies? Oh, Christ." Hernandez took the envelope and opened it. He read the cover sheet quickly, then sat on the edge of the desk and read it more slowly. "They say they've wired the hospital's oxygen system to blow like a huge bomb. They've occupied the Louis Gluck Hyperbaric Chamber and they're changing its name to Fort Franz Fanon. It is going to be their headquarters until the fascist racist murderers who run the hospital cause a meeting of the directors of the hospitals of New York to sign a confession of guilt for crimes committed against the poor and the sick."

Lou waved the sheaf of papers, "They also ask for a written promise to eliminate all private medicine and private rooms, and make all medical facilities available to the poor. If the papers are not signed within four hours, they will blow up the oxygen supply." Lou turned the page. "They also demand free passage for all members of their commando team out of Fort Franz Fanon after the end of the operation."

Lou put the papers on the desk. "So now we know. Christ. Now what?"

Ross was already on the phone to Flaherty. "That's the scoop, Lieutenant. I guess the first thing to do is to see if the Hostage Negotiating Unit is available. I'd do that as fast as possible. In the meantime, boss, I guess we'd better call in the Marines, huh?"

"You and Lou try to take a look at the physical situation. Get the plans to the whole complex. I'll call Police Plaza. Try not to get the hospital blown up while you're waiting—or yourselves, either." Flaherty hung up.

The first uniformed policeman had arrived at the door of the office as Ross and Hernandez were leaving. They instructed him to keep the curious away from the scene, and took his partner by the arm and hurried down the hall. The Chief Administrative Officer of Manhattan Jewish was an unflappable midwesterner who had held his position for only a few months. He still had the midwestern habit of short lunches, and was just stepping off the elevator when Ross and Hernandez rushed down the hall and into his office. He hurried behind them as they presented their badges to his secretary.

In a few minutes they had apprised him of their needs and established his office as the preliminary command post.

"Have you heard anything from the hyperbaric chamber? There's a major operation being performed in there."

"We saw the girl flown in," Ross answered, "But we haven't had a chance to call Gluck. Is there a central desk where they would report an emergency if they could?"

"Yes, there is a central security office number." He reached for the phone. As he waited for it to ring security, he asked, "Is this really serious?"

"We can't tell you for sure at this minute, but . . ." and Arnie told him about Rogovin and the secretary. Simultaneously, Lou took the phone from his hand and determined from security that no call had come in from Gluck.

The administrator was ashen as he put the paper down on his desk. "You think they could be serious?"

"Mister," Arnie answered, "you just can't imagine how many nuts this city can support." He paused, then said, "Listen, let me ask you one. What would happen if this oxygen supply blew up? Can you give us a quick course? Also, what's this Gluck building like?"

The administrator led Ross and Hernandez to a large diagram on the wall. "This is the hospital," he said. He traced a pattern with a pointer, his voice becoming clear and professional. "I have small diagrams just like this one, if that would help." The two detectives nodded, and he went on. "The Gluck building is all brick. No windows and two doors. One here," he indicated the street, "and one here in the corridor of the basement of Waldman." He put the pointer down and cleared his throat. "The oxygen storage unit is in an open lot, completely fenced in, well across the street from the hospital. It's on Ninety-seventh Street, about mid-block."

Lou stood and faced the man. "How much bang are we talking about? Do you have any idea?"

"I'm not a demolition expert, Sergeant Hernandez." He smiled grimly. "But if I had to take a guess, I'd say a hell of a bang, depending on how it started. Oxygen burns fast and hot. That's why the tank is sitting across the street from the hospital buildings. A leak? Escaping gas? A spark? Probably a nasty fire. Possibly even a nasty explosion under certain circumstances. But I would doubt it. Those tanks are built to the very highest safety specifications, as you can imagine."

"Yeah," said Arnie. "I can also imagine what would happen if those tanks were detonated by explosives."

The administrator turned gray and returned to his desk chair. "The pieces of the tank would be like hot shrapnel."

"That's about right," Arnie said.

The man was thoughtful for a moment, then looked up again. "Jim Spencer might know. He's the technician who runs the hyperbaric chambers. He used to be a frogman in the Navy. I'm sure he knows about explosives. And I'm certain he knows everything that there is to know about the oxygen supply and system in the hospital. Shall I call him?" He reached for the phone. He looked up the number in the directory, and dialed it. After a moment the hospital operator picked up the line. "I'm sorry, Mr. Cates, but I can't ring through. There is an operation in progress and they haven't cleared calls yet. It was an emergency."

"Yes, I know. Thank you." He turned apologetically to Arnie, and said, "There was a helicopter case for the chamber this morning. She's still in there."

Hernandez patted his arm. "Relax. It isn't easy, this kind of thing. We know about the girl."

Ross snapped his fingers in annoyance and picked up the phone. In a moment, he was talking to Flaherty again. "Listen, boss, I need your permission to call the Fire Department. I need to know the fire specs and regs on the oxygen tower. Okay?"

"It's all right. I just got off the phone with Shea and Kemmelman," he said referring to the Chief of Detectives and the Assistant Commissioner. "They pulled out all the stops. We're getting the Hostage bunch up to you, and a whole battalion of fire apparatus and the bomb wagon. No sense in fucking around on this, even if it's an eighty-year-old lady with a rotten sense of humor, or that broad you wasted was all alone. You should have help any minute. Have you checked out that chamber yet?" Ross said no and explained. "Go yourselves," Flaherty said. "After you call the FD."

Ross made the call, and was told that they'd have a fireman with the specs in Cates's office in ten minutes. "All right, Roach, let's go. Mr. Cates, there will a large number of policemen here in short order. Tell them where we went." On his way out of the door, Ross stopped short. "Where's Didi?" Lou looked at him. Arnie started to speak again.

Lou put up his hand. "You go to the Gluck building. I'll go see about the girl. Listen, don't close till I get there, right?"

Arnie cocked his twisted eyebrow. "Right, Roach."

# 43

Albert Ruggles dropped Baxter off at the station house and drove through Spanish Harlem over the bridge into the South Bronx. He followed the same route of burned-out tenements and noisy overhead train tracks as he had before. He pulled up to the curb in front of the Mennonite Mission and eased himself out of the car. He walked up the steps and rapped loudly with the metal knocker. In a few moments, the kind-eyed old man who had taken in Mr. Stolzfuss appeared at the door. He extended his hand. "Sergeant Ruggles. Nice to see you. Would you care to come in? Can we fix you something cool to drink?"

Uncomfortable, Ruggles shuffled his feet a bit. "I've come to see Mr. Stolzfuss."

"Please Lord, don't let it be that child," the man said softly, beseeching.

"I don't know. But I'm afraid. For both of them. Where is he?"

"I'll get him. He's reading the Bible." The man turned away. When he came back a minute later, Stolzfuss was with him, bent and much older, looking less substantial than Ruggles remembered him only a few days before. Ruggles stepped inside the door.

"How are you, Mr. Stolzfuss?" Ruggles put out his hand.

The grip was not as firm as it had been. "I am well, Sergeant. I hope you are the same. Do you have news of my daughter?" he said, with the expectations of Job in his tone.

Ruggles fished the ephemeral slip of nylon out of his pocket. "Do you know if this could have been your daughter's?"

Stolzfuss handled the scrap of cloth as though it were hot metal. "It is certainly not among her possessions as I know them. Our girls do not wear such things." He looked sadly at the label. "Of course the store is known to me. If she wished to, she could have had access to this store without my knowledge." He extended the scrap between two fingers and held it out to Ruggles. "Is this all that you have found of her?"

Ruggles pocketed the cloth and said, "It is possible that this and your daughter may have a connection. It's possible . . ." he stopped and cleared his throat. He had decided not to lie. You don't lie to guys like Stolzfuss, he thought. "It may be that she's come to some harm. I'd like to use the telephone. If I can, I'm going to find out if there have been any unidentified girls brought into any of the hospitals in the area."

Ruggles was ushered to the phone, refused a chair and called in first to the precinct. He was passed immediately to his squad commander.

"Christ, Albert, where are you? You better get your ass over to Manhattan Jewish. All hell seems to be breaking loose there. Your buddies Ross and Hernandez are up to their asses in alligators. One killed, Hernandez nicked, I hear. Possible crazies in a bomb attempt. We're sending everything but the janitor. Report to the administration office. Flaherty's gone over there to give them a hand and run the show."

"Okay, Lieutenant. I will. Look, can you just give me a quick hand? Do you know if there has been any hospital or PD turn-ins of young unidentified girls this morning. Possibly hurt?"

"Absolutely. I can quote you one you missed. The NYPD copter squad dragged one into Manhattan Jewish. Flaherty told me about it. Ross and Hernandez saw the whole thing. It was some kid. Had the hell beat out her—gangrene and all kinds of other shit. They don't know if she's going to make it."

Ruggles looked at the phone for a moment, then hung it on the cradle. He sighed and turned to Mr. Stolzfuss. "Will you come with me?"

Stolzfuss read his sad eyes. With a word of thanks to his host, he took his broad brimmed hat from the hall table, fixed it squarely on his head, and walked to Ruggles's waiting car.

Ruggles headed toward the hospital. At 100th Street he was stopped by a policeman who stood before a patrol car parked crosswise in the street, its lights flashing. He showed his ID and badge, vouched for Stolzfuss, and was passed through. There were already half-a-dozen cars, marked and unmarked, in front of the hospital stretching from the corner of Ninety-sixth south to the entrance of Hartz.

Ruggles wrestled with his conscience for a moment, then decided. "Come on. Mr. Stolzfuss. We have to hurry. I have to report." He turned into the door of Waldman because it was closest and went to the information desk. He showed his badge and asked about the girl who had been brought in on the helicopter. Before the words were out of the woman's mouth, Ruggles turned, and holding Stolzfuss by the arm, headed down the corridor where he saw an arrow pointing to the Louis Gluck Hyperbaric Chamber.

# 44

A less competent leader would have been shaken by so many variables cast into the smooth machinery of his plans. Rosario had the indomitable faith that provides the lubrication in such situations. Once he knew that his people were in place, and that the logistical problems had been overcome, it was just as he said, only a little more death to be contemplated. Rosario allowed himself a smile. In the plethora of murder committed in the hospitals of America, it was just another little tick of the clock.

He looked at his watch and walked forward, pushing the cart into the hall. The door of the hyperbaric chamber opened, and a group of doctors and nurses, eight or ten it seemed to him, walked toward him. He smiled fawningly and pushed his cart to the side of the hall. They didn't even seem to see him as they walked by.

He walked forward again, opened the door to the chamber and pushed the cart inside. He was on the level of the chamber below the tanks in which the medical work was actually done. A steel staircase led up a half flight to the operating platform. He pushed his cart to the side and took out his keys. Rafaela Arenas walked into the room, took a key from him without a word, and headed for the door that led through the corridor to the street. She locked the door. He checked his watch a second time. Where was the key lady? He stepped up the stairs quietly. Spencer was huddled over the instruments at his desk.

Spencer's hair stood up on the back of his neck. It was the kind of reaction he had developed in combat situations over the years. He felt as though there were someone behind him. As he started to turn, the phone rang. He answered, "Hello, Spencer. Yeah, Mr. Cates. It's all over. They think that she should stay in the big tank for another forty-five minutes. She'll need at least four or five more treatments—maybe forty minutes apiece. I think she'll live. She's in pretty . . ." He heard a footstep and turned, the phone away from his ear. "Oh, Rosie, it's only you." He smiled and turned back to the phone.

Cates pulled his ear away from the sharp slapping noise. "Spencer? Spencer? What the hell was that?"

"This is the voice of the Army of Redemption. This is the first demonstration that we mean what we have outlined in our demands. We are now in control of Fort Franz Fanon. Will you obey? Or shall we act? You have half an hour before our next contact."

Cates turned around to the uniformed policeman and said, "They say they've got the chamber."

Rosario looked at Spencer, who lay sprawled like a bag of flour on the floor in front of his desk. He was unconscious, but Rosario could see that he was not dead. The bullet had passed through his chest on the right side, but too high to pierce his lung. He was bleeding, but not profusely. Rosario admitted to himself that he had moved the gun a fraction to the right before firing, thus missing the heart. He forgave himself and stuck the gun back in his holster, then he went down the stairs again to secure his equipment.

Rafaela had returned. He reached into the cart and handed her a submachine gun and a clip. Expertly, she melded the two elements and slid back the bolt to charge the chamber, then set the safety. "Go upstairs and check out the chambers," Rosario said. "There may be others."

He walked to the standpipe above Dominguez' head and rapped three times. He waited for a minute till there was a clanking noise from below as the last retaining bolt dropped. Then he took a screwdriver from his back pocket and dug into the rubber seal around the steel plate at his feet. There was a sharp pop as the vacuum was released. He pushed the plate aside. The bottom plate had been removed by Dominguez, and they passed the cartridge boxes up through the hole.

It took fewer than the two minutes that Rosario had alloted to finish the task. Dominguez pulled the box of grenades and the ammunition to the edge of the trap in the utility closet, and dropped through onto the floor. He had intended to take a casual peek down the hall, to see if any activity had started. None was expected for a few minutes at least. He was therefore taken aback when he heard the hurried pounding of feet in the corridor. He picked up the hand receiver and pushed the red button that sounded an alarm on Rosario's set. "Men coming," he said.

"Take them from behind. I'm not ready yet."

"Kill them?"

"If necessary."

Dominguez clipped the unit back onto his belt, drew his automatic and opened the door slightly. He looked to the left. The corridor to the main part of Waldman was empty. Twenty feet to his right Ruggles and Stolzfuss were heading down the corridor to the door to Gluck. Dominguez waited until they were at the end. When they banged on the door, he yelled, "Stop that. Stand still and raise your hands or you will be shot dead."

Ruggles lifted his revolver from the holster in his waistband and spun to fire. Dominguez emptied the nine-shot magazine down the hall. Ruggles was hit twice in the back, and once in the right arm as he turned. He slammed his head on the wall and lay motionless. Stolzfuss was hit once, in the back of the thigh. The remaining bullets whined around the confined space, gouging plaster from the walls. Dominguez withdrew into the closet and locked the door behind him. He threw the empty clip on the floor, reloaded the gun, and called Rosario. He told him excitedly what had happened.

"It's all right, Luis. I'm almost finished. Five minutes. Then you can come in."

Dominguez picked up a grenade and hefted it in his hand. Then he sat on the standpipe to wait. After a while, he just watched the sweep hand crawl around the face of his wristwatch.

# 45

Lou Hernandez couldn't resist the temptation to stick his nose into his mother's room on Morgenstern Four. Her bed was empty. She had been shuttled off to take more tests. He crossed himself and said a quick prayer, then stepped out into the hall. He walked around aimlessly for a moment, then hailed a nurse. "Pardon me," he said, "Have you seen Nurse Rosenberg?"

"Sorry, I haven't. I don't think that she's on in the morning. You might ask at the desk."

The nurse on duty was the floor nurse that he had gotten to know best. She was a tough old Irish lady, with a frizzy pile of silver hair sprouting from a pink scalp. "Well, look who's here. What can I do for you, Sergeant. Mother's off to her tests, you know."

Lou told her for whom he was looking. "She came down here maybe a half hour ago. She was supposed to call back, but she didn't."

The nurse looked at him peculiarly. "I won't even ask what's going on," she said. "I thought I caught a glimpse of her a while ago. She was talking to a nurse's aide."

"Here, on this floor?"

"There," she pointed. "Near the ladies room."

"Take a look in there for me." She looked at him blankly. "Please. It's official business."

The nurse studied him, then walked down the hall. She opened the door to the ladies room and looked around. Seeing nothing, she turned back to the hall. Her trained eye picked up the smear under the closet door. She wanted to scream, but thirty years of experience under difficult conditions had taught her self-control. She opened the door and found the small figure where it had been left, twisted and still, a little blood still trickling from the wound from which the knife protruded. The nurse dropped to her knees and checked for vital signs. They were faint but present. She resisted the temptation to move her, for fear that the intruding blade would rupture a blood vessel or a vital organ. She quickly left the room and hurrying past a surprised Hernandez, took the phone from her desk, dialed a number and said, "Emergency, Morgenstern Four stat. Knife wound."

Hernandez dashed down the corridor to the lounge. He opened the door, looked briefly at the prostrate form on the floor of the closet, and turned on his heel. "I'm on my way to Gluck if anyone asks," he said as he passed the Irish nurse headed back in the other direction.

While Lou was running for the emergency stairs, Arnie Ross was pushing his way through the small knot of people that milled indecisively at the door that led from Waldman to Gluck. A uniformed but unarmed security guard try to fend him off with his hands.

"Police officer," Ross said, flashing his badge. He forced his way forward, the security man babbling in his ear.

"They was shot. Nobody saw. But they heard. It was like two minutes ago."

"Did anybody come running out of there," he asked. The security man shook his head. "Nobody saw nothing."

"Go call the administration office. Ask for a cop—any cop. You tell him that Sergeant Ross is down here, and wants some backup quick." He looked around behind him. "And get these people out of here before somebody else gets wasted. Call your boss and tell him to cordon off this part of the building. I don't want any frigging civilians here. You got that?"

The security man stammered and headed for the phone on the information desk. The small group recoiled from Ross and the door to the corridor.

Ross took his service revolver from the belt holster and checked the chambers. Two were empty from the key lady's face. He pulled two cartridges from a leather holder on his belt, reloaded, and stepped through the doorway. When it was closed behind him, he glanced down the hall. There were two doors on the left and one on the right. He knew from the plan that the two on the left were small offices, one, the farthest, was a suite of two rooms. The door on the right was a cleaning closet.

He inched down the left hand wall to the first door and dropped to his knees. Slowly, he turned the handle, then threw his weight against the door and slid in quickly on his back, his gun thrust out before him above his head. He lay there a moment, checking the half dark room out. Satisifed that it was empty, he regained his feet and walked to the next office door.

Because he was dealing with two rooms rather than one, Ross changed tactics. He stepped into the middle of the hall, took a breath and launched himself, taking the door handle and the door in one motion, so that it swung open under his weight. He somersaulted to his left, assuming that if there were someone in the room he would place himself to his own right. He came up in a crouch, his left arm clutched across his chest covering his heart, his pistol extended in his right hand. When it was clear that there was no one in the entrance room, he crossed it quickly and kicked open the door to the inner office and crouched again.

Ross stood up and took a deep breath. The only place that the gunman could be was in the closet. The men he had shot lay blocking the door to Gluck. He cocked the hammer on the revolver and stepped into the hall. He thought about reading the man his rights and giving him a chance to surrender. "Fuck it," he said under his breath. He fired four times through the middle of the door of the utility closet, starting at head height and working down to the knees. There was no response. He reloaded and fired twice more.

The first shot caught Luis Dominguez by surprise, but missed him. He dropped to his knees and the second and third passed him by, whizzing around the pipes. The fourth caught him in the left shoulder and flattened him against the wall at the back of the closet. He bit his tongue to keep from screaming. By the time Ross had reloaded and fired again, Dominguez had lifted himself back through the trap and told Rosario that he was hit.

"Just a minute more, Luis. Just a minute more."

Dominguez heard Ross's last shots ricochet off of the masonry and screamed into the hole. He waited about thirty seconds until he imagined that the unseen policeman was listening at the door, then dropped two grenades through the trap, rolled away from· the opening and put his fingers in his ears.

Dominguez had anticipated Ross by some seconds. He was standing at the side of the door, pressed against the wall. The sound of the scream had sounded to Ross's trained ear like the bait it was supposed to be. It saved his life. The hollow core steel door flew off of its hinges, fired out of the door frame like some misshapen rocket, slamming against the opposite wall. The concussion gave Ross a nosebleed, and a dozen of the thousand pieces of wire fragments wound into the body of the grenade embedded themselves in his skin. One made a nasty cut above his right eye, which immediately began to bleed, impairing his vision.

Ross backed up, his ears ringing. "What the fuck is going on here?" he yelled to no one in particular. He darted across the now open entrance to the closet and fired three of his four remaining shells. In passing he saw that the closet was empty. A twisted steam pipe gave off a light vapor. He heard another metallic thud and threw himself down the hall in the direction of the two bodies. The grenade didn't roll clear of the door so that the explosion was funneled at the opposite wall again. Without the door to absorb part of the blast, plaster and dust flew in every direction, and black dots of shrapnel pocked the hallway for a space of six feet on either side of the opening. Ross took a quick look at Ruggles and Stolzfuss, determined that they were alive and decided to get the hell out. He turned quietly, then sprinted for the door. He was lucky. The next grenade bounced into the hallway before it exploded. A hail of fragments spread in a cone to the corners of the corridor. He heard the splash against the door as he dove through.

Hernandez barreled through the door of Waldman and ran into the lobby just in time to see Ross, bleeding profusely from the wound above his eye, stumble into view. As he lurched away from the door, the impact from still another grenade disintegrated the glass window in the door and showered particles all over the room.

"What the fuck is going on here, Arnie?"

"That's what I asked. Holy shit. I mean fucking grenades, Roach. Grenades! And Albert is in there with some old guy. Shot up but not dead. We need all kinds of reinforcements. And stay away from that door." Ross headed for the desk phone and called Cates's office. To his relief, it was Flaherty who answered the phone. He filled him in.

"You stay the hell away from the corridor. I'll get some help. The hostage negotiators are on their way."

"Shouldn't I try to pull Ruggles out of there?"

"Stay out, Ross," Flaherty shouted, "or we'll end up having to pull you out, too. Let's find out what they want. Then maybe we can bargain for him."

"It don't do no good to bargain for a corpse! All right. I'll wait." He slammed down the phone, fuming at his impotence.

Rosario was set. He wanted a clear field of vision and movement in the hall. Satisfied that it was empty, he opened the door to the chamber a crack and peered out. Rafaela helped to drag the two heavy men into the chamber and to lock the door again. "Juanita," he said, "get two of them down here. Let them practice their medicine on these, instead of us."

The chubby girl's cheeks glowed with excitement as she ushered two doctors and two nurses down the steel stairway. They were tight-lipped and wide-eyed with fear. Juanita motioned at them with the stubby barrel of the machine pistol. "Go down and do what Rosario tells you to do, killers."

They had been inside of the chamber with the door closed when Rosario had shot Spencer. The nurses had been cleaning and returning instruments to their proper places, and the doctors were finishing the last bits of their repair of Emily Stolzfuss. While Rosario prepared his equipment, he sent Juanita and Rafaela to check the chambers. To his surprise they had returned with the four people that he was looking at.

"If you want to, keep them alive," he said with an edge to his voice. "Of course, one is black and the other one is an old Jew. I guess you'll let the black one die first. It's all the same to me who you kill."

"Now look here, you nut," one of the doctors began, his face flushed to his hairline, "you're the one who shot these people, or at least had them shot. Don't you talk to me about my conscience."

"All right, Doctor," said Rosario, "I won't talk to you about anything." The doctor fell in a heap at the foot of the stairs, gurgling in his throat and clutching at his stomach where Rosario's bullet had hit him. Rosario looked up at the others who huddled in fear against the rail. "Now come down here and deal with these two." He stepped forward and nudged the wounded doctor with his gun. "He comes last," pointing at his colleague.

At first fearful, then grateful for the distraction of work, the doctor and the nurses examined Albert and Stolzfuss. "We need bandages and instruments and drugs and IV materials," the doctor said.

"Good, then drag them upstairs and find what you need. They are cluttering my work space." He watched them, smiling humorlessly, as they pulled Ruggles' giant form up the stairs, leaving spatters of red behind them. "See that they're out of the way. I need the middle of the floor. Juanita, make sure that they haven't touched any of my things."

Rosario looked at his watch. This should be about the right time, he thought. There should be an audience large enough to merit a proper show. Then they could withdraw into what he had already begun to think of as Fort Franz Fanon and wait for the capitulation of the enemy, their humiliation and exposure before the entire world, the detailing of their failures and, by his hand, the beginning of a new day. He hoped he would live to see it, but he had long ago made his peace with death. From his shirt he pulled the picture of his family and stared at it. He felt a pounding in his head, and his eyes started to glaze over as he slipped into the well of his past.

"Rosario, I brought you the radio."

He turned and slipped the photograph back into his shirt. "Thank you, Rafaela." He touched his hand to her lips. "We are ready to start."

Rosario's timing for a show of strength was perfect. In the ten minutes since Ross had scurried through the door, the world had learned about the siege of the Gluck building. And it had become a siege. The half-dozen members of the Hostage Negotiation Squad, all graduate psychologists, were grouped in the administrator's office trying to get some line on the members of the Army of Redemption. They read and reread the angry list of grievances, trying to pick up keys to the possibilities for a peaceful resolution of the siege without further bloodshed. The key to the success of their work over the ten years that the squad had been in existence, was to get their adversaries to talk.

"It's very difficult to rationalize violence in a conversation," the unit commander explained to Flaherty and

Cates. "You can rant and rave for just so long. If you are the least bit rational, after a while—an hour, a day, three days—it becomes apparent that nothing is gained by killing a few hostages except general public contempt."

"Does it always work?" Cates asked.

"Nothing works always." He changed the subject. "Are you sure we don't know who we're talking to?"

"Or how many?" Flaherty added, looking out of the window.

Besides the police personnel in Cates's office, the hospital was swarming with cops. Shea, the Deputy Commissioner, an old cop, had roared up in a squad car to take charge of the overall operation himself.

More than a hundred policemen, half of them in flak vests and carrying shoulder weapons, surrounded the hospital's Lexington Avenue side. All traffic within three blocks of the hospital had been diverted by the traffic squad.

Standing like an infantry officer on the bumper of his car, Shea swept his arm around and directed the group of officers furthest uptown to proceed around the corner to the side door of the Gluck building. He looked down at the diagram of the hospital and tried to figure a third way into Gluck. His thoughts were shattered by the rattle of automatic weapons fire.

The cops streamed back around the corner, bullets kicking up cement dust on the sidewalk behind them. "Jesus Christ, sir," a sergeant panted, "they have some kind of machine gun in a truck by that door. There are three policemen dead or wounded."

Shea sat down on the fender, stunned. To add to his troubles, the media, tuned to all of the police frequencies, and tipped off by the police reporters in the headquarters press room, had started to turn up in force. They represented a threat to his own communications, and increased the chances for more injuries. Television trucks, stopped by his orders, cast out dozens of cameramen and sound men with portable equipment, who accompanied the reporters speaking rapidly into their microphones. Three men from Public Affairs had the bare bones of the story for a briefing proposed in the hope that it would reduce the crush.

"Where's the truck," Shea asked. "Where exactly?"

"Right in front of the entrance to Gluck, sir," the sergeant replied, still breathless with fear and exertion. "Christ knows how long they've been there."

Shea looked at his notes. "Have any of the bomb squad people been to that lot to check out the story about the explosives on that oxygen tank yet?"

"No, sir. They were on Randall's Island. They're suiting up. They ought to be here in a few minutes."

"Well, there isn't much chance that they're going to get a look at that tank with those mothers in that truck shooting at them." Shea frowned. "I'd guess we'd better clean out the truck."

Rosario could hear the chattering machine gun even through the solid walls of Gluck. It was indeed time to proceed. He sat at Spencer's desk. He had Spencer pulled out of the way and lined him up against the far wall of the high ceilinged room with the rest of the casualties. The doctor and nurses treated them with what materials remained from the operation on Emily Stolzfuss, and they had at least been able to stanch the bleeding, and cover open wounds.

Rosario picked up the phone and called Rogovin's office. A policeman answered. "Officer Murphy."

"This is Commandant Rosario of the Army of Redemption. I am calling you from Fort Franz Fanon. I am now going to show the extent of our power so that you may be convinced that we are not to be toyed with. I will be in touch again. In the meanwhile, I will give you one minute to remove all of the personnel you may have on Ninety-sixth Street between Lexington and Third Avenues." He hung up the phone and picked up the small hand radio.

"Martins, are you there?"

"Yes, Rosario. It was wonderful. It was just as you said it would be. It was wonderful. They ran. I killed three. They didn't even fire back."

"When I tell you, you will step out of the truck and do as we had planned. Rafaela will be at the door in thirty seconds." He motioned to Rafaela, who stood at his side at the desk. She moved swiftly across the room and down the stairs to the small corridor to the street. She opened the interior door and trotted down the staircase, inserted a key in the lock of the outer door and waited.

Rosario said, "Look into the street. Is it clear?"

There was a pause and Martins responded. "I don't see

anyone." There was another brief pause. "Wait, I think someone crawled around the corner on his stomach. I have to move forward to see. Al is watching the back." He raised his eyes above the level of the sandbags and saw two policemen in flak vests inching their way along on their bellies with gas grenade rifles, short and blunt, cradled in their arms. "What shall I do? They are coming with tear gas."

"How many?"

"Two."

"Kill them. Then wait thirty seconds more."

Martins put down the radio, picked up the AK-47, lifted it slowly onto the sandbags and waited. When he was sure the police were in his sights, he began to squeeze the trigger. He stopped. They were crawling back the same way they had come.

He put the gun down and watched as they returned around the corner. He picked up the radio and said, "They have gone back."

"Fine, wait another minute, then carry out the plan." Rosario allowed himself a smile of satisfaction. It had been a problem in communications. Very shortly they would be calling to try to stop him. They would want to give him the right number to call. They had evidently set up their command post elsewhere than in Rogovin's office.

In a matter of seconds the phone on the desk rang. Rosario picked up the receiver and listened without talking. "Hello," the voice said. It was just as he had expected. A voice with a bedside manner. The same voice that a doctor uses when he lies about killing your wife and baby. Confident voices, rich with culture and education. The voice of the viper in the Garden of Eden.

"Commandant Rosario," the voice said, "we hope to start a dialogue with you. We have read your paper very carefully and respect your aims. We can imagine that the violence that has occurred thus far has been unintentional. We just hope that we will be able to avoid any further unnecessary injury or death."

"Then kill all of the doctors," Rosario replied. "Or make them stop killing us. Make them stop pulling in poor frightened people and giving them the leftovers from the treatment of the rich, especially their leftover time, when they want to play golf and not treat a poor spic. You want to avoid killing, then do as we have instructed, or we will blow this hospital to kingdom come, and the sparks will light fires all over the world." He hung up.

Let the word trickle down for another minute, he thought. They will want to make contact again before they decide to do anything. Rosario had watched the entire televised proceedings of the hostage negotiation in the occupation of a Brooklyn gun store. It had lasted three days. He had learned many things. He picked up the radio. "Now."

Martins and Al looked around. There was no one on the block. They opened the back door of the van and ran across the sidewalk. They tapped three times at the door which was opened by Rafaela. They locked it behind them and set up the AK-47 at the head of the stairs.

Now, Rosario thought, I will prove my point. He picked up the phone and dialed Rogovin's office again. There was great consternation at the other end when he announced himself. They explained that the number he should call to make contact was the extension in the administration office. It would be open to him at all times. Rosario thanked him ironically, hung up and dialed the other number.

"Yes," the soothing voice answered.

Rosario could hardly suppress a laugh. "I am on your couch? Yes, doctor."

"I am a police officer."

"But you are a doctor, too. I know. I read your publicity. Now we are going to have a little publicity. In an hour I want to see a special editon of the *New York Post* with our demands and our complaints printed—all of them. On the front page. Now, unlike you, I keep my promises. I promised a demonstration. You will determine when it will start. Please, pick a time, just give the word."

"I am sure," said the voice, in its deepest tones, "that you have powers that would amaze all of us, Commandant Rosario. But you don't need to use them to convince us. We . . ."

"Yes, yes, I know, Doctor. You build your power over me by frequent use of my name and title, indicating my importance to you. You soothe, you talk and reason. You avoid my hysterical tendency toward violent acts. I saw you on a talk show. How do you like this?" Rosario hung up, picked up a detonator from among the three on the desk, and sharply twisted the handle. The little magneto sent a charge of electricity coursing through the wire that stopped at the chamber door, ran through the corridor to the street, under the pavement and the roadway, and into the lot. It touched the blasting cap attached to a stick in a box of dynamite that had been buried at the far side of the lot with the oxygen tank. The box was snug against the chain link fence and abutted a six story red brick tenement. When it blew, it took half of the ground floor apartments at the rear. There were six people in the apartments. They died. The old house began to burn furiously, flames spreading up a dumbwaiter shaft, the incinerator shaft, and the stairwell. Even the presence of the fire engine only a block away, did little to stem additional loss of life as the trapped tenants on the higher floors rushed hysterically to the stairs and the window ledges.

There was no contact for fifteen minutes after the explosion. Rosario knew that it would take time to mount a realistic response to his show of force. They would not want to risk a repetition. He was certain that now his demands would be treated promptly and seriously.

In the interim, the Chairman of the Board of Trustees of the Manhattan Jewish Hospital had been driven from Newark where his drug company's factory stood. He was tall and slim with a hawk nose and beetling brows. He was quickly briefed and asked only what he could do to help. The mayor arrived minutes later, listened intently, then began to give orders in his nasal, twangy New York accent.

"Give them what they want. Whatever it is. Has anybody figured out what kind of damage blowing that big tank would cause?"

"Not exactly, Your Honor," Shea replied. "But it would take a big piece of the hospital and Ninety-sixth Street with it. That much is certain."

"Have we got an evacuation plan?"

Shea looked grimly at the window. "People are taking care of that pretty much by themselves." The street below was a bedlam as the inhabitants of the area piled into the street, some carrying their belongings, but most satisfied to escape with their skins.

"Just the same," the Mayor added, "there will be old folks or indigents left behind, or kids. Those buildings have to be gone through. Now what about the hospital?"

"There's not much problem in evacuation of the buildings on Ninety-fifth Street," the hospital chairman said. "They are largely administrative and offices. It depends on the force of the blast. If we had to evacuate the Rosenstein Tower," he shrugged, "I suppose that's possible, too. But to start moving desperately sick people out of Hartz—the risks are enormous."

"Well it beats the hell out of having them killed in a fireball set off by that lunatic. What's his name?"

"Rosario, Your Honor," Shea chipped in.

"Is that all we know?"

"Not any more. Two policemen have been working on the personnel here. We had their files run over from the Twenty-third Precinct. They're in Homicide Zone Four. The man's name is Rosario Gonzalez. He's a hospital employee. Been here for years."

"Great," the Mayor said sourly. "Listen, somebody get the *Post* on the phone for me. I want them to run that edition. It will at least buy us the time to start getting some people out of here." The Mayor turned to Shea and said, "Where are those two cops? How did they let this get so far out of hand?"

"They're still outside of the corridor leading to the Gluck building, sir. They've both been cut up a bit."

"Well I'll sure as hell want to know more about this when it's over." He stalked off to the desk and took the telephone that was handed to him and began to talk rapidly to the Managing Editor of New York's only afternoon newspaper.

# 46

Ross and Hernandez sat disconsolately on the floor not far from the smashed hall door in the basement of Waldman.

The action of the past hour and a half had passed them by, and they could do nothing but patiently wait.

They both struggled to their feet when they saw Flaherty walk in the lobby door with Shea.

"Are these the cooked geese, Flaherty?" Shea asked.

"These are Detective Sergeants Ross and Hernandez, sir."

"I suppose you can imagine that your ass is grass. You've probably managed to bury yourselves and Flaherty. Why did you hold out?"

Hernandez stepped in front of Ross, effectively blocking his red fuming face from the view of the Deputy Commissioner. "We just didn't have enough to go on. As far as the Lieutenant is concerned, sir, well we just didn't bother him with what we thought were unimportant details."

"Well, let me tell you that those unimportant details have cost a lot lives and grief. And before it's over it could be a lot worse. This could cost more than your shields."

Ross pushed Hernandez out of the way forcefully and said, "I can get those fuckers out of there, sir."

"Now how would you do that? Blow up the hospital? I know about you, Ross. I know all about you. Long on guts, short on brains and discipline."

"There's a utility closet where the guy with the grenades is. There's got to be some connection with the chamber from there."

"How do you know that? We've got the hospital engineering staff looking at all of the blueprints, together with a group from the Fire Department."

"I don't give a shit what they're looking at. This guy has a ton of equipment in that Gluck place. He couldn't keep it in the drug lockers or on the middle of the floor, could he?"

"Watch your mouth, Ross," Shea snarled.

"Well where the fuck else could it be but in the crawlspace. He must have been stuffing it there a little bit at a time for years. I can go in and get them out."

"And he'll blow up the hospital," Shea replied.

"Not a fuckin' chance. He's blown his wad. He's got two, three people, right? He's got the big bomb. While he keeps it, he's got the world by the balls. He gets in the funny papers and all that other shit that these nuts lap up. He pulls the trigger, he kills himself first. He's right next door."

Shea looked at Flaherty speculatively, then turned back to Ross. "Just what makes you think he's not a suicidal nut case? Why doesn't it make sense that when you try to hit him, he blows up the place and himself as a final spit in the eye?"

Ross shook his head vehemently, and went on, completely forgetting to whom he was talking. "Aw, bullshit. This man has a case. I read that shit he wrote. He's not your average asshole in this for kicks and publicity. And he isn't some kind of nationalist tool who wants to promote the legitimate aspirations of Staten Island. I think he's out of his gourd. But the problem is he's got a legitimate bitch. No sense in trying to talk him out of it. I think maybe he sees clear sometimes and sometimes he gets whacked out. You know, like having a fit. Oh, you're right enough about his being willing to kill people. But that's 'cause he thinks he's got a higher purpose. But I don't see him blowing the hospital."

"So you're willing to take that chance? To see a lot of people killed?"

"I'll tell you what, mister, you keep dicking around with him and he's gonna kill dozens of 'em a few at a time. He isn't going to blow the joint. But you could get the bulk of the people out of here in the next hour, and all you'd lose is some buildings, and me."

Shea looked Ross in the eye. "Some fuckin' loss that would be." He looked back to Flaherty. "The closet crawlspace, you say?" He clenched and unclenched his hands, teetering in indecision.

"Hey, tell me," Ross said almost conversationally, "how many cops got killed today?"

"If Ruggles is dead," Shea snarled, "twelve. Plus two firemen. I've lost count of the civilians, but it's over twenty. Now shut the fuck up while I think."

"Yes, sir," Ross said, and slumped back down to the floor. Flaherty rolled his eyes to the ceiling, begging for divine intervention. Hernandez just leaned against the wall, tired.

"I'll ask the Mayor," Shea said quietly.

"For permission," Ross asked.

"You know something, Ross," Shea said, "I hope he agrees to this. I'm going to recommend it to him. But I'm not sure who I want to win." He turned on his heel and stalked away. At the door he stopped and turned back. "You wait till I come back."

Flaherty was torn between staying and going, then decided that he'd better stick with the boss. "You've probably cost me my pension."

"Tough shit, Flaherty. If you'd been on the pad like all the other smart cops, you'd be so rich you wouldn't need your fucking pension."

Flaherty turned purple and ran after Deputy Commissioner Shea. As he ran, he fumbled in his pocket for a packet of Gelusil tablets.

Hernandez smiled weakly, rubbing at the wound in his arm, which was beginning to become painful. "Ross, you know what?"

"Huh?"

"You're a meathead."

"Oh." Arnie pulled up his knees under his chin and closed his eyes. "Wake me when the decision comes down from the Almighty."

# 47

Rosario looked at his watch again. The most difficult part of the whole operation was waiting. He had recognized that even when planning it in his mind, and then in the endless dry runs in his apartment. But then he had been able to mesmerize his followers with his talk of a better world, and of self-sacrifice.

As he had conceived his plan, he tried to distinguish between his desire to exact a penalty, to take revenge, and his real concern about the quality of medical care. He was not sure where one began and the other left off.

A month after his wife and child had died, he lay morose in his room, finally able to get a little sleep after the nightmares in which he saw his father and his brothers and sisters covered with running sores, disintegrating before his eyes, crying out to him in hideous pain for help. He drifted into a different dream in which he saw his wife, naked on the bed, her eyes closed in ecstasy, gripping the struts of the brass headboard with her hands. He imagined himself running his fingers over the silky hair under her arms, her thrusting up at him.

He awoke slowly, painfully conscious of a throbbing erection. He squeezed himself. His young body, indifferent to his grief, demanded release. At the moment of release, he had a blinding vision of his wife—dead. He rose screaming from his bed, wracked by spasms of guilt and physical pain, and torn by conscience.

He would torment himself to the point of orgasm again and again, only to stop in a ritual of self-punishment for the crime of surviving alone. In time, he found that when certain others were exposed to his act of immolation, they were drawn to him. He preached against suffering, yet suffered himself. He suffered pain to give others pleasure. Selecting his disciples by intuition, he built his small band. And, he thought as he rose, he brought them to the door of—he was suddenly confused, searching for a definition—victory, he thought, perhaps it was victory.

Juanita was fidgeting with her gun. Martins and Al were staring at the wounded and the doctor and nurses, huddled silent and frightened in their corner against the wall.

"A half hour and the first step in our victory will have been made public. The *New York Post* will be delivered here with a front page telling everybody where we stand and what we demand. It is not impossible that others will come to join us. We have taken the first step in a general uprising against racist murder of the poor!"

They turned to look at him. He offered them one of his somber smiles of confidence. "Even if we are killed, there is no defeat. Our sacrifice will have planted the seed of change, and it will come now. They fear us." He checked their faces, one by one. Death was fine in the abstract, in his apartment. But they had seen death today, and though none of their group had been affected, the sight had taken some of their enthusiasm.

"Juanita, what is left in that chamber," he asked, trying to stir up some distraction.

"Just the girl they operated on."

"I will look." He walked through the steel door and noted the compactness of the chamber itself. Flooded with oxygen at a high enough volume, it would make an impressive bomb. The girl was strapped to a stretcher cart, her flaxen hair shaved away from her forehead where stitches had been taken and bandages placed. A traction weight dangled from a pulley that held her leg, encased in a heavy cast, at an angle in the air. A tube ran into her arm feeding her system with a glucose solution. Rosario sat down beside her and looked at her face. Battered as it was, it was the face of a child. Who, he wondered, could do such a thing?

While Rosario looked down at Emily Stolzfuss, Ross was brought to his feet by the appearance of Deputy Commissioner Shea, the Mayor, and Lieutenant Flaherty.

"Ross," the Mayor said, "the Commissioner tells me you're a wiseass with a good idea. Is it more important to you to be a wiseass or a cop? If you pull this off, we'll forget about. . . . Well, there's no point going into to it. Let's just say that I think you're right. I think once the guy is cornered, he'll give up, or maybe blow his brains out. But I don't think he'll blow the hospital, either. In the meantime, we are evacuating everybody from Green, Leibner, Waldman, the Rosenstein Tower, and the north wing of Hartz. The ambulatory patients are being taken down in the elevators and out Lexington Avenue to Morgenstern. The bedridden are being moved through the basement corridors. The only people that will be left in Hartz are about a half dozen doctors and nurses who are in the middle of open heart surgery. They said they wouldn't leave." He looked at his watch. "We need ten more minutes. The paper is due in fifteen. That gives you five. How many men do you need?"

"None. I need a flak vest, two pistols and maybe an M-16, and a silencer for a pistol."

"How about tear gas?"

"So I can choke to death while I'm trying to get them out of their hole?"

The Mayor smiled. "Shea's right, Ross. You're a real charmer."

Hernandez stepped away from the wall. "I'm going."

"Fuck off, Roach," Ross said.

"Never work without a backup. Even assholes know that, Arnie. You think maybe I can have a flak vest, too, Your Honor?"

"You're his partner, right?"

"Yes, sir."

"I think I'll get you two flak vests, and a straight jacket for him. Okay, don't move till you get the word. I'll be outside, talking to the press. Lieutenant, see that they get the equipment."

As the Mayor walked away Ross said in a stage whisper, "Gee, Roach, maybe we ought to take him. He can baffle 'em with bullshit." The Mayor stopped, then without turning, continued through the door.

# 48

Luis Dominguez licked his dry lips, and moved stiffly. He had lied to Rosario about the condition of his shoulder. "I'm fine," he had said. "It's just a scratch." While it was true enough that the wound was not dangerous, the bullet from Ross's revolver had gouged a chunk of flesh from the upper part of his arm. For a while, the numbness of shock had prevented the pain from overwhelming him, but now he was suffering periods of weakness and nausea. It was odd, he thought, that it had not bled much.

Even when the discomfort was greatest, it never occurred to Dominguez to give up his post. More than any of the others, he wanted to redeem his life through sacrifice. He had nothing to lose. Unlike many in the same position, he saw his life as the only symbol of value in his unhappy world. In some twisted way, he had determined that if it was the only really valuable asset he had, that he would sell it most dearly. He was plagued with recurrent dreams of his own heroism. He was addicted to war movies, often sitting through them four or five times.

He propped himself up against the heavy pipe in the crawlspace with two grenades at his right hand and the machine-pistol cradled in his left. His 9 mm. automatic jutted up from his belt. He felt a wave of pain, and was conscious of being thirsty.

Twenty yards away, and a dozen feet beneath him, Ross and Hernandez talked quietly. "Where's my ordnance," Ross said.

"They're trying to get it from the station house. Relax," Hernandez replied.

"Well I hope the fuck they hurry up."

"It's your own fault. You're the one who made up the damn shopping list." Hernandez slipped into the flak vest, wincing as he pulled it over his wounded arm.

"Shit, I need a little more time to think."

"Well that's what you get for shooting off your fucking mouth. If I get killed in this, Ross, I'm really going to be pissed off at you."

Ross stood and put on his own flak vest, and said, "That's what you always say." He looked at the watch again. "Where is that frigging male *yenta*?"

Lou rolled his eyes. "Watch it, will you, Arnie. The man's the Mayor."

"Big fucking deal." He paused. "Hey, Roach, you think that Didi died?"

Lou paused. "I don't know. . . . Yeah, Arnie, I think Didi died."

They didn't talk much after that. Arnie traced his finger over a crude drawing he had made from his memory of the setup in the hall. They had provided them with a diagram of the pipe stack leading to Gluck, but it was too complicated to be of much use.

Flaherty walked through the door with a metal cylinder in his hand. "It came. Here. It fits this." He drew a .357 Magnum from his jacket pocket and handed it to Ross. "You got three minutes till that paper's supposed to be delivered. Maybe we can stall, maybe we can't."

"In three minutes," Ross said, "either I'll be dead, or this'll be over. In either case, I won't have to listen to any more bullshit."

"Good luck, eagle beak."

"Thanks, Lieutenant. See you 'round. Come on, Roach. I ain't got all day."

Flaherty had seen to it that except for two cops as backup, and himself, the entire ground floor and basement of Waldman had been cleared. The exterior of the building was surrounded by armed men in protected vantage points covering every possible entrance and exit to the building. More than fifty men had volunteered. It was clear that if Rosario pulled the switch, all of the people in Waldman stood a better than even chance of becoming dead. A pumper and a fire emergency vehicle with a crew of ten sat in the middle of Lexington Avenue and Ninety-sixth Street, directly in the path of the blast. The men chatted as though they were on an outing.

"We figure," the fire lieutenant said, "that if there is only a small blast, and we can get to a fire quickly, and we don't get killed, we could do a lot of good."

The Mayor had agreed.

"I think that the hardest thing is going to be to get that fucking door open without the asshole in the closet hearing us."

Hernandez nodded. He crawled along the floor to the edge of the door and looked at it critically. He motioned at Ross with his finger. "Listen, there's plenty of clearance between the bottom of the door and the jamb. Just push this glass out of the way quietly, so it doesn't tinkle. I'll slip the catch."

Lou waited till Arnie was through using his suit jacket as a broom to move the fragments. When he was done, Lou took off his necktie and looped it over the door handle. Ross took the end of the tie, and Hernandez pushed a plastic credit card from his wallet into the door catch. He pushed gently and the catch recoiled against its spring and disappeared into the door. Lou nodded, and Arnie pulled gently on the end of the tie. The door opened noiselessly. Lou leaned forward to keep pressure on the spring, and then, when the door was ajar, slowly released it. Lou took off his shoes and placed one of them between the door and the jamb. Ross took off his shoes as well, and pulled the door open further. Both men slipped into the corridor on their hands and knees, leaving the door held open by the shoe.

They edged quickly down the slick surface. If the man were in the closet and he threw a grenade, they would have no chance in any case. Therefore, they would have to assume that he was up in the crawlspace. Lou sat with his back against the wall. Arnie swallowed, made sure that the silencer was firmly screwed onto the heavy revolver, and that it was fully loaded. Then he stepped silently, in a crouch, past the closet, looking in as he went. Knees shaking, he sat down on the other side. He crouched again, then stood directly before the closet, taking a quick fix of what he could see. He motioned to Lou, who joined him.

Their course of action was clear. Arnie would have to get to the standpipe, climb it, and get through the hole, gun first, without being spotted. Even, Arnie thought, if the man in the crawlspace were looking down the hole, he might be able to get him with the silencer. Arnie shrugged. He was out of time anyway.

He put his finger to his lips. Lou lay on his back with

the M-16 beside him. Arnie stepped quickly into the opening of the closet with his revolver pointing up at the trap. He lowered the gun, there was no one in it. Lou slid forward into the closet, still on his back, and leveled the rifle over Arnie's shoulder, effectively covering his ascent. Noiselessly, Arnie pulled himself up through the maze of pipes and stood bent. Lou got to his feet, keeping the rifle pointed at the hole. Ross winked and popped his head and upper body through the trap with the gun extended. It was his good fortune that Dominguez did not see him first. Ross guessed that he would be closest to the entrance to Gluck, and that that entrance would be where the standpipe was.

As Dominguez became aware of Ross, he began to tighten his fingers around the butt of the machine pistol and to extend them to the trigger guard. It seemed to him that he was moving in slow motion. He was totally unaware, of course, of the soft plopping sound. The top of his head disappeared, and he slumped forward.

Ross waited for a moment till his eyes became accustomed to the dark. He saw that the crawlspace was empty except for a few ammunition cases, and Dominguez' corpse. He reached under the trap and waved for Lou to come up, reaching over to take his rifle.

When Hernandez arrived he found Ross already at the base of the plate at the bottom of the standpipe. "That's where. Half a turn on that bolt and we're in there."

"We don't know how many, or anything," Lou said.

"Listen, you go get Flaherty and some reinforcements," Ross said in an urgent whisper. "Once we're in there, it's all over."

"Arnie, you could get a lot of people killed."

"Just go get 'em." Ross watched Hernandez leave. He checked the time. According to the agreement with Rosario, the paper was to be delivered at the street door in less than a minute. Ross reached up and slowly turned the bolt, already half-loosened. It slipped off, and the heavy plate fell against his palm. He broke into a sweat as he struggled to keep it from falling. Noiselessly, he lowered it to the floor and felt the cool breeze of the air conditioning on his face. He could see the institutional green of the ceiling up above him. If he stood, his head would extend above the level of the floor into the hyperbaric chamber. He heard rustling beneath him, and glanced across at the trap to the closet. Hernandez' head and shoulders were emerging. He made an okay sign at Ross with his fingers.

The voice was clear above him. "All right, Rafaela, you can go to the door now. Tell Martins and Al to keep a careful watch while you get the paper. Juanita, watch them carefully."

There was a clicking noise that sounded like a telephone being removed from the cradle. Ross strained his ears, but could not distinguish the words. He thought he had heard that there was someone already waiting at the door for the paper, and that were to be three knocks. He motioned to Lou, then stretched his body out so that he was near the trap.

"Listen," he whispered, "in a minute—one minute— when they knock three times on the outside door with the paper, force the door, shoot, do something." He turned back, and Hernandez dropped out of sight. Arnie leaned against the standpipe and thought about nothing but the second hand on his watch. When he thought that a minute was up, he eased back the hammer, and stood up, facing what he supposed was the middle of the room. As he did there were shots from the other end of the hall.

Juanita Marques saw Ross before he saw her. She screamed, "Rosario," and fired wildly across the room. One shot caught Ross in the side of the neck and snapped his head back. He spun and without aiming pulled the trigger three times. Two of the bullets skidded harmlessly off the walls, the third destroyed Juanita's knee. She shrieked and tumbled to the floor among the wounded. Ross tried to shake off the effects of his wound and lift himself through the portal into the chamber. Juanita, gasping in agony, managed to prop herself on her elbow and lift the machine pistol toward Ross.

Through the haze of his pain, Albert Ruggles reached with his two great hands, putting one under Juanita's chin and the other at the back of her head. He snapped his hands in opposite directions. She fell backward dead, her neck broken.

In the hall at the door, Rafaela screamed as a dozen bullets tore into her midsection. Rosario could hear the chatter of the AK-47. But he knew that once the door had been breached, the chamber would fall. He spotted Ross out of the corner of his eye, and pegged a shot at him. Ross dropped below floor level.

Rosario took the detonator and a box of grenades into the big chamber with Emily Stolzfuss, and bolted the door shut. He waited quietly as the noises of death rattled through the corridors of Gluck.

Hernandez watched over his shoulder as two cops lowered Ross, complaining and struggling, back to the basement corridor, and to medical treatment. Other hands were fast passing the wounded doctor and Ruggles in the same direction.

Impasse. Rosario sat in the chamber and looked dispassionately at the girl on the cart. He reached for the phone that hung on the wall, and dialed the administrator's number. The Mayor himself answered.

"You have broken your word," Rosario said. "I am not surprised. You should not be either. There will just be more death and more pain. I am not defeated. I will blow up your hospital and all the world will know why. You will have killed our bodies, but the idea of the Army of Redemption lives on. Go on television, Mr. Mayor. Make them bring me a set. I can look through this thick window. Go on television and tell the people what I want them to hear. Read them my declaration. If you do not, I will take the detonator I have in my hand, and blow up your hospital."

The Mayor put his hand over the phone. "What the hell is going on down there," he asked Shea. He was quickly briefed. "We've got to stall him," he said to Shea. "Get someone to bring him a TV set. I'll do it. Get one of those network guys in here, and get me that damn manifesto. I'll read it. It'll buy us time."

"Mr. Mayor, do you hear me? Do you want me to detonate the bomb now?"

"No, no, certainly not. I am arranging the TV broadcast as you asked."

"You cheated me before."

"I didn't. There is a paper. It was printed."

"Have them bring it to the window," Rosario demanded.

"All right, but if we meet your demands, then will you let us dismantle the bomb?"

Rosario hung up. He waited for a few minutes, staring morosely at the door. For the first time since he had begun the venture, he felt a small lack of direction. His purpose was still clear, but his next steps were not. In all probability, all of his followers were dead. He had lost still another family. Where would he go, assuming that he were let free. Would he be captured and spend the rest of his life in a cage? There was a knocking at the window, and he stood warily edging toward the round porthole. A man held up a paper. The headline was real enough, "Manhattan Jewish Under Siege By Insurgent Radicals."

The man backed away from the window. Rosario held up the detonator and pretended to turn the handle. The man flinched and ducked out of the way. Rosario laughed. They had wheeled a television set to the window so that he could see the Mayor, peering through his bifocals and reading from Rosario's list of grievances. Satisfied to listen he sat back on the stool and put the detonator down. He pulled the pistol from his waist and cocked it, then sat back and listened with his eyes closed.

Jim Spencer was the last of the wounded to be removed from the chamber. He was fully awake and in considerable pain. He kept trying to get the attention of a policeman, but was constantly being hushed and told that he would be all right. He was too weak to make much noise. He finally caught the eye of the tall Puerto Rican who seemed to be in charge. He motioned the man to bend over. He was having trouble talking. "He's in the chamber, isn't he?" Hernandez nodded. "Turn up the oxygen," Spencer choked out. "Do it slow. He'll start to see double. Then he'll pass out."

"How about the kid in there?" Hernandez asked urgently.

"No permanent damage as long as it doesn't last too long."

"Where's the . . ."

"Green handle, by my desk, second one three turns, watch the dials. . . . About one pound every ten seconds . . . third dial. . . ." he faded and passed out.

Hernandez got to Shea at the command post and outlined the idea.

"Try it. There's nothing much to loose. If it goes, it goes."

Rosario was conscious of the fact that the Mayor was drawing close to the end of his missal. He stood resolutely and took the detonator in his hand. He heard a sound behind him and turned quickly, clutching the detonator. It was the girl. She was looking at him. She blinked and her eyes frosted with fear. She moved her lips creakily trying to make a sound come out. He could see that she was very young. Her face contorted in pain.

"Please don't hurt me any more, mister."

"What?" he asked.

"Please, mister. Do you want a blow job?"

"What did you say." He looked at her, dumbfounded and confused. Her face was swollen and bruised, her leg in a cast. She rambled in pain and the after effects of anesthesia.

"I'll suck you good, mister. Do you want to fuck me? Please don't hit me anymore. You can fuck me, please, mister. Just don't hurt me."

Rosario wanted to scream. His head throbbed and he felt nauseous. He backed away from the girl against the cool curved steel wall of the chamber. He was not a monster. He wanted to cry. She kept begging him, pleading that he should not hurt her again. Offering her body.

Colors danced before his eyes, his head reeled. He put his hands to his ears, dropping the detonator to the steel decking. His heart pounded in his chest but he was unable to shut out the sound of her pleading. Please, he heard. No more. Fuck me. He screamed to drown her out, louder and louder as he screamed to his pillow. By the time the atmospheric pressure had reached sixty pounds per square inch, four times normal, Rosario's head was bursting. The girl babbled on. He staggered over to her and screamed, "I won't hurt you. I won't hurt you."

"Please," she begged. "No more, please." She reached out weakly with her hand and clutched at his sex.

With a shriek of horror, Rosario Gonzalez pulled away from the fulfillment of his nightmares, pulled the gun from his waistband and splattered his brains over the wall of the Louis Gluck Hyperbaric Chamber.

# 49

Later that night, Eddie Biggs strolled across the dirty floor of the Port Authority Bus Terminal to the newsstand. He bought himself a big Reggie bar and a copy of *The Daily News* and sat down to wait for the late bus from Allentown, Pennsylvania.

He relaxed against the bench, chewing slowly on the candy bar, stopping every so often to suck on a tooth.

He read about the big shootout at the hospital, which took up the first dozen pages of the paper, together with graphic pictures of the dead and the maimed. It was not until the middle of the tabloid that he came to the story, which would have been big news otherwise, that a girl had been found beaten nearly to death in the Jersey Meadowlands, and would have died except for the quick action of the New York Police and their helicopter. The girl had been miraculously saved twice in one day. Once in the Meadowlands and once when, inexplicably, the leader of the radical band had committed suicide before her eyes in the hyperbaric chamber where she had been operated upon.

Eddie Biggs stood up casually and threw his candy wrapper on the floor. He left the newspaper on the bench, and began to saunter toward the exit of the building. He had about seventy dollars. If he could get three blocks to the hotel, and pick up his threads, he would just hop on the next bus to anywhere. But he sure would have to get out of town. If that chick ever lived to tell on him . . . Well, shit, he thought, shame on me.

Armed with the description that Emily Stolzfuss had been able to provide, and with Eddie Biggs's name, Marvin Baxter parked his car on the Thirty-ninth Street side of the Port Authority Terminal and pulled down the visor to show his shield.

He was met at the door by the head of the security squad, and five of his men. "Okay," the chief said, "you know the drill. We comb the place. All the men's rooms. You know what to do. Don't miss any corners. I want every pimp and bad dude in this place rousted and in front of my face. Anybody who comes within ten miles of his description goes downtown."

Baxter and the chief took the south side of the building. Eddie hadn't quite made the door when he spotted them. He turned on his heel and walked casually toward the ticket windows. He looked up at the bus schedule. The next bus left in five minutes for Red Bank. "One to Red Bank, please," he said to the indifferent man lolling behind the barred window. The man barely lifted a hooded eye. "Shit. Wake up, man. My bus leaves in five minutes."

"That'll be four dollars and sixty cents." Biggs pushed the money on the counter, grabbed the ticket and moved swiftly toward the escalator to the departure floor above. Torn between the need to avoid attention and the need to make the bus he walked in a stilted, cramped fashion that the experienced security chief caught out of the corner of his eye.

"Right there," he said to Baxter. "There's something on his mind besides catching a bus."

They walked swiftly in Eddie Biggs's direction. Eddie had nowhere to go but up. If he could just hop on that bus, he thought, he'd be all right. He galloped up the escalator steps, hotly pursued by Baxter and the security man. There was another security guard at the entrance to the platform from which the buses left. Eddie ran into him knocking him to the ground. He kicked him savagely in the face and ran out to the platform.

Baxter drew his gun as he ran to the platform, watching for a chance as Eddie Biggs wove among the people who were either waiting for, or descending from buses. Realizing that he could never fire a shot on the platform, he holstered the gun and ran full tilt after him.

Eddie Biggs laughed over his shoulder. The bus to Red Bank was already moving. At worst, before they could stop it, it would be out of the building and onto the street, and he could lose himself in the crowd, or a thousand doorways. He jumped onto the slim bumper of the bus and with his finger tips grabbed at the protruding plastic light covers. How many times, he thought, had he hitched rides on the Fifth Avenue bus that way. You just hang on where it says, "Danger—Do Not Ride."

The bus swung around the curve down the ramp. He saw Baxter snarling in frustration. He hardly realized it when the bus brushed him against the wall. He lost his footing and hung by his finger tips, kicking his legs trying to regain his purchase with his feet. The bus gave a final lurch and cast him off into the roadway. He started to lift himself, but it was too late. The front wheel of the incoming bus from Allentown, Pennsylvania, passed over the midst of his body—tearing a terrified shriek from his throat—and crushed him like an ant.

# 50

It was a sticky August morning when Abner Stolzfuss made his second trip to New York. He confessed to himself with some humor that he had read extensively in *Genesis* 18 and 19 since his last arrival. But all things considered, while the big city had certain aspects that reminded the serious Bible student of Sodom and Gomorrah, it seemed that New Yorkers had sufficient redeeming features to prevent instant consumption by Heavenly fires.

In his reference to the Holy Book, he had also dwelt upon *Luke* 15. It seemed to Abner Stolzfuss, upon reflection, that prodigality, be it of a son or of a daughter, was in the eye of the beholder. Forgiveness of a strayed lamb was a theme played through both Testaments. And if it ground against his hard shell of belief and habit to accept his daughter back into his fold, no one else in the community was able to perceive it. As he saw it, Emily had been more sorely tried than he had thought possible. He had never asked her what happened. She had never told him. But he saw her scars and her pain. He had sat at the side of her bed for the first week after the battle of the Gluck building. He smiled to himself again. In a wheelchair. His leg still throbbed.

He fondled the plain, sturdy wooden cane between his calloused hands as the cab drew him from Newark Airport through the Lincoln Tunnel and thence across New York to Manhattan Jewish. He enjoyed the view and the bustle, recognizing that he would not see it again. He paid the driver and descended painfully to the sidewalk in front of Morgenstern. Leaning on the stick, he made his way to the cashier's department at the back and asked for his daughter's bill. Without a glance at the preceding pages, he turned to the last sheet. He read the number and paid the startled cashier in hundred dollar bills. A small enough price to pay, under the circumstances, he thought.

Emily was on Morgenstern Six. She seemed very small to him when he came to the open door of her room. In part, it was due to her substantial loss of weight, and the pallid complexion caused by her weeks of hospitalization. In part it was by comparison with the man standing beside her bed.

"Nice to see you, Mr. Stolzfuss. I see you're here to pick up the little lady."

"*Ja.* So, Sergeant Ruggles. I see that you don't stay in bed, either."

"They didn't hit anything very vital. The worst I came out with was a broken rib. I must admit I don't sit down so good now." He grinned and rubbed at his buttock.

"I don't walk so good." Stolzfuss tapped his cane. "But today, I feel good. We are going home. *Ja,* Emily?"

The nurse helped Emily to her feet and let her hobble across the floor to the wheelchair on her good leg and the walking cast that had been put on her leg the week before.

"How about that, Mr. Stolzfuss?" the nurse asked. "The doctor says she'll be running like a deer in two to three months."

"The young heal fast, thank God." He shook hands with Ruggles and the nurse and walked beside Emily as the attendant pushed her chair toward the elevator.

"Wait till you see what we've done Emily. Mama and I are moving out of the big house so Abraham can move in. We're building a *Grossdaddy's* house just next door. For me and Mama and you and the younger girls." He paused a moment and looked at her. She sat quietly in the chair.

"I know that it's going to take awhile for you to feel better and get back to farm work. I wondered if instead of wasting your time at foolishness sitting around the house, you might not be able to continue your schooling a bit."

She turned and smiled shyly. "You mean it, Papa?"

"Why not?" He wiped at his nose with a large linen handkerchief. "Perhaps you could become the bookkeeper after me." The elevator arrived, bringing them to the ground floor. Stolzfuss continued, "And of course, with that leg so, you couldn't walk to the school. And I can't be wasting too much time from my work. So I thought perhaps to get you a trap and a mare of your own to get about with."

Emily Stolzfuss left the Manhattan Jewish Hospital holding her father's hand—for the first time in her memory.

# 51

It was not until September that Mama Hernandez really began to look a little more like her old self. She sat in the garden of the house by Jamaica Bay shelling peas into a pot.

Arnie and Luis sat in chairs across the small lawn drinking beer. Their guest, Dr. Rogovin, still wore a souvenir of his meeting with the Army of Redemption in the form of a sling for his arm.

"I still don't understand how somebody named Burke can be Jewish," Mama said.

Rogovin smiled. "Mrs. Hernandez," he stopped at her frown, "Mama, I mean. It's pronounced Burke, but it's spelled Boecke. And besides, he wasn't Jewish."

"Listen, Mama, you should just be grateful that it was his disease you got, and not the one from Mr. Hodgkin." Arnie rubbed at the new scar on his neck and finished his beer. He'd only been off duty for three weeks. The Deputy Commissioner had personally delivered the Mayor's citation to him and Lou. All in all, not a bad ending.

"Crazy, huh, Saul?" Lou said.

The doctor nodded in agreement. "That's medicine, pal. All of the symptoms of Hodgkin's Disease—all. Look, let's face it, Boecke's Syndrome isn't funny. Cortisone is not a funny drug. But, it's an absolute cure. And the way Mama is going, we're all to weigh three hundred pounds before she's finished."

Margarita Hernandez wiped her brow as she stepped into the garden from her den. "I can't stand it anymore. Everybody in this place is supposed to be some kind of invalid, and all I hear is a lot of talk about diseases and sickness."

"Yeah," said a piping voice from the kitchen. "Well, all I ever hear around here is the sound of teeth gnawing on

248

food. Doesn't anybody ever get tired of eating in this house?"

Didi walked out into the sunlight, still a little frail, but after a month in the sun, much better than when she had come out of the hospital. "You better eat some of that chicken soup in there, Sarge, it's good for your neck."

Arnie drained the glass of beer and licked his chops. "I wish it was good for something else."

## ABOUT THE AUTHOR

Nick Christian is the pseudonym for a business-man whose interest in international investment banking and corporations has taken him from Tokyo to Athens and from SaoPaulo to Addis Ababa. But regardless of his momentary destinations he always returns to the excitement of his home city, New York, where the ferment and intensity of life have given him the inspiration and the background for this series.